STILLWATER

PRAISE FOR *STILLWATER*

"Darcie Friesen Hossack's Lizzy grabbed hold of my heart right from chapter one. A fierce hero at war with her upbringing, with her father's ideology, and with the society she does not yet have the power to escape, Lizzy inspires me. She functions as an "Every Girl" figure, refusing to be kept down by a social order forever working against her. Lizzy continues to be what her culture tells her she cannot: her strong, independent, empathetic, curious, intellectual self. *Stillwater* reminds me that even with damaged wings, we can learn to fly. We must. Go, Lizzy!"

ANGIE ABDOU, author of *In Case I Go* and *This One Wild Life*

"*Stillwater* is a compelling exploration of family, liberation . . . and food. Hossack tempts us with recipes, some appealing, some intriguingly bizarre, and yet tells a story so riveting that readers will prefer to turn the page rather than pause and head for the kitchen."

ANDREW UNGER, author of *Once Removed* and *The Unger Review*

"*Stillwater* is a delicious story of simmering cultural tensions that boil over during the pandemic. In turns irreverent, funny, deeply moving and heart-wrenching, this novel offers a window into the worlds of both Seventh-day Adventist and Mennonite believers who evidently mix about as well as oil and water. Darcie Friesen Hossack writes of these conflicting worldviews with both deep affection and unflinching honesty. At the centre of the story there is Lizzy, an unforgettable character who finds relief and escape from her strict upbringing within a whole other worldview: science. But the real heart of this story is food, food that defines each culture and cleaves it from the other, even to the point of tearing a family apart. Food as an act of defiance and rebellion. Food as solace and comfort, as refuge. By including the recipes for the many tasty and quirky foods she writes about, Hossack hits home that recipe, just as much as taste and smell, is a form of cultural and familial memory, and that, at the most fundamental level, we really are what we eat. This is a novel that will quite literally leave you hungry for more."

GAIL ANDERSON-DARGATZ, two-time Scotiabank Giller Prize finalist

"Darcie Friesen Hossack's latest work of literary fiction is an exquisitely gripping novel of unsettling injustice and the origin of courage. *Stillwater* is a profound exploration of the strength formed by struggle and the hope born of despair. Like the faint agony and rediscovered power of a freshly healed broken bone, this beautiful and complex story explores the pain and promise of a young woman's path to independence."

AMBER COWIE, author of *Last One Alive* and *Loss Lake*

"*Stillwater* opens a fascinating window into the world of Mennonites and Seventh-day Adventists in western Canada, and of family life and strife in those communities. Darcie Friesen Hossack's novel, like her acclaimed short story collection, *Mennonites Don't Dance*, has writing that is precise and sensuous, grounded in the corporeal and earthly, even as her characters are pulled and pushed into the realm of the spiritual or quasi-spiritual. The tension between these two—the real and corporeal, and the spiritual—forms the scaffolding of the novel. Caught in the middle are Hossack's characters, especially the protagonist, Lizzy, a young girl whose journey towards self-determination is the arc of the story. *Stillwater* is a coming-of-age tale set in a particular world, vividly imagined and finely drawn. "

DAWN PROMISLOW, author of *Wan*

STILLWATER

A Novel

DARCIE FRIESEN HOSSACK

TIDEWATER
PRESS

Published by Tidewater Press
New Westminster, BC, Canada
tidewaterpress.ca

978-1-990160-20-2 (print)
978-1-990160-21-9 (e-book)

LIBRARY AND ARCHIVES CANADA CATALOGUING IN PUBLICATION

Title: Stillwater : a novel / Darcie Friesen Hossack.
Names: Hossack, Darcie, 1974- author.
Identifiers: Canadiana (print) 20230145639 | Canadiana (ebook) 20230145647 | ISBN 9781990160202 (softcover) | ISBN 9781990160219 (EPUB)
Classification: LCC PS8565.O756 S75 2023 | DDC C813/.6—dc233

Printed in Canada

For Dean, who told me so.

PROLOGUE

Remember the day you punched the wall? You were tall enough to miss my head so your fist left a hole in the plaster. For as long as we lived in that house, I used it to measure my growth. Dad, I'm here with you now as the nurse comes in to check your oxygen and listen to your lungs. When she's finished, she draws your covers back over you, and you're so small you barely make a shape.

Some days I go home and sit in my empty bathtub. Everywhere else is too big, and I need to feel the walls around me. They keep me from breaking apart and scattering. Although, if I did that in there, I might just slip down the drain.

I'll remember to put the stopper in next time.

In the bathtub, with the door closed and the light off, I'm underneath our basement stairs again. You never once found me there. Is it because you never looked? I wonder that now. Maybe you were glad when I disappeared. When you no longer had to harden yourself to make sure I didn't grow up too soft.

This morning, I drove past our old house and remembered the day the washing machine was full of blankets and became unbalanced and made a terrible noise. When Mom, Zach and I all came running down the stairs, there you were, sitting on top of the lid, laughing and trying to keep the machine from shuddering its way across the room.

That should have been a good memory. But you got angry. You

thought we were laughing at you. You didn't know all you had to do was open the lid.

I still have the *Messages to Young People* you gave me for my baptism. The same copy that was given to you for yours. I brought it with me to school, Dad. It's the only thing I have that belonged to you, otherwise I would dig a hole and bury it in our old backyard, next to all the birds and other things I found dead or killed, having lost their breath of life.

There are more more things down there than you know. The neighbours' cat that got hit by a car and the neighbours didn't care. The casserole Zach made that you said tasted like sin. Mom's wedding watch and the pretty blue church shoes you bought me once when you took me to the mall, and then got mad because I liked them too much. They're all under the rhubarb. The shoes are still in their box. I never wore them. Not even once.

You know what I buried at Stillwater.

Part One

KELOWNA

NUTEENA

"Have you found yourself a recipe yet?"

Lizzy, seated at a farm table on the eating side of Stillwater's kitchen, looked up just as Mrs. Schlant bent to check inside one of two industrial-looking ovens. Having already decided not to like anything about this place, she thought how easy it would be to Gretel the woman inside and shut the door.

"I've been doing math," Lizzy said, imagining a nice, crispy skin—something a Seventh-day Adventist should know nothing about.

Nevertheless, she picked up the cookbook the director's wife had offered and flipped a few pages, looking for recipes for her home economics assignment. Recipes she was told she could cook for her future husband and his guests. All the traditional Adventist dishes were there—walnut patties in mushroom sauce, spaghetti and gluten balls—along with a few she didn't recognize. On those pages, Lizzy stuck a series of Post-it flags, until she finally came to one she knew she had to have. She took out a recipe card from the front pocket of her backpack, set it on the table, and printed NUTEENA at the top. Before she could get started on the ingredients though, her mother opened the mudroom door, just off the kitchen, and let herself in, along with a cold breeze.

"Still snowing out there," Marie said, stomping her feet. "I'm afraid Daniel still has the summer tires on. And I don't even have the right shoes. Caught us all by surprise, I guess."

"October's early for snow in the Okanagan," Mrs. Schlant agreed, already moving on to her next task.

Marie shed her jacket onto an iron hook. "Lizzy, you'd like the bakery and the homeschool, I think."

When Marie said things like that, Lizzy felt as though her mother had never listened to a thing she said. But since Lizzy needed Marie on her side, she kept quiet as her mother stepped out of her shoes, arranged them neatly on a black rubber tray and stuffed her feet into a pair of crochet slippers from her jacket pockets. The slippers, a polyester checkerboard of yellow and brown yarn, looked like two over-ripe bananas, and Lizzy offered up a years-old prayer to keep Marie from slipping.

Crossing the expanse of green and white linoleum between them, Marie unlooped the hand-sewn mask from one of Lizzy's ears. She pressed her cold cheek against Lizzy's warm one, then brushed the bangs from her face. "Take that off," Marie said. "It's rude."

Lizzy, who had leaned into the softness of her mother for just a moment, replaced her mask. Annoyed, she batted away the attention, picked up her pen and clicked the nib in and out a few times. At that, Mrs. Schlant made her way over to see which recipe Lizzy had chosen to copy into her scant collection.

"I thought you might choose that one," she said, smoothing an invisible crease in her apron. "What others do you have already?"

Lizzy reached into her backpack and withdrew a Ziploc baggie containing the dozen or so recipes she had already gleaned from here and there: the potluck ladies at church, Mrs. Wroblewski down the street from them in Kelowna, her mother's recipe box.

Mrs. Schlant unzipped the bag. "Sweet and Sour FriChik?" she said. "I don't think I've tried that one."

"Mom invented it for Sabbath lunches. It's her specialty," Lizzy said through layers of cotton that she had stitched together in sewing class, and for which she had received a C-minus. As she spoke, she lifted her feet off the floor and snugged her heels onto the front edge of her seat.

"Then it must be good," said Mrs. Schlant. Lizzy saw her mother blush.

"Back when Mom was my age, she used to make it with actual chicken," Lizzy said, which was nothing more than a matter of fact.

"Oh," said Mrs. Schlant, replacing the card in the bag and setting it on the table with a little push. "Well, I see."

Lizzy tipped her head to one side for a better view of the director's wife. She was a sturdy woman, more in her bones than her flesh; older than Lizzy's mother, but not by much.

"And pork," Lizzy added. "Sweet and sour pork was your favourite, wasn't it, Mom? My grandpa—they lived on a farm, you see—used to let her choose which pig to kill."

Lizzy, who'd never met her grandfather and never would, given that he had died when Marie was a girl, had no idea whether that last part was true. It had the hoped-for effect though. Mrs. Schlant's hands fluttered upwards to her chest, where she fiddled with the topmost button of her blouse. "Oh," she said again, clearly appalled by the thought of handling anything that "parted the hoof." After all, pork was at the top of the Leviticus list of forbidden foods.

Mrs. Schlant settled herself and pressed a hand onto Marie's shoulder. "My goodness. But I guess we all have a past, don't we?"

Lizzy could almost feel the hot glow of her mother's mortification. To keep from laughing out loud, she fake-sneezed into her mask, grateful it was there to conceal her smile. If only Lizzy could tell them both about her secret after-school job at a butcher shop. But then her father would find out, and that would be the end of that and a whole lot of other things, like ever leaving the house again. Worse, it could be the final push he needed to move their family here.

"I know what you mean about having a past," Lizzy said, recovering quickly. "Once, I ate almost an entire box of no-name Oreos.

Double Stuff." That day, Lizzy's father had come home, found lard in the ingredients listed on the side of the package, and declared the cookies—and her—unclean. She'd been made to fast on nothing but vegetable broth for a week.

"*Oba*," Marie said. "We don't need to talk about that."

Tomato juice, potato water, cornmeal, Lizzy wrote, along with their measurements. *Peanut butter, oil, soy sauce . . .*

"Dad won't like seeing you sit like that." Marie whispered, "Or this," again snapping the elastic of Lizzy's mask.

Lizzy slipped her feet back to the floor, crossed her ankles as she had been taught at home and at her church school, but left her mask in place.

Combine the first 14 ingredients in a blender until smooth . . . With her recipe card complete, Lizzy set down her pen and pressed the heels of her hands against her forehead to uncrinkle tension brought on by the thought of having to cook.

Marie, who had been waiting patiently, picked up the card. "Nuteena?" There was a note of wonder in her voice. "You'll get an A for sure with that one."

Nuteena—once a beloved canned item by the same name—had been discontinued by Kellogg after they'd bought the Adventist-owned Worthington brand a number of years ago.

Marie turned to Mrs. Schlant. "Do you remember when they stopped making this? In Kelowna, we were afraid there'd be riots."

Lizzy had heard the stories. The couple who drove the mobile ABC—Adventist Book Centre—had parked their semi-trailer and truck at the SDA Academy. Word had gotten out, and a swarm of anxious wives had shown up clutching backyard wheelbarrows by their handles. Three cases were as many as anyone was allowed. Most of the families they knew were still saving their last cans, along with their best can openers, for the Great Tribulation—the time when faithful Sabbath-keepers would have to head for the mountains with their Ellen G. White libraries and vegemeats. Mrs. Wroblewski, their neighbour in Kelowna, had opened a can for Lizzy once, and she could still taste the finished product, as salty as it was beige.

Lizzy agreed it was a good start to her recipe box assignment, but even Nuteena would go only so far in the one class currently dragging down her GPA. GLUTEN STEAKS, she wrote on another card.

While Lizzy copied, Mrs. Schlant drifted to the other side of the kitchen, emptied a burlap sack of carrots into the sink and began to scrub at their skins with a brush.

"Do you know why we leave the peels on, Lizzy?" she called over her shoulder.

"Most of the vitamins are there," Lizzy replied flatly, not surprised when her mother shoved up her sleeves to help.

Lizzy decided to take advantage of the opportunity to reward herself for her own culinary efforts. She dragged her backpack around from the back of her chair onto her lap, opened its main compartment wide and unsleeved her most prized possession: a used college microscope, lately purchased using sixteen ten-dollar bills, a lifetime of birthday money from an aunt and uncle in Saskatchewan who Lizzy had never met. She had noticed a dried smear, presumably of raw Nuteena batter, on the open page of Mrs. Schlant's cookbook, and she wanted a closer look.

Lizzy expected her mother to tell her this wasn't the time or the place. When she didn't, she set her microscope on the table and snuck its power cord into a nearby outlet. Then, using the blade of a scalpel kept in her pencil case, she scraped a flake of the substance onto a glass slide and set it with a drop of water. She positioned the slide, flicked on the illuminator and adjusted the focus until the matter came into view. She had hoped to find some kind of exotic flour mite trapped in the mixture, like a specimen preserved in amber. But no. There was nothing more interesting than flecks of peanut in the smear. She switched off her microscope light and watched the two women push carrots end to end through a juicer until they had exsanguinated enough to fill three large pitchers.

As though the whirring of the machine had been a signal for the whole community to gather, the other members of Stillwater began to file in. Some came from elsewhere in the house. Others, including a troupe of children with carrot-coloured eyes, appeared from outside.

Lizzy's father, along with her younger brother Zach, soon followed, having been on a men's tour of the facilities. With them was an older teenage boy who balanced on one foot, ankle over knee, to unlace his boots.

"I told you it's quite the setup they have here, isn't it?" Lizzy's father said, cheeks flushed or maybe a bit frostbitten. He shucked off his shoes and Marie, hurrying over, scooped them up to arrange next to her own. "The bakery, Marie. The bread. And did you see? There's a pair of old washing machines they've refitted since I was here last, just to juice apples. Comes right out the drainage hose during the spin cycle."

Lizzy made a covert gagging motion for the benefit of her brother.

"Take a look at this, then." Marie fetched the cookbook from under Lizzy's elbow.

Daniel took the book, offhandedly at first, until he saw what it was. He then lightened his touch and held it like a relic. Uninterested, Lizzy zipped up her recipe cards, tucking them into the front pocket of her hoodie, and packed her pencil case and textbooks into her backpack.

"Where did this come from?" Daniel said.

"Loma Linda University. Department of Dietetics, 1999," said Mrs. Schlant, with a carrot in her hand. "I was one of the students in that class." She went over and tapped the book with the end of the vegetable. "There are hardly any copies out there."

"Loma Linda," Daniel said. "Now, Lizzy, there's something for you to think about. Loma Linda's one of the best medical schools in the world, you know. And it's *ours*."

"Not interested," Lizzy muttered.

Daniel stared at her mask and flicked it with his fingers. "Now," he said.

"There's a pandemic, you know. And they're all wearing masks at Loma Linda." She tried not to think about how many people breathed and coughed in this kitchen every day.

Daniel ignored her and turned to Mrs. Schlant. "I keep telling her no one is going to need a zoologist when the Tribulation starts. But nurses and dieticians . . ."

"Maybe *I* could become a dietician," Zach ventured. "Do they get to cook?"

Daniel returned the book to Mrs. Schlant. "You'll have to do very well in school if you want to go there. I'm sure it's a difficult program."

As though on cue, the Stillwater women fell into a choreography that quickly had plates down from cupboards and mismatched casserole dishes pulled from hot ovens with scorched mitts. As they moved, the long, mid-calf bells of their dresses swished, and Lizzy realized she was the only girl or woman there dressed in pants. Her father caught her eye, and she could tell from the look on his face that he was thinking the same thing.

"Put this away," Daniel said, tugging the cord of Lizzy's microscope from the wall. Marie was the one to take it, along with Lizzy's backpack. As she did, one of the women stepped in to scrub the table and two others set down dishes and food. With the women still on their feet, the men took their seats. Lizzy realized, too late, that she had been expected to stand, and quickly scrabbled to her feet.

"Don't worry about it. Everyone takes time to learn," said the boy from the door. "I'm Joel, and you have something on your face."

Lizzy brushed her fingers over her cheeks. "Hilarious," she said, and Joel shrugged.

As the men settled in, the children, including Zach, gathered around a smaller table to the side, next to a kumquat tree warming itself in the afternoon sun. Each of the children was poured a tall tumbler of carrot juice.

Before sitting, the women quickly peeled off skins of plastic wrap that had covered the dishes. Steam lifted, revealing stacks of whole-grain pancakes, alongside dishes of hashbrowns and Stripples—vegan bacon from the ABC—that looked as though they'd started off crispy before losing their nerve. To spread over the pancakes, there was oily peanut butter in vintage gold-coloured Tupperware, along with glass jars of chunky applesauce, lightly pink from the retention of their peels.

Finally, the women, including Lizzy, took their seats.

There was a hymn sung in poorly tuned unison. Director Schlant, Stillwater's founder, was the first to speak. "Before we dig into this good food, I'd like to thank our guests for coming all the way out here from Kelowna today," he said, to murmurs of agreement all around. "Of course, we'd already met Daniel here enough times to judge his character. But after having you with us, Marie, Lizzy, Zach, I think each one of us will agree that we'd like to see you join us here. So let me just say welcome, and we hope the feeling is mutual." The entire table turned and pressed upon them a collective, if somewhat uneven, smile.

Daniel's face split open into a Cheshire grin, while Marie, Lizzy noticed, inclined her face toward her lap. She'd missed a perfect cue.

"Um, thanks," Lizzy said in her mother's place. "But I don't think we've decided. Dad hasn't even decided yet whether he'll get the vaccine when it—"

"Well, we do certainly feel welcome," Marie interrupted, rearranging her fork and knife before putting them back exactly where they'd been.

From under the table, Lizzy felt her father's sock-covered toes dig into the bones of her foot. She removed her mask, shoved a forkful of pancake into her mouth, and swallowed it dry before realizing that everyone else was waiting for the director to pray.

After prayer, which petered off at the end so that Lizzy had to look up to find out whether it was over, conversation turned to business.

"We took a look at last year's sales from the greenhouse again," said a man at the other end of the table. "We could probably get away with planting double the edible flowers and herbs, just for the contracts we already have."

"One of the clothes dryers is acting up again, if one of the men can come and take a look," said a woman near Lizzy, who smelled strongly of fabric softener. While perfumes were frowned upon, even among less dedicated Adventists, Downy was considered a good, functional scent.

One forkful at a time, Lizzy and Marie ate, soon falling into a common pace.

"Is there any salt or pepper?" Lizzy asked, pushing her fork through a perfectly bland pile of hashbrowns.

"Pepper excites the animal passions, dear," said Mrs. Schlant, handing Lizzy a salt shaker. "Salt is fine, and cinnamon for baking, but Ellen G. White says our food should be prepared free from strong spices."

The director cleared his throat and wiped his mouth on a starched napkin.

"That's right, Lizzy. Now, Daniel, we hear you might be willing to share some of your hospital skills," said Mrs. Schlant, tipping a second helping of Stripples onto his plate. Lizzy's father was a nurse, who would've been a doctor, he often said, if he'd been able to pay for more school. He would have gone to Loma Linda, in fact, which was responsible for churning out doctors for the Lord.

"I've worked in old folks' homes, mostly. I'd say it's the best place to practice because there's a little bit of everything." Daniel was rewarded with a round of enthusiastic murmurs and nods.

"We can certainly always use someone with medical knowledge," said the director. "Someone who isn't just quick with the medicines, forgetting that God gave us good fruits and vegetables and sense. And Lizzy, you have your father's interest in science, I hear. Perhaps you could assist with the younger children."

Lizzy lowered her fork and wrapped her fingers, overhand, around its handle, tamping down an impulse to stab. "I'm in Grade 11, but I'm already taking a bunch of Grade 12 classes this year."

"I see," the director said, forking up another mouthful of peanut butter and pancake. "Well, perhaps your education could take a new direction."

"That doesn't make any sense. Why would I do that?" Lizzy said and once again felt her father's foot.

"It does make sense, Lizzy," he said. "You just have to think about it a little longer. And you'll have plenty of time for that while you help your mother pack."

Lizzy tried to count to five. "What do you mean, pack?" she said, without even getting to two.

"It's okay, Lizzy," Marie said, reaching for her hand. "We can all talk about this once we're home."

Silence fell from one end of the table to the other. Only the children, off to the side, kept up a happy chatter. When someone finally spoke, it was the director again. "I think what your father means, Lizzy—" he said but was interrupted by Joel.

"You know, I wasn't sure about this place, either. The first time you see all these people out here with their sprouted wheat and carrot juice, living together under the same roof, it looks kind of crazy. But I came, and I can tell you I've learned a better way."

Joel sounded like a salesman. But after he had spoken, the director himself reached around a man seated between them and clapped Joel warmly on the back. "Our boy here is being modest," he said, beaming. "Do you know that the church in town found him living in their basement? Eating nothing but potluck leftovers when he could get them. And at night, when the building was locked up? He'd make his way to the upstairs library and read our dear Mrs. White. By the time someone noticed, he'd gotten through everything from *Messages to Young People* to *The Great Controversy*."

Joel patted the director's hand good-naturedly even as he peeled it away. "It's true," he said but didn't elaborate.

"Excuse me," Lizzy said, her chair scraping loudly against the floor as she stood. She was still clenching her fork and deposited it into a vase of silk flowers as soon as she reached the front foyer before continuing up a flight of shag-carpeted stairs. At the top was a U-turn: bedroom, bedroom, bedroom and a bathroom to the right.

Lizzy shut herself behind the last door and turned the lock. Inside, the smell of bleach stung the delicate membranes of her nose. There was a small window above the bathtub, providing light as Lizzy lowered the toilet lid and sat down on a rug-hooked cover the colour of yellow cough drops.

"I cannot live here," she said out loud, just to hear the sound of her own dissent.

"Lizzy?" came Marie's voice from the other side of the door.

Lizzy, startled at first, untwisted the lock and Marie let herself in to perch on the edge of the tub. She'd brought her purse with her, and from inside its opened mouth fetched a clump of cherry-flavoured hard candies. She broke one off from the cluster and offered it to Lizzy, taking another for herself. The same cherries had been present at every scraped knee and after every harsh word from her father since Lizzy was a little girl.

Lizzy picked away a ball of lint before putting the candy in her mouth, welcoming the painful pinch of saliva that followed, and the sour-sweetness on her tongue. "Do you have any aspirin in there?" Her head hurt, and she wasn't sure when it had started.

Marie drew back a little. "Are you sure you need one? You know how your father feels."

Lizzy nodded, and after digging again in her purse, Marie offered a single pink chewable from an envelope kept secret inside the purse's lining.

"Really, Mom? Children's?"

"You can have another in twenty minutes if it's not enough," Marie said, checking her watch. "We don't ever want to over-medicate. People get into trouble that way. Your father . . ."

Lizzy closed her eyes but only needed to count to three. "I don't think aspirin is what they mean," she said, pushing the candy into her cheek for safekeeping while she bit down on the tiny pink tablet.

Her mother, purse settled in her lap like a cat, began to pick at the sides of her fingers, where she tended a perennial thicket of hangnails.

"So what do you think, Lizzy?" Marie said, tearing off a square of toilet paper to stick to a drop of blood. "Couldn't you see us here, though?"

Lizzy sat up straight. "Can you?" she said, incredulous. "I thought you and I only agreed to come here so we could talk Dad out of it."

Marie's face fell. "I don't know. Don't you think it's nicer here than you expected? What about Mrs. Schlant giving you her recipes and what-not-all? Besides, Dad doesn't think the Cotton Glenn is going to give him much of a choice."

"Yeah, but maybe they're right, Mom. I mean, we have all of our other vaccines. Dad, too. And besides, they don't even have someone who can properly teach science and math. What would I do for school?"

Marie made a familiar sucking noise as she chewed away a stubborn snag of flesh. "Would it be so bad to spend a little more time with us before going off to university?" Marie said.

"If I go to UBC in Kelowna, I can live at home for four more years, maybe more," Lizzy said. "And what about Zach, Mom? Did you see all those other kids with their carrot eyes? People don't live together like this, all in the same house. It's not normal."

Marie's hands dropped onto her bag and her shoulders slumped toward them. "It's not normal to you, Lizzy," she said after a full measure of silence that grew louder with every tick of Lizzy's mental clock. "But I grew up around lots of aunts and cousins, you know. And sometimes I might like to have other women around to talk to."

"Mom, you have friends back home. And me. I talk to you."

"I don't tell you about everything," Marie said. "But if you still want me to talk your father out of this, you just let me know." She snapped her purse shut, stood, and let herself out, leaving the door open to the landing.

Lizzy was left with a bitter taste in her mouth, along with the cherry candy still dissolving on her tongue. She tore off a square of toilet paper, spat out the candy and slipped it underneath her into the water below.

That's when she heard it. Someone clearing their throat.

"How long have you been spying on me?" Lizzy said, even before she saw him.

"I live here," Joel said simply, coming out from one of the bedrooms.

Lizzy crossed her arms, wishing she could puff herself up to appear larger and spikier than she was.

"I didn't mean to upset you earlier. And I'm not spying on you now." Joel leaned close to whisper. "Your mother is the one who's listening."

"Good. And you didn't upset me," Lizzy said, her voice wavering a little now at the sound of Marie's slippers shushing down the stairs.

Joel came into the bathroom and squinted at Lizzy, as though considering something, then crouched down and reached into the cabinet under the sink. He took out a glass bottle and a jar of cotton wool and set them on the counter.

"Look. I can tell you've already decided not to like me—"

"I don't have to—" Lizzy said. "I mean, I haven't decided anything."

"Just that you're too good to be here. But it doesn't matter." Joel tipped the open bottle over a wad of cotton. "Your mom will probably manage to talk your dad out of this for you, even though, from what I can tell, he'll probably make her pay for it. And you can keep on doing whatever it is you do. Biology, is it?" He squeezed out the excess of what Lizzy could now smell was rubbing alcohol into the sink. "I'm going to touch you now. If that's okay."

Lizzy drew back. "Excuse me?"

"Okay, look. I tried to tell you before at the table, but you have something blue, just there," he said, pointing at Lizzy's forehead. From a hook next to the sink, he passed Lizzy a pink-handled mirror. He swept back her bangs, and Lizzy saw what must have been apparent to half of the people at the table, even through her hedge of overgrown bangs. A smear of ink.

Lizzy checked her palm for the corresponding blob of blue and felt her cheeks prickle with heat. "I can get it," she said, quickly licking her finger when Joel moved toward her with the cotton.

"No, you'll just smear it." Joel bumped away Lizzy's hand and took the mirror. Before she could stop him, he tipped back her head and touched the cotton ball with alcohol to her face.

NUTEENA

2 ½ cups tomato juice
1 ½ cups potato water
½ cup cornmeal
1 ½ cups chunky organic peanut butter
2 tbsps vegetable oil
1 tbsp low-sodium soy sauce
Pinch each of dried sage, thyme, marjoram and rosemary
¼ tsp garlic powder
¼ tsp onion powder
1 tsp table salt
1 tbsp Lawry's seasoned salt
¼ cup gluten flour
¼ cup whole wheat flour
2 cups rolled oats
1 ½ cups whole wheat breadcrumbs

Heat oven to 375°F. Combine the first 14 ingredients in a blender until smooth, then transfer to a large bowl. Fold in oats and breadcrumbs.

Grease five 2 ½ cup-sized tin cans and fill each with 1 ¾ cups of the batter. Place cans in a deep casserole pan and then into the oven. Fill casserole dish with boiling water to ¼ of the way up the sides of the cans. Cover the cans and dish with foil and allow to steam for 1 to 1 ½ hours or until the mixture is set. Remove cans from water and let cool completely. Keep covered and refrigerated, then let Nuteena come to room temperature when ready to remove from cans. Makes a total of 60 slices.

BEET ROLL

Marie adjusted the waistband of her skirt, a consequence of Mrs. Schlant's pancakes. Too much bran always made it tighten. So, for that matter, did Lizzy and Daniel whenever they disagreed. And since both of those things were true today—too much friction and too much fibre—it was difficult to know which to blame for the tightness that had begun to cinch her insides like the strings of a purse.

"How about we play a game while we drive?" Marie offered toward the backseat of the car, where Lizzy and Zach silently, if not patiently, passed the time. Both shook their heads and Marie turned back to face the road.

It had only been an hour or so since they had driven away from Stillwater. Already, though, daylight had become gritty and turned to dusk.

Without a word, Daniel switched on the headlights. They needed to be cleaned, Marie thought. Even on high beams, they barely spilled enough light for something to come into focus the moment it became too late to swerve. It could be a deer, Marie imagined. Or a rock the size of a chesterfield, slipped from an unstable bank. Or it could be one of those cheerless, soiled people who seemed, for no reason—thumbs in, they carried nothing—to drift between towns along the shoulder of the road.

"Anyone need to get out?" Marie asked a short while later when a glow on the horizon told her they were nearing the city of Vernon. If she were in charge, they'd pull over at the Dairy Queen on the highway. That's what her own father used to do when she was a girl and he had taken her into Swift Current with him, whether it was to buy a used tractor or just to knock on watermelons together until they agreed on the perfect one.

"Zach? Lizzy?" she said over her shoulder as the Dairy Queen came into view. "Bathrooms?"

"I'm okay," Zach said.

Lizzy, reading by booklight, didn't reply, and before long they were swallowed back into an evening that seemed to have grown darker for every minute they had driven under streetlights.

Alongside an inky pool that was Kalamalka Lake, a bank of lights sped toward them. Marie sucked in a gasp of a breath, holding it until a logging truck carrying a jumble of stripped-down trees had passed. "That one was close," she said after they swept through its wake.

"It was fine, Marie. Or maybe you want to take over and drive us the rest of the way?"

No matter how long she lived in British Columbia—more than seventeen years, now—Marie had never been able to get used to its roads. She had learned to drive on the Prairies, with its stick-straight lines. BC was all ups and downs and hairpins that jumped out of the middle of nowhere and seemed to appear in a different place every time. And then, today, there was the weather. The snow from the morning had melted, but the temperature was dropping again. The water it left on the roads could freeze and turn into black ice.

"Mom, do we have anything to eat?" Zach said, and Marie relaxed a little at the sound of his voice.

"Why don't we see what Mrs. Schlant put in our bag?" Marie reached between her feet for a paper grocery sack the director's wife had handed to her on their way out of Stillwater.

"You'll find a beet roll on top," Mrs. Schlant had said. "It's a new recipe, so next time you're here, you'll let me know what you think."

Marie had promised she would. As she felt inside the bag, her head was nearly on her knees when the front passenger tire of the car thumped over something on the road.

"Cripes, anyway!" Marie said. "That could've been a . . ." She settled herself back down. Reason told her it was just a clump of ice, shed from the mud flap of a semi that had come over Roger's Pass. But ever since she'd read a story about a mother out east who had placed her infant son in a brown paper bag and left him on a highway, Marie imagined an abandoned baby under every bump in the road. "Everyone okay back there?" she said, giving herself an excuse to count her own children.

"We're fine," Lizzy said and turned a page.

Marie found Mrs. Schlant's beet roll. Keeping a slice for herself, and one for Daniel, she passed the rest back to Zach.

Marie faced forward once again and touched her hand to her belly where her own seatbelt should have been fastened securely across her hips. For months now, the mechanism to pull the strap down had been stuck, but whenever she pressed Daniel to take a look, he told her that he'd get to it soon. "If the Lord decides it's your time, Marie, a seatbelt won't add an extra minute to your life," he said. To which Marie replied, "Maybe He gave us seatbelts so He can worry about other things." Which was as good as making sure it would never get fixed.

To keep her mind off the road, Marie bit into her beet slice, expecting, despite the name, to taste jam-filled sponge, and maybe a hint of something that resembled cream, reminiscent of the delicate cake and sweetened preserves her mother used to make. Instead, the beet roll lived up to its description. If they did end up at Stillwater, the food was something she would have to get used to. And she couldn't see how there would be many opportunities to go into town to get a little something sweet.

But when she passed Daniel a slice of what amounted to cooked beets rolled up and baked into dense bread, he ate his and reached for Marie's, too.

Marie wiped away a few crumbs from her skirt before digging into the bag of yarn she travelled with. With a few twists, she began to cast chunky knots off the end of an oversized crochet hook, and her breath, which had risen high and tight into her throat, began to deepen and slow.

"You haven't said much about the place," Daniel said after a while, reaching across the space between them to touch Marie's hand.

She flinched and dropped a stitch. Even in so little light, Marie was self-conscious about her hands. As she saw them, they were all rough and red from years of scrubbing pots and potatoes. Just flesh, skin and knuckles with circular wrinkles like elephant knees.

"Oh, well I . . ." she said.

"I know it's a big change," Daniel said, returning both hands to the wheel. "But once we all get settled in there, it won't take any time at all for it to feel like home. Don't you think so, kids?"

From the back seat, a glutinous silence stretched out until Zach, finally, gave it some slack. "They have a nice kitchen," he said, allowing Marie to dip her crochet hook back into the scarf she had begun to make. "And Mrs. Schlant knows a ton about food."

The yarn slid and looped its way through Marie's fingers, reminding her of the way they'd felt the first time Daniel had ever touched them. Slender and elegant. Piano hands. Even though her fingers had always been too short to span an entire octave.

From behind, Marie felt her daughter's feet push into her seat. A reminder. "Lizzy, do you want a scarf that's long enough to wrap a few times or just once?" she asked over her shoulder, casting for a reprieve.

"What colour is it?"

"You saw when I packed it this morning. It's that purple."

Lizzy was quiet for a moment. "Maybe just make it for yourself?"

Kilometers passed without anyone saying another word. The dark shapes of mountains and trees continued to unspool along the sides of the road.

"So do we think we could get ourselves out there by the end of the month?" Daniel said, more sternly than before.

"Mom," Lizzy said.

"Well," Marie began. "You know, those kids there. The school isn't what we might have hoped. Less than we thought. And when I tried to give the children each a candy, they looked at me as though I'd offered them an onion. It's not right for kids to not at least want a little sweet."

"I see," Daniel began to grip and ungrip the wheel. Little strangling sounds of skin against plastic filled the silence. "So, because a few children don't want your pocket lint, I should what?"

"We don't even know what will happen at work. Everything could be fine. Some people say this is all still going to go away, so why don't we just wait and see?"

For a moment, Daniel lifted both hands off the steering wheel, then slammed them back down.

"There is a lot to like out there." Marie used her most placating tone. "But maybe we should wait a little while. Lizzy could finish up her schooling where she is, and we could see whether things get a little better for you at—"

Daniel's fingers flexed open, his knuckles flashing white in the dark. Only the heels of his hands were touching the wheel, and Marie mistook it as a gesture of surrender.

"It's not even all that long until she's done," she added, leaning against the passenger door. "I bet she could finish by the end of this school year, with all the extra classes she's been taking. Isn't that right, Lizzy?"

"That's another eight months, Marie. I don't have another eight months. Lizzy, this sounds a lot like you. Did you put your mother up to this?" He strangled the wheel a little tighter.

"Is this seriously a done deal? I don't know if you saw, Dad, but all of those children's eyes orange from all that carrot juice. And, really, that many people all living in the same house? It's weird."

Marie lifted her hand to her mouth and tasted yarn as she bit away a shred of skin next to a nail. Lizzy had nicked the taut string of Daniel's patience and she could almost hear her husband's thoughts taking shape as she continued.

"Dad, I won't learn anything out there," Lizzy said, leaning into the space between the front seats. "I could teach every class in that place."

Marie, hands ravelled up in purple yarn, gently pushed Lizzy back.

"I'll tell you what, Lizzy," Daniel said. "School isn't everything, and it worries me that you think it is."

"Fine, then. I'll just become a housewife." She switched off her booklight with a tiny click.

In the silence that followed, it began to rain, small, spattering drops that quickly became half-frozen splashes drumming wetly against the hood and roof.

"Kalamalka Lake," Marie said, just under her breath. "Duck Lake. Wood Lake." She counted the various waters between Stillwater and home. By feel rather than sight, she dipped her crochet hook back into the scarf. Okanagan, Kalamalka, Duck, Wood. One, two, three, four. *Over, dip, over, draw.* Marie knotted their names into the yarn of the scarf. Soon, however, she had to unravel several rows she couldn't account for.

Around a particularly tight bend, Marie slid sideways and, unrestrained, grasped Daniel's arm to steady herself. "I'm glad we're almost there," she said with a nervous laugh.

Silence.

"Dad, you're speeding," Lizzy said, and after a moment, Daniel slowed to just under the limit.

The car lurched over a frost heave and Marie was lifted slightly out of her seat. Her hands flew out in front of her as she landed, and the seat seemed to count every unnecessary ounce against her.

Mennonite thighs, Marie thought, trying to regret the *varenyky* and cream gravy of her childhood. She had already been soft by the time she met Daniel. Two children later, and even though she had agreed to a vegetarian lifestyle, her belly had taken on the consistency of punched-down bread dough.

Marie relooped her yarn and tucked back a tendril of hair that had escaped from the bun at the back of her head. No longer light brown or dark blond or even grey, now it had become a shade that, whenever she washed another clump of strands down the shower drain, reminded her of the dead mice she found every autumn in the kitchen glue traps Daniel set inside her cupboards.

"Marie, why don't we try some of that bread next?" Daniel said. The rain had stopped, although the road remained splashy with puddles. "Lizzy, I'm sure a future biologist will appreciate this. At Stillwater, they make their bread from sprouted grains. We can use the rest for tomorrow morning's toast."

Marie could tell he was offering an olive branch and said a little prayer that her daughter would accept it.

"That's botany," Lizzy said.

"Why do they sprout it?" Zach asked, accepting the loaf Marie passed back. "Does it have better flavour that way?"

"You guys tell us," Daniel said.

From the back seat came a crinkle of paper, after which Marie felt the remaining loaf slide over her shoulder from behind. She took it and removed two slices, handing one to Daniel and keeping the other for herself. She was still working hard on her first bite when Zach offered an opinion.

"It's like loofah!" he said with a note of horrified wonder.

Marie's stomach flopped.

"Think of it toasted with some margarine and honey," she said, encouraging him to say something nice.

"Honey on loofah is still loofah."

"Nutty. That's the word. It's nutty." She reached back into the bread bag and was about to offer everyone a second slice when Daniel gently lowered the bag back into Marie's lap.

"What about you, Lizzy?" Daniel said.

"It tastes healthy. But Mrs. Wroblewski's bread is a thousand times better and it's healthy, too. And we don't have to move to a commune to get it."

"Kids, you know if it were up to your mother, we'd eat nothing but white bread. Fried white dough. Boiled white dough. And white gravy over it all."

He was laughing, but it felt like a trap. He and Marie had long ago agreed not to confuse the kids with ideas from a different time in her life. It was a promise Marie had occasionally broken, when she found a particularly good watermelon to share with the kids, by frying up small batches of *rollkuchen* to accompany it when Daniel was at work. Mennonites always ate *rollkuchen* with watermelon in the summer.

"Not everything about where I came from was so bad," she said, having nearly managed to keep the thought tucked in. "The kids might want to know about where they came from someday."

This time when the car went over a heave in the road, Marie's body lifted and came back down with a painful thump.

"The only thing anyone needs to know is where they're going," Daniel said, the words falling like hot coals from his mouth. "And if you keep up with this, I can't be responsible for where that might be."

Marie slipped her yarn-tangled hand behind her seat to find her daughter's foot, surprised when Lizzy reciprocated with her own hand. She wanted to reach for Zach, as well, but knew she couldn't do so without being noticed. "If the two of you could just agree," she said softly, toward her lap.

"Mom, it's okay. We don't have to talk about it anymore," Lizzy said and pinched her nails into Marie's palm.

Marie felt Daniel's foot twitch on the gas. "Well, let's just get home, then," he said.

"Fine with me," said Lizzy.

Daniel picked up speed. Faster and then faster, round curves and through gullies while the road, it seemed to Marie, threatened to slide out from beneath them at every turn. Her hands had begun to tremble, and she slid them under her legs. She had a habit of reaching for the door handle when startled, and if something made her do that now, without a seatbelt, she would spill right out onto the road. It was uncomfortable, though, sitting on her hands. Her hangnails caught on the polyester of her skirt. She had no lotion in the car to soothe the dryness that caused them. She longed to be home, massaging Vaseline into her fingers while seeing the kids off to bed. Or home in her mother's kitchen, where hands that handled lard never needed a pump of Jergens. Or simply back at Stillwater, where Mrs. Schlant kept a glass bottle of something that smelled of rosemary next to the homemade soap on every sink.

Wood Lake was finally alongside them, with its too-fast bend in the road up ahead. Marie reached for her seatbelt and gave it a tug. It clunked inside the housing and refused to be moved.

"For God's sake, Marie," Daniel said and his arm flew across her. He grabbed the seatbelt and yanked it hard three times. "There," he said as a shard of plastic cracked away from the door and the belt suddenly unspooled.

There was too much slack in the shoulder, but Marie clicked the latch in gratefully and snugged the belt tightly around her waist.

"Dad, let's just get home safely," Lizzy said as the rain returned as slush. "We're already really close. It'll just be a few minutes extra if we go slow."

Marie began to hum. A squeak of a sound at first, and barely audible. But as the notes seeped from her, they grew louder until they finally flattened out into a hymn her mother had taught her to sing whenever she felt far from home. *Nearer my God, to Thee, nearer my God;* thin and thready, like a bow dragged across the strings of a dried-out violin.

"For crying out loud, Marie," Daniel said. "You'd think I was trying to kill us." And though it hadn't seemed possible to Marie that they could go any faster, he coaxed yet another measure of speed from the car, whose frame began to rattle.

"I don't know if God would want you up there if you sing like that," Daniel said. It was an attempt at a joke, and Marie rewarded it with a little laugh.

"Well, I just think—" Marie said but didn't get to finish.

Daniel accelerated into the bend and Marie was shoved against the inside of her door like a load of wet laundry as the road and mountains spun around them. For a few seconds, her chest felt tight, and her head clunked heavily from shoulder to shoulder.

Something struck Marie's side of the car with a terrible noise. Glass from the passenger window shattered and was followed by the sudden shock of coming to a full stop. Marie's body, only half restrained, was flung forward and her hands, raised to protect her face, smashed into the windshield before falling into her lap.

At first, Marie didn't recognize the cold that began to climb toward her knees as water from the lake inched its way up her legs. Not even as it began to lift them, and she pushed them back down with hands that made crunching sounds like bags of loose marbles, the kind she used to take outside on warm summer days.

"O, mein Gott," she said, lapsing into Low German as the water reached her waist and recognition crept in. "Daniel?" she said, with

water at her neck, but when she turned to look for him, he was gone. "Zach? Lizzy?" she said and inhaled a breath that filled her nose and mouth with lake.

BEET ROLL

    1½ cups warm water
    ¼ ounce active dry yeast (1 packet)
    ¼ cup honey
    3 tbsps baking margarine, softened
    3½–4 cups whole wheat flour
    ½ cup wheat bran
    ½ tsp kosher salt
    2 medium beets

Sprinkle the yeast over top of warm water and set aside in a warm place to proof for 5 minutes. Transfer to the bowl of a stand mixer fitted with the dough hook attachment. Add honey and margarine. Mix in 2 cups of the flour and the salt until moistened. Beat on medium speed for 3 minutes. Add more flour, just until dough pulls away cleanly from the sides of the bowl. .

Turn out and knead on floured surface, adding remaining flour, until dough is smooth and elastic, about 10 minutes. Place dough in large greased bowl and cover with a clean tea towel. Let rise in warm place until doubled in size, 30–45 minutes.

Meanwhile, cook two medium beets in salted water until tender to the tip of a knife. Rub away the skins using a paper towel. Chop into small dice, and mash those slightly with a fork.

Lightly grease a sheet pan. Punch down the dough and roll it out to the size of the sheet pan. Spread beet over the surface, leaving room along the edges. Roll up like a jelly roll and transfer to the greased baking sheet. Cover loosely with a tea towel and let rise in warm place until doubled in size, 30–45 minutes.

Preheat the oven to 350°F. Uncover roll and bake 40–45 minutes or until roll sounds hollow when lightly tapped.

HAYSTACK COOKIES

Lizzy clicked her seatbelt and rolled down her window the moment the car stopped spinning, exactly the way she had been taught in swim classes at the Y. "Mom!" she coughed and pulled herself through the open window. As the car began to sink, she whipped her legs into an eggbeater. "Zach!" Her nose stung as inky black lake water rushed in. Paddling in place, Lizzy's jacket and jeans threatened to drag her to the bottom.

"Dad!" she cried out, but from all around came nothing but the sound of small waves breaking in on themselves.

"I have Zach," Daniel called out from a short distance away.

"What about Mom?" Lizzy shouted, pivoting in the water to face the sound of his voice.

At first, she couldn't see them, but then light filtering up from the car's headlights below showed the silhouette of Zach's arms wound tightly around their father's neck. Unlike Lizzy, who Marie had sent to the pool every summer, Zach had never learned to swim.

There was a pause, and a spluttering snuffle from Zach, before Daniel replied. "I think she's already gone to shore," he said. "Can you make it by yourself, or do you need me?"

"Mom!" Lizzy called out again. She waited for a reply and shouted one more time. "I don't hear her."

Daniel, with Zach coiled around him, put his back toward Lizzy and began to swim away.

Lizzy leaned after him into a heads-up front crawl. Her hands and feet already felt wooden from blood that was rushing away. She stopped after just a few strokes. "Wait. I have to check."

"Lizzy, you come with us right now," Daniel yelled back, but Lizzy had made up her mind. Paddling back to the underwater lights, she took several deep breaths and plunged under the surface, down toward the car. It had settled no more than six feet under, and swimming to its depth was easy with the additional pull of her sodden clothes. Once there, however, she found the front passenger-side door jammed. The window was broken, though, and she reached in to feel for Marie.

At first, Lizzy thought she felt her mother's hair, but it was nothing but yarn. She returned to the surface, shedding her jacket along the way, then dove again. She went straight for her father's side of the car and pulled open the door. It was darker inside, and when she waved her hand through the water, feeling for where she had last seen her mother, her hand bumped against something. When she closed her fingers around it, it felt like stones wrapped in meat and string. They were her mother's hands, and the cold, butcher-shop feel of them cracked open a hot yolk of panic inside Lizzy's chest and nearly forced her to take a breath.

Feeling her way to her mother's arms, Lizzy braced her feet and pulled until she felt a pop. But Marie's body didn't yield.

The seatbelt. It was cinched tightly across her mother's waist.

With another breath from the surface, Lizzy swam down one more time. Catching her leg on what might've been a twist of metal as she undid the seatbelt, she gathered Marie under her arms and pulled. This time, Marie's body floated free of its seat, and Lizzy, struggling with the additional weight, kicked away from the car toward the surface. Up, up, up, until they burst into the air to the sound of a siren in the distance.

"I can take Mom from here. Stay right beside me." Daniel was there and he slipped his arm alongside Lizzy's, doubling the hold she had on Marie. "You can give her to me."

"I don't think I can." Lizzy's voice shook with cold, and her limbs felt frozen, as though her arm might break if she tried to let go.

"Okay, then let's do it this way," he said, and instead of taking Marie, he grasped Lizzy under her free arm and over her chest. And together, he swam them back to shore.

Once there, Lizzy knelt barefoot in the rocks and sand, dimly wondering where her shoes had gone as she pumped on her mother's chest. *Stayin' alive. Stayin' alive. Uh, uh, uh, uh. Stayin' alive.* The words played in Lizzy's ears to the beat of the compressions, just like she'd been taught in her classes by the side of the pool. Sixteen beats. A breath. And then repeat. Until she couldn't anymore, and Daniel took over. Finally, Marie coughed and just as an ambulance raced to a stop on the road above, he rolled her onto her side to drain the water from her lungs.

"I'll go in the ambulance with your mother," Daniel said. Both he and Zach were wrapped in mylar blankets, being fussed over by a second attendant. "There's another one coming for you and Zach."

"No," Lizzy said. "I'm going with Mom."

Already, the second set of spinning lights was coming toward them, followed by what Lizzy could tell was the police.

For once, her father backed down, and soon Lizzy was seated in the back of the ambulance, wrapped in a blanket of her own.

"You need to let me look at that," said the paramedic, who looped a blue medical mask over his face.

Lizzy turned toward his voice but didn't reply.

"Your leg. You're bleeding pretty bad."

Lizzy didn't understand. All she felt was cold and numb, but when she touched her fingers to her thigh, the heat of her own blood brought the gash in her skin into focus. "Oh. Okay."

"I'm just going to put a pressure dressing on that, and they'll close it up when we get to the hospital."

Lizzy had never sped through Kelowna so fast, and yet the rest of the way felt slow, as though they were still underwater. On the gurney, Marie breathed into a plastic oxygen mask and occasionally opened her eyes. "She's bleeding?" Marie said, her voice muffled behind the plastic.

"It's nothing, Mom. Forget about it." Lizzy leaned closer, and when she moved her foot, her toes slipped through Marie's blood, dripping from the purpled and shattered links of her fingers.

Kelowna General Hospital loomed over the ambulance as the paramedic—did he say what his name was?—pushed open the door and stepped out. The hospital dominated this stretch of Lakeshore Road. It was near her mother's favourite beach. Strathcona. The one they used to take picnics to as a family. "I like being near the hospital when we're by the water," Marie would whisper to Lizzy. "Just in case."

Lizzy had never been inside KGH. Daniel preferred to take care of fevers and scrapes on his own and had even set and splinted Lizzy's leg when she broke it falling from a branch of their backyard plum tree. After that, Daniel cut down the tree and burned it stick by stick.

"Is she . . ." Lizzy said to a nurse who came to fetch her, as the paramedic and driver wheeled Marie inside.

"She's breathing and awake. That's what we like to see," said the nurse, whose voice behind a mask and face shield seemed kind. With a squeeze of Lizzy's hand, the nurse gave her a matching blue surgical mask.. "And I hear we have you to thank."

"Can you feel that?" asked a young doctor.

Lizzy watched as he threaded a curved needle through the gash in her leg, stringing it back together with thread. But every time a voice or an alarm sounded, her attention was whisked away from the angry-looking meat.

"No," Lizzy lied. Although the doctor had injected a nerve block, she could feel each time the surgical-steel sliver punctured her skin, both as it went in and came back out. Twenty-seven times for twenty-seven knots that now bristled in a jagged line down her thigh.

Clipping the last thread, the doctor waved down the same nurse who had brought Lizzy in. "Are her parents around?"

Instead of answering, the nurse crouched by Lizzy, who was dressed in a pair of pink scrubs and green paper slippers. "I just asked, and your mom is going into surgery now. Your brother is being looked over just on the other side of the room. And I'm not sure where your dad has gone—maybe to find out about your mother—but he did say your neighbours are on their way to pick you up. Does that seem right?"

For the first time all day, Lizzy sighed with relief and let her body sink into her chair.

When she was cleared to go, Lizzy found Zach and they were each given a plastic bag with their wet clothes. Marie's things were there, too. Not her dress. But half a purple scarf, trailing a snarl of yarn that someone had disentangled from her shattered hands. "We couldn't find your father to give this to," said the nurse. "But your neighbours are in the waiting room now. I'll take you."

"We don't need a babysitter," Lizzy said. "I'm sixteen."

"I know. But maybe just for tonight, you need some friends."

More than anything, though, Lizzy wanted to be alone. Not alone, perhaps, but invisible, and Doris Wroblewski was a woman who, with one look, could see right inside her.

"I brought you some haystack cookies," Doris said, reaching into her coat pocket for a paper bag. "I was making them when we got the call from your dad."

Zach, who hadn't said a word since Lizzy found him, suddenly brightened. "I'll take one," he said and went on chattering about the food they'd eaten that day.

"Lizzy?" Doris said.

But Lizzy had nothing to say.

HAYSTACK COOKIES

11-ounce package butterscotch chips
1½ cups semi-sweet chocolate chips
3 tbsps peanut butter
1 cup cornflakes
12-ounce bag chow mein noodles

Line a baking sheet with waxed paper. In a large glass bowl, mix together butterscotch chips, chocolate chips, and peanut butter. Microwave at 50% power for 1 minute. Stir and microwave in 30-second intervals, stirring each time, until smooth (about 3 minutes total).

Break up the noodles and fold into the mixture until until well coated.

Using a cookie or ice cream scoop, scoop about a ¼ cup of the mixture at a time onto the baking sheet. Set aside until set, about 2 hours. Store in an airtight container for up to 2 weeks.

BANANA SANDWICHES

Daniel was still cold. Coming from the chapel, where he had knelt alone until his knees ached, he pulled down the hospital mask that had been forced on him when he'd been brought into the hospital. His nose pinched at the familiar smell of antiseptic in the room. He scraped the chair from next to Marie's bed closer to the window, away from where she slept, but the distance didn't help remove him from what he'd done.

"Got any room under that blanket?" he said to Marie, softly, the way he used to when they were first married. Now, though, he turned away from her face, puttied by the morphine in her drip, and looked out the window toward Strathcona Park. It was nothing but a patch of darkness at this time of night.

As a family, they had picnicked there a few times. All four of them under a tree, biting wordlessly into sandwiches that Marie and Zach had filled with bright pink Wham, diced and stirred together into a salad with margarine and celery. Zach had asked for an ice cream from a truck. After that, Daniel refused to take them back. "If you can't be satisfied with what I provide, then we'll just stay home."

He still stood by that decision.

In her hospital bed, Marie shuddered and made a whimpering sound, and Daniel looked back toward her. Above her head, saline and glucose dripped down a clear plastic tube into a vein in her neck, combining with a metered drip of pain meds fed to her by machine. Marie's hands, the surgeon had explained, had been too damaged to take a line.

"Your wife will be on pain medication for several days, at least," the surgeon—whatever her name was—had said. "But it's important it be for as short a time as possible. By morning we'll want to see what kind of function she might have, although we won't know anything for certain until the swelling goes down." Her tone became more formal. "Please pull up your mask."

The surgeon lady asked whether Daniel had any questions, and he had simply covered his nose and mouth and shaken his head. It wasn't because she was a woman, he told himself. In his own work at the nursing home, he'd seen that they were as capable as he was. It was just that women had more important, more womanly, things to do. And that came straight from the Bible.

"How is she?" asked a nurse whose one squeaky shoe had alerted Daniel to her approach.

"She made a sound a minute ago but went right back to sleep," he said, adding that Marie's respiration and heart rate were unchanged.

With the click of a button, the nurse made a minor adjustment to the electric syringe pump. "No sense her feeling any of this until she has to." She checked the catheter bag pinned to the side of the mattress, sloshed it back and forth a little, and made a note.

"Your wife is stable, Mr. Fischer. You shouldn't be here. You know we can't allow visitors. But you can come closer for a minute if you like. There's no holding her hand, of course, but she'd feel you here."

"Okay, thanks," Daniel said but didn't move.

"Or," the nurse said, not missing much more than a beat, "you can go home and get some rest yourself. We'll call you." She finished her notes and left the room.

Daniel waited until the squeak disappeared all the way down the wing before he got to his feet. Although he stood up slowly, his head felt light and his vision grew dark around the edges. He pushed the heels of his hands into the sockets of his eyes until the blackness began to sparkle. "Photons," he could hear Lizzy telling him as he lowered his hands and blinked the sensation away.

Coming closer, Daniel touched Marie for the first time since the car. Her hands, bandaged and stained with discharge, were suspended in sheepskin slings. Trembling, he touched one with just the tips of his fingers but stopped when her sleep became unsettled again. Instead, he slid down to sit on his heels and reached under the blanket until he found her foot. Her toes were cold, the way he had always known them to be, and that was reassuring in its way. But as her skin began to warm to his touch, he quickly let go.

"I'm sorry I let you put that seatbelt on," Daniel said. He stood up to go, then. He needed to have a talk with Lizzy.

Outside the hospital's main exit, a taxi idled. "I suppose you're Mrs. Covington," the driver said when Daniel slumped into the backseat.

"Whatever. I'm here and she's not," Daniel said. He wanted to get home and change before showing up on Walt and Doris' doorstep. "Lacey Drive off Hollywood Road."

"As you wish," the driver said, waving his hand with a princely little flourish that, because it reminded him of Zach in a way he was always quick to dismiss, put Daniel on edge. The driver muttered something into his radio and started the meter. Ten minutes later, Daniel fished a soggy twenty-dollar bill from his wallet, passed it forward and stepped out in front of his house where, for the first time in almost fourteen years, not even a porch light was on to welcome him home.

Daniel walked up to the door. He reached for his keys before remembering that they were still in the car's ignition. Marie kept a spare under a rock in the backyard. But by the time Daniel thought of it, he had already changed his mind.

Four doors down and across the street, Doris and Walt Wroblewski's house was the pale green bungalow on the corner lot. Set well toward the back of its yard, its wide apron of front lawn reflected the girth of the actual apron worn by the woman of the house. Daniel hesitated, then knocked.

"Daniel," Doris said, opening the front door and filling it completely. She was one of the deacon ladies who had gotten the church to lock its doors and hold services online. As though the need for fellowship was outweighed by a few people coming down with sniffles and coughs.

Daniel had hoped, more than expected, that Walt would be the one to answer the door.

"I apologize for coming so late, but I can take the kids now," Daniel said, forced by the woman's presence to take a step back and down. "In fact, you didn't need to trouble yourself this much. They could have taken care of themselves if you had dropped them both at home."

Without giving space for Daniel to regain an equal footing, Mrs. Wroblewski crossed her arms and took hold of her wrists. "It *is* late," she agreed in that Australian accent of hers. "The kids are having a late supper at the table. Why don't you come in and ask what they'd like to do. Maybe eat a little yourself."

Daniel bit down until he felt a flash of nerves deep in the roots of his molars. *Such a nasty woman.*

"Just so you know, they're in pajamas already," Doris said, making space to let Daniel follow her inside. "I always keep a room and nightclothes made up for anyone in need. And I've gone ahead and told them there's nothing to worry about concerning their mother. That is the news you've come with, I hope. Because if not, letting those two have a good night's sleep would be the kindest thing you can do."

"Marie's fine," Daniel said to her back.

In the living room, Walt Wroblewski looked up from a book with a well broken spine. The man and his reading chair, the betters of which Daniel had often seen waiting on curbs for pickup, were the only unkempt items in the house.

"Daniel," Walt said with a nod and a smile, an unlit cigarette dangling from the corner of his mouth.

"Walt," Daniel said. The two of them exchanged a handshake while Doris disappeared into the dining room.

"Lizzy. Zach. Your father's here," Daniel heard her say.

Zach peered around the corner, tipped back and teetering on the back legs of a wooden chair.

"Get your things," Daniel said, crossing from one room into the next, where he righted his son with a clunk.

Across the table from her brother, Lizzy sat in front of an untouched plate of food. She looked up at Daniel, then returned her attention to the raft of craft supplies Mrs. Wroblewski had set out.

"They're not little kids," Daniel said to Doris.

Lizzy pushed her plate toward the centre of the table and, as quick as that, Zach reached out and claimed the open-faced sandwiches for himself. It was Marie's fault for teaching him to eat whenever he had feelings.

"Want some?" Zach said, his mouth full. "Mrs. W taught me how Adventists make sandwiches in Australia."

That was another thing. When Zach was worried, he gabbled on like a goose.

"Well, we don't make just the one kind of sandwich there, but this one's certainly a favourite," Mrs. Wroblewski said.

Most of the time, Daniel forgot to notice the woman's accent, which, in his mind, counted as a strike against her. Australians were loud and Canada already had Americans for that.

"What's in it?" Daniel asked as an unholy aroma reached his nostrils.

"Miracle Whip with tomato and banana slices," Zach said, swallowing a bite. "The trick is to keep it under the broiler until the Miracle Whip bubbles and the sugars in the bananas start to caramelize."

Daniel touched his hand under his nose, and Walt, still in the living room, boomed into laughter at the end of Zach's description. "That's the nice thing about the church," he said. "Everyone brings their own culture."

Daniel couldn't remember the last time he had seen Walt at church on a Sabbath. The man seemed to prefer spending Saturdays in his chair. He was like that even before it closed. Daniel liked him though; he was a good neighbour.

"That's nice, Zach, but we'll go home and I'll find something for us to eat there. Come on, Lizzy."

Zach slurped up a slug of hot banana that'd slid from bread to plate, then stuffed the bread into his mouth, too.

At first, Lizzy didn't respond.

"Now, Lizzy."

Lizzy picked up a paper doll from the collection on the table. They looked old. From the 1960s, maybe, with their bouffant updos and wardrobe in shades of avocado and assorted squash.

Lizzy selected a paper dress and folded its tabs around the doll. When she was finished, she carefully tore off the doll's head and picked up another.

"Lizzy, let's go." Daniel said, and Lizzy froze in the middle of the next beheading.

"Actually," Doris said. "You should know that two detectives came by, and I told them we'd be responsible for Lizzy and Zach through tomorrow morning, at least. That way you can be available for your wife."

Daniel stood, and what he didn't match in the woman's width, he made up for in height. "I'm sure there were no detectives, just officers, Doris. No crime was committed. And now that I'm here, your help is no longer required. Besides, no one is allowed in the hospital these days. They just assume we're all infected. Even you," he said.

"Dad, don't." Zach got up to stand between them. "She's just trying to make sure all of us are safe." For the first time, Daniel saw that he was shaking.

"She's allowing the government to interfere with faith, that's what she's doing. Next they'll round us all up."

From the living room came the sound of Walt's recliner snapping closed.

"Okay then," he said, coming to place a hand on Daniel's shoulder. "I'm going to have a smoke outside. Maybe you'd like to join me. The oven's been on half the night, and God knows it takes more than a bit of snow to cool down my wife's kitchen."

"I don't—"

"Just some fresh air, then," Walt said and led Daniel out the back door.

Under a porch light, cigarette butts floated in a coffee can half full of melted snow. Daniel watched as Walt bent down, poured off most of the liquid and relocated it to a more sheltered position.

"Here, I think you need one of these more than I do." Walt took a a cigarette package from his shirt pocket. He held up a hand when Daniel began to protest. "I'm an old man, Daniel. I see things." He pointed down the block in the direction of Daniel's house, the back-yard of which was clearly visible. He tapped out a cigarette from the pack and gave it to Daniel, before striking a match against a square of sandpaper tacked to the door frame. It took a few tries, but soon the phosphorus head flared to life. He seemed pleased. "Damn matchbooks, strip always wears out too soon," he said.

Daniel accepted the light and drew a column of smoke, warm and familiar, into his lungs, before expelling it into the air in a dense cloud of relief. He hated how much he needed this, but it was hard to be a man and not have a vice. Harder than it was for women, which was why he never let Marie or Lizzy badger him about it.

Walt lit his own cigarette and reached back into the house, returning with a big, old dog bed he set down on the concrete step. He lowered himself into it and invited Daniel to join him. "Old girl's been gone for years."

Daniel, after sizing up the bed, sank into it, and the two men smoked in silence for a while. Walt was the one to break it.

"That girl of yours." He took a final drag and dropped the butt into the coffee can, where it went out with a small sizzle.

Daniel waited.

"As soon as she didn't have to be in charge anymore, she collapsed. Didn't stop shaking for the first hour we had her here. And I'll tell you, it wasn't from the cold."

Exhaling smoke through his nose, Daniel nodded. "It was a shock for all of us, that's for sure."

"And the boy," Walt said. "He started off acting like nothing happened. But I've never seen a kid eat so much. So here you have one that's barely said a word, and the other, even with his mouth full, hasn't stopped talking except to swallow. You saw what happened as soon as you got in Doris' way, though. Zach is right on the edge, I'd say. A little time with us might be good for everyone's nerves."

Daniel gathered a ball of spit from his tongue and used it to extinguish the last millimeters of embers. "They'll be fine after a good night's sleep. At home. Kids bounce right back," he said, tasting his own father's words in his mouth, bitter but true.

"Well," said Walt. "You've always been one to act on what you think."

Daniel found Marie's hidden key under a flowerpot in the backyard and sent Zach to his room to get ready for bed. He kept Lizzy in the living room and sat down next to her on the couch.

For a minute, Lizzy kept herself apart, until Daniel, still feeling the calm of Walt's cigarette, wrapped his arm around his daughter and sighed. He had almost forgotten how good it felt good to hold her. It wasn't something he did very often, anymore. Men got into trouble that way, with women and girls mistaking warmth for something else. Even now, he felt Lizzy stiffen under the weight of his arm.

Lizzy pulled away and slid herself against the arm of the couch, separating them by an entire seat cushion. "You said she'd gone to the shore. You were driving like a maniac. Mom was scared. We all were. And why? Just because Mom likes to sing, and I don't want to live in a cult?"

"That's enough, Lizzy," Daniel said, grabbing Lizzy's wrist and feeling it crackle in his hand.

"Go ahead. You almost killed Mom already. You might as well break my hand, too."

Daniel took a long, slow breath and let go of Lizzy. "I would never hurt you."

"I could have drowned along with Mom."

"I didn't mean for you to go down there."

"No, you just meant for Mom to stay where you left her." Lizzy started to cry. Not the hiccuping tears of a girl, but furious sobs that wracked at her shoulders.

"Stop that," Daniel said.

I'll give you something to cry about. His father's voice, clear as if he had climbed out of his grave and hissed in Daniel's ear.

"Stop what? Having feelings about Mom almost dying?"

"Zach is going to hear you. Lizzy, I was only thinking about you and your brother. Getting you to safety. That's all, and that's what Mom would've wanted. And if you go and tell her what you've been thinking, these lies you've been making up for yourself, with her injuries the way they are, you'll only end up hurting her recovery. So, I'll make you a deal. Unless you give me a reason to take it back, we'll stay here in Kelowna for as long as we can. But I'll need you to help me take care of your mother. Do we have an agreement?"

BANANA SANDWICHES

    4 slices whole wheat bread
    2 ripe bananas, peeled and sliced
    1 large tomato, sliced
    ½ cup Miracle Whip
    Salt, pepper

Preheat oven or toaster oven to the broiler. Spread bread slices with half of the Miracle Whip and arrange on a baking sheet. Top with tomato slices. Toss bananas in remaining Miracle Whip and arrange on top of tomatoes. Sprinkle with salt and pepper. Place under broiler until Miracle Whip bubbles and starts to become golden and caramelized.

CHOW

Black was the way Lizzy's father preferred his toast. *Toast should be black because that's where the flavour is.*

To Lizzy, the smell of burning bread, and the occasional smoke alarm, had been her weekday wake-up call for as far back as she had memories. It meant her mother was in the kitchen and her father wasn't yet home from work. And it meant that even if everything wasn't always right with the world, everything was at least in its place.

Over the last few days, however, with Marie still in the hospital, Lizzy had inherited most of the things her mother did for the family. To be honest, she welcomed an excuse to get out of bed early. Since the accident, she had been having bad dreams.

This morning, with her father's toast proverb repeating in her mind, Lizzy gathered up three almost-empty bread bags from the fridge and shook assorted heels, dotted with little blue-green colonies, onto a baking tray. With her microscope at the bottom of the lake, they weren't much to look at, but they also weren't anything that couldn't be scorched away or covered up with a little jam.

"Don't take this the wrong way, but I'll help with the cooking," Zach had offered the other night, when he'd found his sister making a list of chores that began to spill onto a second page. "But not breakfast. I don't burn food on purpose."

Lizzy spun the oven dial to broil and slid the tray under the element. She left the door ajar, crouched in front, and within minutes, a hot, dry breath spilled from inside and crackled against Lizzy's face as she kept watch over the bread, ready to pinch out embers with a pair of tongs.

Zach was the first to join her. Daniel, who still hadn't returned to work, had yet to make a noise.

"Is Dad awake?" Lizzy said, and Zach nodded. He was carrying an old bear of hers that he'd rescued from its banishment to the basement in a black plastic bag of other childish things. "What's Hermione doing up here?"

The bear, with its nubbly brown fur, saggy bum and deeply scuffed hard plastic eyes, had hardly an original stitch left after being loved right down to her stuffing and sewn up so many times. In fact, by the time Lizzy had turned six, she had begun to perform the surgeries herself. Hermione had become her partner in crime after she transplanted a velcro pouch into the bear's abdomen and used it to hide things from her father. Tiny library books or a pair of clip-on earrings. She still had the curved needles she had used for making the mattress sutures she had perfected by the time she was nine. The same kind the doctor had used to stitch up her leg.

So when, still crouched in front of the oven, Lizzy noticed a small seep of blood begin to soak through the front of her nightgown, just over her right thigh, she knew what to do.

"Get out the jam, okay?" Lizzy said to Zach, setting the toast on the stovetop and gathering up the soiled patch of fabric into her fist.

Passing her father in the hallway, Lizzy slipped into the bathroom and closed the door. Under the sink was a first aid kit, and with that, she sat on the edge of the tub and swung her feet inside. From the kit, she took out a bottle of iodine. They had hand sanitizer, too, but iodine was the only disinfectant her father trusted against open sores and wounds, including the canker sores Lizzy often got inside her mouth.

Lizzy carefully peeled back her nightgown and stripped away the bandages from the hospital, discovering a pair of popped stitches. She dripped iodine from the bottle into its cap and, biting down on the meat of her thumb, carefully dribbled it into the jagged snag of angry flesh. She dipped a curved needle into the same bottle, dangling it from a length of thread, then began to feed the needle through her own skin, tying one two-hand square knot, followed by another. When finished, she covered the area with fresh gauze and tape, and blew her nose, gooey with snot and tears. She rinsed the tub and scrubbed the blood from her pajamas under cold water, like every girl knew to do, then wrapped up her used dressings in a sheet of newspaper, kept in a basket next to the toilet for the disposal of menstrual pads. Thankfully, she thought, this would llook enough like that that her father wouldn't unwrap it to check.

Lizzy hurried to her room to dress for the day. When she returned to the kitchen, her father was sitting across from Zach at the table, waiting. The toast was cold and neither of them was speaking.

"I need your bank card today," Lizzy said, stacking toast onto a plate and taking it to the table. "I told you to get the jam, Zach." She nudged her brother, who tried to hide the bear under his armpit. "I can heat these up again, Dad."

Zach fetched a jar of strawberry jam from the fridge, one of two dozen he had helped their mother fill in the summer, after a day spent picking in the field on KLO Road. Lizzy had been there, too, doing homework at a picnic table. And again later in the kitchen, as they rendered the berries down along with a waterfall of white sugar poured into the pot from a paper bag.

"This is the last of the bread. So I'll need to shop today," Lizzy said. "And Mom will need some things before she comes home, too. Is the hospital letting her go soon?"

Daniel reached for his wallet and tossed his bank card onto the table between them. "Your mother will be home when she's home," he said and took his toast to go. "I have to drop by the home today. Apparently, they expect me to start back on Monday."

When the front door clicked, Lizzy put a pot on the stove and took a box of Cream of Wheat down from the cupboard. "There's brown sugar behind Mom's diet chews," she said. Cream of Wheat, according to Lizzy's mother, was Sunday food, which probably dated to when Marie was still Mennonite and didn't know about going to church on the Sabbath. Today was Thursday, but once the cereal was cooked, Lizzy and Zach sweetened their breakfast and ate. They washed and dried the evidence and returned it to the cupboard, and Lizzy pushed the remaining toast down to the bottom of the garbage, where she covered it with two handfuls of wet eggshells from the night before.

"What about school today?" Zach asked. They had already missed Monday and Tuesday but had gone yesterday afternoon.

Lizzy lifted her shoulders and let them drop. She'd already had to cancel this week's shifts at the butcher shop.

"I need to stay home and clean. Dad left me a list. But you should go. I'll do my chores and maybe I can make it for classes tomorrow."

"You could come this afternoon."

"No. I have to go to the store."

"I mostly just have gym and Bible class after lunch. I'll come back and go with you to make sure you get actual food."

Lizzy knew her brother was supposed to be in math after lunch. But the idea of a long walk to the store on her own was enough to make her pretend she believed him.

For the next three hours, Lizzy vacuumed and mopped the floors. She cleaned along the baseboards with an old toothbrush dipped in vinegar, dusted furniture with a wet cloth followed by a dry one and washed all of the laundry in the bathroom hamper.

By the time Zach returned, she was sticky with sweat and she'd popped another stitch.

"You need a shower," Zach said, making a face.

"When we get back."

Before the two of them left, Lizzy went to her room and fetched her library card from her underwear drawer and tucked it into her back pocket, along with her father's bank card. She also took five dollars in loonies and toonies from a Mason jar she kept hidden under a camouflage of socks and bras.

For the most part, the coins were ones that Lizzy had palmed from a bowl her father kept by the front door, where he emptied the contents of his pockets each morning after work. She never took more than a single coin at a time, often just a quarter, but it was enough that every few months they would accumulate into a full jar of change. In the case of Lizzy's current jar, it was nearly time to seal and put it up with ones hidden away in her secret pantry beneath the basement stairs.

"Here," Lizzy said when she and Zach were halfway down the street. She held out the coins and dropped them into her brother's mittened palm. The corners of his mouth twitched toward a smile— the first she'd seen since the Wroblewskis'.

By the time they reached the strip mall with its Cooper's grocery store on one end and the library in the middle, both Lizzy and Zach were covering their ears with their hands to keep out the cold. The store's automatic doors opened and a blast of warm air that smelled of cinnamon buns invited them inside.

"Mask," Lizzy said and pulled two new surgical ones from a box she'd taken from the hospital.

"Maybe we should bake something," Zach ventured, picking up a plastic shopping basket for himself and another for Lizzy to carry. "Mom deserves to have something nice to eat when she comes home."

"Whenever that might be."

Beyond bread for toast, and the ingredients for a buttermilk bran muffin recipe Zach knew by heart, Lizzy didn't know what else to buy.

"Do we want a watermelon?" she said when they reached the produce section.

"It's October. They'll taste like cucumbers, and we have to carry everything home," Zach said, handing her a bunch of bananas instead. "Look them over for tarantulas so you can tell Mom."

Lizzy checked between each yellow arm and declared them spider free. "People in the hospital eat Jell-O," she said when they entered the pudding aisle.

"They don't carry the vegetarian kind here. We'd have to wait for the ABC truck to come back through town."

Lizzy selected a box of cherry flavour and another of orange anyway. "I'll make it when Dad's not home. Mom doesn't care about pig knuckles," Lizzy said, making a mental note to lose the grocery receipt on the way home.

By the time they were finished, Zach had also gathered up two boxes of dry spaghetti, a carton of brown-shelled eggs, an onion and a bottle of soy sauce—they already had Veja-Links in the pantry, he said—for the "chow" he planned to make for supper that night. Lizzy, meanwhile, chose powdered doughnuts, ginger ale and two Twix bars—items Marie snuck home for Lizzy whenever she was sick and home from school.

At the library, Lizzy accepted a small stack of books she had put on hold for pickup the day before, wishing she could go in. With the books in a plastic grocery bag of their own, she and Zach walked back down the hill and turned onto Hollywood Road, a busy enough street that intersected the two major arteries through the city, draining traffic from one to the other. Halfway home, without a word, they slipped into a corner store, setting off a jangle of cow bells overhead.

"Plain or French Vanilla?" Lizzy said, handing her brother a paper coffee cup and keeping one for herself.

"Vanilla," Zach said. He took the cup and filled it with hot chocolate, leaving room for a splash of real cream. Lizzy filled her cup in threes: French Vanilla, syrupy coffee from the bottom of a neglected pot, and the last of the cream. In this way, one cup at a time, Lizzy had been teaching her brother the art of keeping secrets.

Lizzy and Zach sipped their drinks as they walked along the shoulder toward home, past the public school where kids in masks would be doing their best to sit six feet apart. Passing vehicles hugged close to the centre line as they approached Lizzy and Zach, giving them the safety of a little extra space. So when Lizzy heard the crunch of tires on gravel behind them, she knew before she looked. Falling half a step behind, she saw Zach scramble for somewhere to hide his cup.

"Just let him see it," Lizzy said as she joined him to face a taxi that had come to a stop on the side of the road. "You know it's worse if he thinks we're trying to hide."

Lizzy lifted her gaze until she saw her father through the windshield, mask under his nose. Daniel glared back, but didn't open the door, didn't move or even nod. He simply stared into her with the intensity of a bone saw. Then, when he seemed satisfied, he flicked his hand for the driver to move along.

"He's really mad, isn't he?" Zach said as the taxi signalled left. He held out his share of the shopping bags. "He could at least have taken these."

Lizzy was still watching the cab, and before it disappeared down Lacey, saw that someone else was in the back seat. "Was that Mom?"

Lizzy should have left the Jell-O and chocolate bars on the side of the road, but in her hurry to get home, she forgot what she was carrying. Even the receipt was still there when they rounded the house to enter through the backdoor by the kitchen. Zach set down his bags.

"I can still make it to gym class," he said, although Lizzy was sure he only went as far as the side of the house.

Lizzy, with the other half of the groceries and her bag full of library books, walked up to the door.

Minutes passed, and before Lizzy could find the courage to go in, her father came out. He pulled a plastic chair toward her and sat down, dragging another alongside for Lizzy.

For a while, the two of them sat and looked at each other, Daniel staring and Lizzy trying not to blink. It was a test. It was always a test. Dry eyes, her father believed, were a sign of guilt.

"How's Mom?" Lizzy finally said.

At the sound of her voice, her father seemed to deflate as though pricked. He shrugged, a small, jerky motion that looked more like a nervous twitch than a sign of uncertainty.

"She says she's in too much pain to be at home." He paused to swallow. "But her doctor says there's nothing more they can give her. I tried to tell her she just needs to have a better attitude and let the tissues heal. I see it in the nursing home, you know. If they let their minds go, then . . ."

Lizzy didn't have to ask what happened next. "Is she in bed?"

"I couldn't listen to her talk like that. I put a chair in our room. You go see what she needs."

Lizzy moved to get up, but Daniel reached for her wrist. "Just sit another minute. We hardly ever get to do this."

Lizzy lowered herself back into the plastic chair, but her father seemed to have nothing more to say. Not even about the Jell-O boxes that had slipped out of their bag.

Not knowing what else to do, Lizzy reached down and crumbled a few leaves of crispy basil from a pot on the ground. The plant had died in the cold, but the leaves still smelled of summer as they broke apart in her hand. Next to the pot was a mug from inside the house. Lizzy picked it up, and even over the scent of basil came another—the roasted chicory from her mother's last cup of Caf-Lib, left out from before their visit to Stillwater.

Lizzy was about to slosh the contents onto the grass. Before she could, though, she noticed a sudden flutter inside the mug. There, caught in the surface tension of the liquid, unable to gain a foothold on the smooth ceramic, was a moth, beating one dry wing against the glaze. She paused, knowing it would be pointless to help. The moth would never fly again after losing so many of its flight scales, which lay dusted like glitter across the dark brown surface of the liquid.

Still. Lizzy leaned toward the edge of the lawn and carefully poured out the Caf-Lib, and the moth along with it. Feeling her father's eyes on her, she used a corner of the mask she'd shoved into her pocket to keep from further injuring the insect as she coaxed it upright, until it was standing on its own. She didn't wait for anything like a miracle, though. Nature, as it always did, would take its course.

"When Zach comes back, tell him to put on a pot of soup for Mom," Daniel said as he looked, now, through Lizzy's shopping bags, separating the sweets from the rest. "You can ask Mrs. Wroblewski whether she has any agar agar you can use." He kept the Jell-O but handed back the rest. "Just this once. Because you did a good job in the house."

Lizzy fetched Zach from the side of the house and and together they left their father outside. With Zach at the stove, stirring a pot of soup, Lizzy set the temperature of the oven to 150°F, and the timer for an hour before she arranged her library books on the baking tray she'd earlier used for toast. Her dad had let her get away with *Are You There, God, It's Me, Margaret,* a title Lizzy returned to whenever something was wrong. Even now that she was too old.

She'd had her own copy once, up until her father had thrown it out. Maybe he hadn't noticed it today, among her other choices, which included *The Anatomy and Mechanics of the Human Hand,* and *Fundamentals of Hand Therapy.*

After setting the books in the oven to sterilize, Lizzy washed her hands and selected a blue bowl for her mother's soup, adding a straw instead of a spoon. Although they hadn't been allowed to visit Marie in the hospital, the look on her father's face outside just now had told her much of what she needed to know.

Zach poured the soup—vegetables and stars—into the bowl, and Lizzy set it on a hot pad. She was about to take it to the bedroom when Daniel came inside. He placed one hand around hers on the outside of the bowl and leaned close to whisper.

"Just remember," he said. "You'll only hurt her more if you tell her."

With that, he let go and a slosh of hot soup spilled onto Lizzy's skin.

Because her father worked nights and slept during the day, Lizzy's parents' bedroom was kept dark by sheets of aluminum foil taped over the window. No lamp was on, and it took a moment for Lizzy's eyes to adjust. When they did, she found her mother sitting on a kitchen chair.

"Mom," Lizzy said. "I brought you soup. Zach made it. Well, he heated it up. He didn't have time for scratch, so it's from a can. It has some noodles." She set the bowl on the nightstand and licked onion-and-celery-tasting broth from her skin as she made her way to the window, where she peeled back a corner of foil. Her mother had always preferred natural light to a lamp.

Coming back round the bed, Lizzy saw, for the first time, the pins and wires holding together her mother's bones.

"I . . ." Lizzy said, startled at first. She could still feel the meat and bone of that moment in the water, like the refrigerated animal parts she worked with at the shop. "How long have you been sitting here?" Lizzy asked, trying to guess how long it had been since the taxi.

Marie was slow to answer. "A while," she finally said, raising her arms a few centimeters before lowering them back down to hover just above her lap.

Not knowing what else to do, Lizzy held up the bowl of soup and guided the straw to her mother's mouth for a sip.

Marie stared in Lizzy's direction for a few moments before her eyes seemed to focus.

"*Dankscheen*," Marie said, speaking the Plautdietsch that Lizzy wasn't supposed to understand. Her father, with his High German, had never wanted the three of them to have a secret language. Nor had he been willing to learn.

Marie looked pale, and Lizzy touched her mother's forehead with the back of her hand. "*Feehls dü die schlajcht?*"

"No, not sick. I just need to lie down."

Lizzy helped her mother stand and pulled back the top comforter. "*Dankscheen*," Marie said again.

ZACH'S CHOW

    1 pound spaghetti, cooked
    1 pound frozen shoestring French fries, baked
    ½ small onion
    4 large eggs, scrambled
    1 can Veja-Links, drained, halved lengthwise and then sliced
    ½ tsp garlic powder
    Soy sauce
    Salt/pepper

In a large wok over medium-high heat, toss together first 6 ingredients until hot. Season to taste with soy sauce, salt and pepper.

DEVILLED HAM

"Lizzy!" Marie called, sitting up in bed. It was three o'clock in the morning and Daniel was at work. The sleeping pills had helped carry her this far, but she wouldn't be able to make it another hour.

Lizzy arrived in the doorway, half asleep. "What do you need, Mom?"

"I'm cold," Marie said, but in fact her nightgown was slick with sweat, and the whole room felt hot and damp.

"Those blue pills you gave me taste like dirty pennies."

"I can throw them out. Dad wouldn't want you to have them, anyway. The pain medicine should be enough to help you sleep. It's dangerous to take the sleeping pills with them."

"You sound like your dad. Dr. Vickers prescribed these. He says they're the best thing for women who've had a difficult time. And he's from the church, so he knows what he's talking about."

Dr. Vickers was their family's GP, when Daniel would let them go. "Can't take the morphine drip with you, I'm afraid," Dr. Vickers had said when he'd come to make his final rounds. Without the drip, what relief there was failed to stretch to the edges of a full six hours that was supposed to be eight.

"Dr. Vickers prescribes a lot. The pharmacist kind of freaked out when I went to pick everything up."

"Your father thinks I'm just supposed to pray. So who am I supposed to believe?"

"I know Dad has his own ideas. But Dr. Vickers is a a loon,

Mom. Can't we just do what the surgeon wrote down? Pain meds for a little longer, but not the sleeping pills or muscle relaxer?"

"Is it time for my Dilaudid?"

"That's so much stronger than codeine, Mom. It's hydromorphone. A hundred times stronger than morphine."

"Good," Marie said, pain cracking its way through her bones. Her fingers began to curl against the pins holding them in place, and in response, the sutured skin suddenly felt struck by a match.

"Lizzy!" Marie cried out, and moments later her daughter returned from her room, a cosmetics bag held tight in both hands.

"You should really wait another hour or two. I'll sit up with you."

"Please," Marie said, hot, desperate tears slipping from her eyes. Finally, Lizzy knelt beside the bed, withdrew a single white tablet and held it out like an offering.

Marie bent forward a little and pressed the tip of her tongue to the palm of her daughter's hand. She bit the tablet once, twice—she wasn't supposed to—and swallowed without water.

Half an hour passed before the medication began to erode the edges of Marie's pain. "I think I can sleep now," she said. "But maybe don't go." And Lizzy, who had half stood to leave, crawled into her father's side of the bed.

When Marie woke again, the taste on her tongue had softened a little and a cereal bowl sat on her nightstand with a plastic picnic spoon—all Marie could manage on her own—sunk into what had become a cold porridge of bloated Os.

"You didn't eat with the kids."

Marie jumped inside her skin.

"You didn't eat with the kids?" Daniel said again, and this time it was a question.

Marie hadn't seen him there at first, next to the dresser, on the chair from the kitchen.

"I . . ." she said, Marie checked the clock behind the bowl. 9:00 am, it said, seeming to shine a spotlight on another white tablet. Lizzy must have gone to school today.

"How are you doing? Do you need an Advil? You haven't been wanting anything stronger, have you?" Daniel said, and Marie resisted the urge to look again at the bright white tablet.

"An Advil would be nice." When Daniel went to fetch it, Marie gently touched a fingertip to her tongue and dabbed up the pill. Her mouth was dry, and she had to tip a spoonful of cereal milk onto her tongue to make it go down.

"Good for you," Daniel said after offering a single pill and a sip of water he brought from the kitchen. By the expectant look that followed, Marie knew he wanted the bed to himself.

"How was work last night?" Marie stalled, but even before she could give him the room, he went round to his side of the bed, rolled himself in and started to snore.

In the kitchen, evidence of Lizzy and Zach's morning lay scattered: shoes by the back door, a few blackened toast crumbs across the countertop, a forgotten math textbook—Zach's, of course. And Marie's recipe box, part of Lizzy's home economics project. Her homework had been saved from the lake by a bit of grace and the Ziploc sandwich bag stuffed in the pocket of her hoodie.

The recipe box was an encyclopedia of Mennonite dishes, each written in the hand of Marie's mother, an aunt or her grandmother in the traditional, Mennonite way—*enough flour to make a soft dough, a dessert spoon of baking powder, a cup* (which could be either a teacup or a water tumbler) *of sugar*. With no proper measurements, you had to have grown up Mennonite to understand them.

Marie had added cards with Seventh-day Adventist dishes, and she hoped those were the ones Lizzy had continued to collect for school.

Today, Lizzy had left an old card sticking out from between the others, and Marie twisted her neck to see what her daughter had chosen. It was one of Marie's favourites, and Lizzy had added her own pencil mark in the margin. *Luke Chapter 8, verse 33.*

It took a minute, but when the scripture came to mind, a laugh scratched its way past the dryness of Marie's throat. *When the demons came out of the man, they went into the pigs.* She used her elbow to tuck Devilled Ham back among the other cards, hoping Lizzy hadn't copied that one, though she wouldn't put it past her. The look on Mrs. Tilley's face would probably be enough to make Lizzy's entire week.

Alone in the house, except for her sleeping husband, Marie sat at the kitchen table. She was still tired. Exhausted. And the Dilaudid no longer seemed to help the way it had in its first few days.

Friday, Saturday, Sunday, Marie began to count out on her broken fingers. A few days ago, Lizzy had said most of her pills would run out soon. But how soon was soon?

Monday, Tuesday, Wednesday . . . She lost track.

Lizzy should've . . . She stopped herself. Lizzy probably didn't know how these things even worked. Daniel had only rarely allowed Marie to take the kids to the doctor and didn't even like antibiotics for a case of strep, preferring sliced onions plastered to the soles of their feet to draw out toxins. And lately, deworming paste for horses, purchased from a church member who owned a ranch.

Marie would have to find a way to see Dr. Vickers. Today. She regretted not having thought of it sooner, and not keeping Lizzy home from school. Lizzy, after all, could dial the taxi. Lizzy could keep her company. She could help her know what to say when they got to the clinic. And then . . .

Listening down the hallway for a continuing snore, Marie looked at the family's phone. Ancient, green and anchored to the wall, it was nothing like the cordless kind in everyone else's homes, phones that allowed a person to go into any room they'd like and close the door. Or the smartphones everyone carried with them. Theirs was a toad squatting on this narrow table, along with a fat old phone book and a jar of pens and pencils. For all the times Marie had hinted to Daniel about something more up to date, she wondered whether the point of this one was to make sure no one in the house could ever have a private conversation.

Now, though, there was no way Marie could even turn the dial. Instead, she made her way to the front door and slipped her feet into a pair of boots. Using her elbows, she twisted the lock and then the doorknob, and let herself out of the house. The Wroblewskis were just a few doors down. At this time of day, with people at work and kids at school, hardly anyone would see her in her pajamas.

"Marie," Doris said. "Come in, come in. It's cold. I was just on my way out the door to see you, dear."

Marie stepped inside and smelled the warmth of one of Doris' casseroles. "I need you to drive me," she said.

"Of course. I'll just put these in the fridge, and we can warm you up with a bit of something first," Doris said, sweeping her way into the kitchen with two dishes of her Special K Roast, one stacked sideways on top of the other. "I made these for you. Zach will know what to do with them."

Marie accepted a seat at Doris' table and a blanket from her couch.

"Saw a peculiar thing the other day," Doris continued, putting a kettle on the stove. She fetched a packet of English biscuits from her cupboard and set them on the table. "I wasn't sure whether to bring it up, but did Lizzy go and get herself a job? She'd been talking about wanting one, but I didn't know if maybe her father wouldn't like it."

Marie opened her mouth and closed it. The bitter taste was suddenly back. "I don't think so."

"Well, I thought I saw her in the butcher shop. You know, the one next to the produce market I like down at the end of Hollywood. I looked twice, but since there's nothing in there for our sort, I kept on my way. And before you ask, that was at noon two days ago. The day I brought the applesauce cake by."

Marie didn't remember an applesauce cake and wondered whether Daniel had thrown it out. He and Doris had never gotten along.

Taking down an economy-sized jar of instant coffee, Doris set it next to her biscuits and filled up a kettle. Moments before it could whistle, she plucked it from the stove and poured them each a mug of hot water, leaving the top third empty for a splash of real cream. She added a paper straw for Marie. "Now, where is it you need to go?"

Soon, Marie was dressed in clothes from a bag of donations. Doris collected them on behalf of the Adventist Disaster Relief Agency, and Marie, it seemed, was a disaster herself. She was grateful, though. The dress Doris picked out was still warm from the hot iron she had run over it.

"I'll come in and sit with you," Doris said, pushing her car door open and rocking herself twice for the momentum she needed to exit the vehicle, too small for her by half.

All the way here, Marie had rehearsed a response to that very offer. "The walk home will do me good," she said with conviction she did not feel. "You go on, I can manage."

"I can come back for you when you're done. I'll just get some groceries and turn right around." Doris came round to the passenger side, opened the door, and Marie accepted an arm to lean on.

"No, no. It's just a little checkup he wants to see me for. I'd nearly forgotten all about it. I'm sure he'll tell me fresh air is all I need." Another lie. Marie had no intention of walking home. She did intend to walk, just a block, to the pharmacy. She didn't need an audience for that. Doris should not have to keep her secrets. And what if she didn't approve?

"If you're sure," Doris said, looking anything but. "But let me help you with this." She fetched a fresh mask out of a Ziploc in her purse and slipped the loops around Marie's ears.

"I'm sure," Marie said, her voice muffled behind the paper.

At the clinic, a woman inside saw Marie through the glass and quickly got up to let her in.

"Thank you," Marie said and made her way up to reception. She stopped and bit her lips. "I don't have an appointment, but . . ." Up until then, she had not considered what she'd do if Terri, the practice manager, told her there was no room in the schedule and sent her away.

Terri looked up from a ream of paper on her desk. Like Dr. Vickers, Marie knew Terri from Sabbaths and potlucks and the annual Revelations Crusades at church.

"Marie! I heard what happened." Terri stood and leaned across the counter. She lowered her voice to a whisper. "It's as bad as it looks, isn't it?"

"I don't have an appointment," Marie said again.

Terri sat back down and pulled up the schedule. She pressed her lips together and shook her head. "Look. Don't tell the doctor that you're not on his calendar, and I'll put you in a room next."

When an older woman came out of an exam room a few minutes later, dressed in one of the silk saris Marie saw around town from time to time, Marie took her place and found herself enveloped in the woman's scent, earthy and full of spice. Marie closed her eyes and breathed deeply. She had always wanted to go to India, which was often featured on the Missions Wall of the Mennonite Brethren church back home, or on a series of slides presented by returning missionaries. Why, she wondered, would anyone from a place that brightly coloured want to come and live somewhere as cold and colourless as Canada?

When Dr. Vickers came in, Marie's head was bowed in

almost-sleep. It was the crinkle of exam table paper beneath her that finally caught her attention.

"Have you been back to see the surgeon?" he said, apparently for the second or third time.

Startled to find she hadn't been listening, Marie shook her head. She was supposed to make an appointment with her but hadn't yet.

Dr. Vickers rolled up in front of her on his stool and held out his hands, palms up, into which Marie cautiously lowered her own. He looked them over with only the lightest of touches, then patted her on the knee.

"Well, it looks to me like everything's healing up nicely," he said. "No infections there, but you'll need further X-rays to make sure things are knitting properly on the inside. You're still having pain, I suppose?"

Marie swallowed hard, and her chin began to quiver.

"It still hurts. All the time. And not like anything I could ever have imagined."

"I see. Is it any better than when you left the hospital?"

Marie mouthed the word "no," unable to give it sound.

"Worse?"

Marie shrugged, uncertain. "I don't know if it's worse," she managed to whisper. "But who can cope with it all the time?"

"I see," said Dr. Vickers, looking over her file. "Well, we should add some fentanyl, then, shouldn't we, if you're okay with that? We can try for a month. Sometimes all it takes is to give the brain a rest from thinking about what hurts, and when it's done that, there's no more need." He pulled a pen from his shirt pocket and took out a pad from a locked drawer.

Marie didn't recognize the name but nodded in agreement. She wanted whatever it was.

"We can do this one with a little sticker that goes on your belly. The medicine passes right through your skin so it's with you all the time, more like the drip from the hospital, except that was only morphine. This is like the Dilaudid. Much stronger." He rolled back toward Marie a little and seemed to survey the available flesh. "If it's as bad as you say, we'll keep up with the Dilaudid tablets for now, too. How are your moods these days? Sad? Anxious? And are you sleeping?"

When Marie left the exam room, it was with a small sheaf of papers pinched between her wrists. Seeing her, Terri quickly came over to help, sucking air through her teeth as she scanned the various scripts.

"Go straight to the IDA with these, and then right home. The ones for pain aren't all that easy to replace if they go missing, and Marie, there are people who'd knock you over to get them. Some of these other ones, too. Ativan. That's like Valium. Is someone waiting for you outside?"

Marie nodded—another lie—and the same woman who'd opened the front door for her earlier opened it again to let her out.

Outside, the air smelled bland after the spice of the exam room. There was rain on the horizon, still some ways off, in clouds that hung low over the rounded tops of the mountains. Marie couldn't tell, but with any luck, they were headed in another direction.

Marie walked across the parking lot and down to the sidewalk along Highway 33. The IDA was only a block down, and four lanes of highway traffic across. There was a pedestrian crossing farther along, but that would double or triple the distance. Thinking of nothing but getting to the other side, Marie stepped off the curb.

At the same moment, she was snatched back onto the sidewalk. "What do you think you're doing, Mom?"

Startled, Marie turned to find Lizzy, who had shouted over over a wave of oncoming traffic.

"How did you get here?" Marie said, barely making the connection between herself and the cars and trucks that were already whizzing by.

At first, Lizzy didn't reply. "Mrs. W. She came to find me at . . . at work. It's just a few blocks but she drove me here so I could still catch up with you."

"It was just a little checkup," Marie said, dismissive, although she let Lizzy tug her a little farther back from the road. "What work? Doris said she thought she saw you."

"Mom, I can call a taxi. Or we can go inside and call Mrs. W. She said she'd wait by the phone."

"I need to—Dr. Vickers wants me to get a few things from the drugstore."

Lizzy's jaw stiffened for a moment and she bit her bottom lip. She was like her Aunt Toots that way, even though Lizzy couldn't possibly remember her. After all that happened back then, Daniel had decided, and Marie agreed, that it was best if the kids never knew.

"Okay. But this time follow me," Lizzy said, and the two of them, with Lizzy's arm looped through Marie's, hurried across the road, balancing for a few seconds on the centre median to let a small school of cars go by.

"Why don't you go look at the magazines? I'll bet there's something good to read over there," Marie said when they reached the store, and Lizzy pushed open the door. "Or meet me over at McDonald's. I'll join you when I'm done here."

Lizzy looked doubtful. "Don't you think I should be with you? I mean, if you have new stuff, I'm going to have to know what to do."

"Fine. But don't act like you're listening."

"All of these? At the same time?" said the pharmacist, after Lizzy helped fetch the slips of paper from inside Marie's purse. The woman sorted through them a few times. "Have you had all of these before?"

"The white pain ones. And the blue night ones," Marie said. "And the ones for my muscles."

"Okay," the pharmacist said, exhaling loudly. "We're not all that busy today, but I'll need half an hour at least," she said, checking her watch. "The safe won't open for another ten minutes, and I'll have to see if we have enough of your patches in there. And look, you should really think twice about taking the Zopiclone and Ativan with these. Any of these, actually."

Stepping away from the counter, Marie lowered herself onto the edge of a nearby blood pressure chair and waited for her name to be called. Her hands were crackling inside again. "Go pick out some chocolate bars," she said to Lizzy, nudging at her purse.

Lizzy waved it away. "I have money."

Marie's name was called while Lizzy was still wandering in the store.

"These stay on your skin for three days. Don't touch the glue part with your fingers, and if you do, wash up right away. After three days, put the used one down the toilet. I don't care what anyone says about medications ending up in the water supply. You don't want this getting away from you and someone stepping on it." She piled the boxes into a white paper bag, along with a handful of bottles whose contents she also described.

"I don't want to use insurance," Marie said, and without Lizzy nearby to help, slid her purse onto the counter. The pharmacist, clearly uncomfortable, found the money Marie told her was pinned behind a tear in the lining. Paid up, Marie was left with nothing but a toonie and a jumble of smaller change.

"All of these can compromise your immune system," the pharmacist said, just as Lizzy reappeared. "The Covid vaccines aren't approved yet, but I could give you a flu shot right now if you haven't had one."

"No, I don't think . . ." Marie said.

"Mom. You should. Please. Really, just please."

Outside, the smell of French fry oil drifted from the McDonald's across the parking lot. It had the whiff of being a little too used, but Marie didn't mind: a little rancid fat had never stopped her and Lizzy from sharing a large order, followed by an apple pie. Today, however, she wouldn't have enough cash. They'd have to walk home now, too. And at that thought, Marie began to droop.

"I spent everything I had on those prescriptions. I didn't want your dad finding out."

"It's okay, Mom. I'll pay. Let's go in."

"Are you sure?" Marie said, grateful when Lizzy linked arms and guided her across the lot and under the golden arches.

"I just need the washroom a bit," Marie said. And when Lizzy looked unconvinced, "I can do this by myself, at least. What do you think I do when you're at school all day? Or wherever it is you go."

Lizzy relented, and when Marie pushed her way into the bathroom, an automatic light switched on. She selected the farthest stall and worked up a lather of sweat before managing to lock herself inside, where she collapsed, fully clothed, onto the horseshoe-shaped seat of the toilet. She'd bunched her skirt into her lap to keep it from falling into and wicking up the water below. She needed to pee but cinched her bladder against the idea of getting out of the pantyhose Doris had helped over her legs and up her hips like sausage casings.

Marie closed her eyes and took a breath, expanding it into the sides of her ribs instead of the front of her chest. It was a trick she had learned a long time ago, to steady a sometimes-skipping heartbeat. It also served, if only a little, to clear her head. If she could manage to do this on her own, then Lizzy would stop judging her. After all, they were just simple stickers, right? She imagined them being like the coloured stars and smiley faces she used to put on the pages of children's piano music when she taught lessons back home in the village.

Marie used her teeth to rip her way past the staple that fastened the open end of the white paper pharmacy bag. A few minutes later, she slid a box of stickers into her lap and, using her teeth again, found she could open the flap. She didn't think she would actually find smiley faces in assorted colours inside, but her heart sank when, instead of stickers arranged on an easy-peel sheet, five little envelopes, tightly sealed around every edge, fluttered out. Three landed on the floor, but the ones that fell into her lap felt just as out of reach.

"Lizzy?" Marie said, at the sound of someone coming into the washroom.

"Sorry, no," replied a woman's voice. "Do you need me to get someone for you?"

Marie opened her mouth to speak. "There's a young girl by the PlayPlace. My daughter. Her name is Lizzy."

"Lizzy. Got it," said the woman. "I'll go get her. Mia, you go pee next to the nice lady, and mommy will be right back."

"Wait," Marie said as the bathroom door swung closed again. An upside-down, caramel-coloured face with a soft pouf of hair appeared under the gap in her stall. "Hi, honey, hi."

The girl smiled, then made a silly face by fanning her fingers out from her cheeks. That's when Marie saw it happen. Mia's fingers curled like petals into her palms and her hands fell away from her face. As the little girl reached for the nearest envelope, Marie put out her foot and covered the envelope with the toe of her shoe. Sweat trickled down the river of her spine as she did the same with her other foot. Just as Mia turned her attention to the remaining sticker, the bathroom door swung open, and Mia's mother returned with Lizzy.

"Mom?"

Marie doubled over and swept up all three stickers, heaping them onto her lap, surprised that she'd gotten her hands to do it. "I need some help," she said, wishing she had chosen the handicap stall on the end. She hadn't wanted to keep it from someone in need.

In the next stall over, Mia began to pee. A minute later, both mother and daughter were washed and gone, and Marie had forgotten to thank the woman for her help.

Lizzy, after rattling the door, got down on her belly and slithered under the gap.

"We need to make sure we have them all," Marie said, as another trickle of sweat snaked its way down her spine and into her waistband. It was just the stress, she told herself, and then, as Lizzy counted the envelopes against the information on the box, Marie repeated, as best she could, what the pharmacist had said.

"I'll be careful," Lizzy promised, tearing open one envelope and fishing out a flat square of plastic, clear except for the word "fentanyl" in green, along with a dose: "25mcg/hr."

Marie stood as Lizzy lifted the front of her dress, the hem of which she gently tucked into the band of Marie's bra.

Lizzy rolled down a bit of beige waist, as well, and touched her fingers to a section of Marie's belly. She wiped it dry of sweat with the sleeve of her shirt, pressed the sticker into place, and snugged the waistband back over top.

"We'll want to check on it, maybe put some medical tape over top to keep it stuck once the pantyhose are off," Lizzy said as she untucked Marie's dress and shook it back into place. "I think the sweating is a side-effect of the Dilaudid you've been taking. This might make it worse."

Marie began to sit back down, spent. Lizzy stopped her, but not before Marie's hem touched the water. As they left the bathroom, Marie could feel the cold wet tapping against the backs of her legs. She followed Lizzy to a table where one schoolbook was open to the middle of a chapter. Other books were stuffed into a pair of matching carpet bags Marie recognized from their basement. One of them was used to hold Marie's clothespins, and the other for single socks whose mates had gone missing. Marie couldn't remember Lizzy carrying them, but she must have.

Marie looked around them. Other mothers, younger and tired-looking, were there with their preschool children. The PlayPlace was closed, and notices outlined expectations that parents keep their children seated while they ate. She envied those women, overwhelmed as they looked. She'd been tired, too, when it had been her turn with little ones, but there was nothing like the feeling of a pair of little-girl arms wrapping themselves around you, the smell of fried apple pie on their breath. Every woman in the world deserved to have a daughter.

Lizzy went up to the counter before the new drug had any effect on Marie. She returned with a tray laden with cheeseburgers, fries and Cokes. Or were they milkshakes, maybe, to go with the apple pies?

Marie watched as Lizzy peeled back the papers from around their cheeseburgers and held one out for Marie to take a bite. She was halfway through a strawberry shake when she finally repeated her question from the sidewalk. "So, are you going to tell me about this job of yours?" she said, careful to not stare Lizzy down the way Daniel did whenever he wanted an answer. She was an honest girl and didn't need more than an opportunity to tell the truth. She took another bite and waited, while Lizzy slowly chewed the last of hers and swirled a French fry in a puddle of ketchup.

"It was Miss Taylor," Lizzy said. "Her brother, he's not SDA. He owns the place, and she thought I could earn some money for university and learn more about anatomy at the same time. She told me to ask you and Dad first, but Dad would never have . . ."

Miss Taylor was the academy's biology teacher. She was Lizzy's favourite, and Marie liked her too, but this—working where unclean meats were prepared—if anyone from the school came to know, would be another strike on an already long list of reasons half of the parents wanted the teacher dismissed.

"Look. They gave me this," Lizzy said as she pulled a package wrapped in butcher paper out of one of the carpet bags. She carefully tore the tape and rolled the package open to reveal a pair of chicken feet.

"We can't cook those at home," Marie said, looking over her shoulder for anyone they might know.

"They're not for cooking. I wanted to learn more about the tendons and ligaments in hands, and I borrowed books, but this is the closest I could get as an actual analog to dissect. You wouldn't believe how many similarities there are."

Marie smiled, despite herself. Although she had never had Lizzy's interest in science, she—though never Toots—had always joined her father on butchering day at the farm, each taking a severed pig's foot and tugging on its ligaments to make the trotter walk in mid-air.

The fentanyl was starting to erase the sensation at the edges of her suture lines and pins. At the same time, a flood of warmth rose upwards to her shoulders and into her head, until it felt both heavy and light. She liked the idea of Lizzy enjoying something she used to do when she was young. "Okay, but do that away from home," she said, closing her eyes and floating forward on a deep and easy breath. "You know how your father would react if he knew."

DEVILLED HAM

    2 pounds diced ham
    1 cup mayo
    1 ½ tbsps Dijon mustard
    ½ tsp hot sauce
    1 tsp Worcestershire sauce
    1 tbsp white vinegar

In a food processor, pulse diced ham until it is finely minced.

In a large bowl, combine the ham with mayo, mustard, hot sauce, Worcestershire and vinegar. Combine well and refrigerate for two hours or more. Serve as a dip with crackers, or as a sandwich filling.

SPECIAL K ROAST

By the beginning of December, Daniel was already on his last chance at work.

The initial warning, a first in his career, had come six months ago, after a wave of deaths, allegedly from the virus. "The government is thinning the herd," is all he had said.

Mrs. Beverly, the home's head nurse, had sat him down in her office. "You frightened Mrs. Tataryn half to death with that nonsense." The warning she put in his file hadn't amounted to much just then. After all, he had worked at Cotton Glenn for more than thirteen years, ever since he'd finished nursing school at the local college.

But Daniel could hardly be expected to keep quiet about the facts. Mr. Shellenberg, whose mind wandered in and out of dementia, was the next to believe. Followed by the family of a frail old duck who began to refuse her medicines.

"And just who do you suppose is the government's Angel of Death around here? Me?" Mrs. Beverly had demanded. "We're nurses. We help people."

"The drug companies must be testing their vaccines, or whatever they're cooking up, in the nursing homes. I'll bet Trudeau is letting them. And with all these people dying around the world, then the UN will have no trouble getting everyone to roll up their sleeves," Daniel had said.

Not long after, Daniel had made his first visit to Stillwater.

Everyone from the local Adventist churches knew about the commune. Admired their dedication, even. But few had the conviction to give up their worldly ways, place their whole faith in the message given to Ellen G. White, and join them there.

Today, with three of the practical nurses having tested positive, Daniel had been demoted to making sure the residents came down to breakfast. Those who could, anyway. The more than ordinarily infirm, or the just plain stubborn, had to have trays carried straight to their rooms.

"I have your breakfast, Mr. Schellenberg," Daniel called out as he knocked on a door at the very end of the hall, next to an alarmed exit that could only be accessed by use of a code.

"Mr. Schellenberg," Daniel repeated, and knocked again.

It was important to announce oneself. Not just for the residents, who might feel intruded upon. But because some of them seemed, truly, to have opened the doors to their minds and gotten the devil in them. In fact, Daniel thought as he waited for any indication that the old man had heard him, that might be God's honest truth: that as soon as a mind began to go, it made up a guest room and sent out an invitation.

"I'm coming in, then," Daniel said, and pushed open the door.

Mr. Schellenberg, once a respected deacon in the church, was sitting up in his bed, arm cocked behind his ear, hand loaded with a pile of shit, the rest of which was probably still in his pants.

"I knew it would be you," the old man said, narrowing his rheumy gaze. "You've come to inject me."

"Put that down," Daniel said, a taste rising into his mouth like mercury. He was still holding the breakfast tray, on which was balanced a pink plastic tumbler of apple juice and a bun stuffed with a scoop of scrambled tofu and a few uncrispy Stripples. "I won't warn you again, sir."

"You've come to experiment on me," said Mr. Schellenberg, his voice pitching toward hysterical. "I won't let you!"

"Sir," Daniel said. "I'm not the one who wants to do that. Now put your hand down and we'll get you cleaned up so you can have your—"

Even before Daniel could complete his sentence, he flipped the plastic meal tray on its side as a shield, allowing the food to fall to the floor. When the tray caught what had been flung toward it, Daniel threw it down, as well.

Mr. Schellenberg was reaching back into his pants.

In an instant, Daniel had the old man's wrist clenched tight in his hand, as the wet stench of cold excrement stole its way into his nose and mouth.

Mr. Schellenberg's fingers opened, and a loose putty of shit fell from his palm to the bed.

"Filthy old bastard," Daniel said under his breath. With his free hand, he snatched a lap blanket off the bed as Mr. Schellenberg began to whimper, using it to pick up the pile and drop it to the floor. As he did, he felt a sickening little snap within the circle of his grasp.

Mr. Schellenberg cried out once and collapsed back onto his pillow as a fellow nurse walked into the room.

"What's happening in here?" she said, rushing to the bed when she saw for herself.

"He did it again," Daniel said, holding up Mr. Schellenberg's soiled hand as evidence. Ella, he knew, had also been the target of more than one of the old man's attacks.

"But why is he—?" Quickly, she pressed her fingers against the side of Mr. Schellenberg's neck and seemed relieved by what she found.

"I didn't kill him," Daniel said, then whispered, "But I wouldn't put it past him to pretend."

Ella's eyes widened. "Okay. I see. Why don't you go get yourself cleaned up then, and I'll take care of Mr. Schellenberg." Softly, she placed her hand over the one Daniel still had wrapped around the old man's wrist. She began to peel away his fingers, and Daniel, responding to the warmth and softness, relaxed his grip and let go.

That's when they both saw it: a ring of bruises encircling Mr. Schellenberg's wrist that were already ripening into plum-coloured stains.

"It's okay," Ella said. "Go on." And Daniel did. He went out and down the hallway until he reached the men's change room, which he shared with a roster of orderlies and a couple of cooks. He opened the door with his clean hand and pushed it closed behind him. Past a small bank of lockers, he made his way to the washroom, turned the faucet to hot, and began to cleanse the stinking muck from his skin. He washed. Once. Twice. And, still feeling unclean, washed again, the water growing hotter until his hands were raw and beginning to swell.

Steam obscured the mirror in front of Daniel as he turned off the water and reached for a paper towel. While he dried his hands, the fog began to fade, revealing brown flecks on his scrubs where his breakfast tray shield had failed to protect him. Shit was on his collar; it was on his sleeve as well. And when he turned his head, he found that a smear had transferred onto his mask and neck, left there by the struggle to pin the old man's hand to his bed.

"Disgusting," Daniel said, dipping a length of paper towel into a fresh stream of hot water. He loaded it with antiseptic soap and scrubbed until he, too, was purple and bruised.

"Lord, if I ever get like that, I'd rather go in the ground and wait for you to find me on Judgement Day," he said. He slipped off his mask, reached for a pair of scissors in a jar of combs by the sink and, instead of lifting his scrubs over his head, slit them from waist to neck and let them drop to the floor.

"Daniel, I need to talk to you." It was Mrs. Beverly. No doubt she had already been to see Mr. Schellenberg and found him docile. That's the way it happened with these folks. Always the innocent ones. Never the problem.

Daniel went to his locker and slipped into fresh scrubs.

"There's no one in here but me. You can come in," Daniel said, loud enough to be heard through the door.

"Daniel," said Mrs. Beverly, letting herself in. "Why don't we sit?"

Daniel accepted her offer and the two of them took a seat on a wooden bench in front of the lockers.

"You know I like you. You're a good nurse. And we need all the nurses we can get right now. But Mr. Schellenberg will have to go to the hospital for an x-ray. Do you understand how complicated that is these days? Tell me what happened."

Daniel told it exactly the way it had been. "Their bones snap at anything. You know that. I barely touched him."

Mrs. Beverly crossed her arms lightly under her chest. "We can't afford to lose any staff. But Daniel, now that a vaccine has been approved, we'll be requiring all our staff to get it. We can't go on risking our patients unnecessarily."

"You know those are time bombs," Daniel said. "It's all about population control."

"What are you talking about, Daniel? We're nurses. We know better than that."

"They're going have you spreading super-strains to everyone who doesn't comply. And you don't know what will happen to you in a few years. Your DNA—"

"Stop it, Daniel. The vaccine has been tested."

Daniel clenched and unclenched his hands. Marie used to argue like this when they were first married. Until she took some ladies' studies at the church and learned to stay in her place. "So they say."

"*They*, Daniel? You didn't used to be like this. What's happened to you?"

Daniel felt a twitch in his shoulder. "Damn it, woman. Doesn't your husband teach you anything? It's Revelations. The Mark of the Beast. They're going to force us to choose allegiance to God or the State. You get that vaccine, and you've made your choice."

"That's enough. I'm suspending you for a week for what you did to Mr. Schellenberg. I expect you to take this time and put some thought into whether this is really the road you want to go down. When you come back, I'll arrange for your vaccination. Interior Health wants everyone working in long-term care done by the end of the year."

Daniel tightened his fist. The woman deserved it, but he aimed at the door of his locker instead. "Then I guess I won't be coming back."

Outside, Daniel intended to take the Black Mountain-to-Rutland bus home from work, as he had done since the night of the accident. But when he reached for the change he'd scooped up last night, along with his keys and a button still attached to a length of thread, he came up short.

Lizzy, he thought. For at least six months, now, he had been pretending not to notice that his pockets were lighter when he filled them at night than when he emptied them in the morning. He should have put a stop to it right away but, to be honest, it had amused him to guess what the money might be for. Now that her microscope had gone to the bottom of the lake, she might want another of those. Or maybe the money was for university, if he decided to let her go.

He should replace the microscope for her, he thought. In fact, that's what he'd do. He would stop by the library and use one of their computers to find a used one online. He didn't like to give out his banking information that way, but really, what did it matter when everything about a person was kept in a cloud, anyway? Although hadn't he heard that even the libraries were closed now, too?

The bus came, and Daniel held out just over a dollar in change. Not enough and no exceptions.

"Nice day for a walk," the driver said as he closed the door, leaving Daniel standing on the shoulder of the road.

Daniel muttered a curse under his breath, in German—High German, not that unintelligible nonsense Marie had wanted to teach the kids. Cursing in his father's language was different, somehow, than swearing in the English God's Angel had spoken to Ellen G. White. *"Deine Mutter schwitzt beim Kachen,"* Daniel added, this time hearing an echo of his father's voice, growling beneath his own. *Your mother sweats when she shits.*

Startled at himself, he decided to use the walk home to pray. "Thank you for this opportunity," Daniel said, looking one way but not the other before he crossed the highway. By the time he reached the other side, he had decided that the long wind down Black Mountain into Rutland was a blessing. After all, he hated the mix of people who rode on public buses. Their variously washed bodies. The masks they smugly wore.

"Thank you for these orchards," Daniel said, walking by an orchard that was barren, now, except for a few wizened apples that still clung to the odd branch. "And for surrounding me with the beauty of your creation." He drew in a long breath of sour-sweet fragrance, of apples fermenting on the ground. A moment later, though, his gratitude was punctured by the furious rumble of an engine, followed by a stink of hot resin from the brakes of a semi roaring down the hill.

"Scheisse," Daniel said, again hearing his father's voice.

Son, get back in that barn and don't come out until you've killed that calf. The calf had been sick for days, from the moment it dropped out of its mother. And Daniel's father didn't believe in calling up the local veterinarian for things they could deal with themselves. Daniel had asked anyway.

It's time you learn that's not how we make money around here.

Daniel stopped to shake out his nerves and to look out across the valley. He had loved this panorama when he'd first started work at Cotton Glenn, and still had to admit that the nursing home was in a particularly lovely setting for its purpose. From up there, the residents and staff could see Okanagan Lake shimmering in the distance. In season, its surface was notched with individual and small flocks of sailboats, alongside that old red-and-white paddle-wheeler that had made its way under the bridge in other summers, carrying tourists up and down the lake, docking near enough to the hospital for unwary passengers who didn't know not to eat the shrimp.

From the nursing home, half of the city and its vineyards could be seen, going about its daily business. Daniel didn't approve of the vineyards. Their wine. But even Jesus had called Himself the vine, and His people the branches. "Although," he said aloud, glancing heavenwards, "You know most of those folks at the home are about ready for you to prune them."

Daniel's mind went to certain residents who did nothing, it seemed, but stare into the mid-distance, day after day, often year after year, until the Lord Himself got tired of it and took them home. "I didn't mean to hurt the old man," he continued. "No one should have to put up with that kind of thing, though. Or this other crap that's going on. We all need to learn that You are our shield. Not these vaccines of theirs."

By the time Daniel made his way down Black Mountain and into the Benchlands, to Hollywood Road and then, finally, Lacey and home, he was two hours later than he should have been and had forgotten about going to the library. The microscope would have to wait, although it might have been helpful if he could bring Lizzy a printout of what he bought. He needed to talk to her. Now. This time, she would just have to understand.

Even though she would be in school now, Daniel more than half expected to find her inside the house, conjured by his own, renewed purpose. Instead, he found shoes, scattered like breadcrumbs in the entryway. He kicked a few aside to make a path and found that the kitchen, too, was a mess. He picked up a cold piece of toast and scraped a smear of margarine onto it from a knife abandoned on a plate. It's not as though she's lived up to her end, Daniel thought, taking a bite. Look at what I've let her get away with. Honestly, if it was this hard for Lizzy to clean as she went, maybe by now she would be grateful to put an end to their agreement.

"Marie?" Daniel called out. He couldn't think of a reason she shouldn't be up and about by now. He had even brought their clunky old television out of the hall closet and set it up in the living room so she could watch movies if she wanted. They had an old VCR and an assortment of VHS tapes from the ABC. "Marie?"

Finding her asleep in their bed, Daniel sat in the chair against the bedroom wall so he could take a moment and think. He didn't like to find people napping during the day. There was no reason for it if they didn't work at night. Still, it was good to see the pinched skin between Marie's brows flattened a little in sleep, and hear the long, slow sounds of sleep-breaths, instead of the short, sharp gasps that needled him whenever she was awake.

Halfway through one of his thoughts, Marie's eyes opened. There was a moment of alarm in the look of her, as though she wasn't certain of where she was, but when her focus settled on Daniel, he saw her relax. It was good to know he could still be that for her: her anchor in whatever storm. It had been a long time since she'd seemed to want him for anything.

Maybe, he thought, his mind reaching back into the stream of his mountaintop prayer. Maybe all of this is part of Your plan. And if that's true, then one day, all four of us will thank You for Your terrible mercy.

"Could I have an Advil?" Marie said, instead of asking him about his day.

"Are you sure the pain is still bad enough for that?" he said. "Some discomfort isn't a bad thing. It means you're healing."

Marie nodded, and Daniel got up. He went out into the hallway, to the closet where the TV was usually kept, where he also stored the family's medications. Inside a safe to which only he knew the combination, along with important papers, was a plastic basket containing blister packs of children's Gravol, store-brand pink liquid for indigestion, and the Advil. He shook out two tablets, put one back and returned to Marie.

Daniel thought about telling her what had happened at work, but when he tried, the words got stuck in his throat. He had never lost a job before, had never hurt a resident before, even unintentionally, and the sting of it swelled deep beneath his skin. "I should get some sleep," he said. As Marie got up, he slipped out of his scrubs, went round to his side of the bed, and slipped under the covers.

He wanted to call Marie back. Something happened at work today, he wanted to say. I didn't mean it. I don't mean a lot of things. You know that don't you? Instead, Daniel closed his eyes and pushed the words away. It was a gift of his that, no matter what was going on, he was always able to sleep.

No more than a couple of hours later, Daniel woke to a house that creaked with silence, his mind full of thoughts that seemed to be crawling over one another to get out of his head. He sat up, checked the time and scratched his scalp, hard, with both hands. It was just past noon.

Out in the house, the kitchen was clean now, and in the fridge, Daniel found a stack of casseroles—Doris' Special K loaves by the look of them. Lizzy and Zach's shoes had been sorted into the closet where they belonged.

Doris Wroblewski had been here, and Marie was gone. Daniel opened his jaw to keep from biting down on a tooth that was already sore. Sometimes it felt like Doris, for the way she came in and had her way with things, was as much his wife as Marie. And if that wasn't a reason to clench his teeth, he didn't know what was.

Daniel's intention had been to walk to the Wroblewskis' and look for Marie there. But when he got outside, he turned, instead, toward the school. It was lunchtime, and if he hurried, he could catch Lizzy and have a talk with her before her next class. He could tell her about work, about Mr. Schellenberg and Mrs. Beverly and how it was a good thing it had finally come to this.

At the same time, he would tell her he knew how hard it had been on her these last couple of months, taking care of everything at home. He would tell her she could still go to university. She'd just need to be patient. Her whole life was in front of her, so what was a year or two when moving to Stillwater was so clearly God's plan for the whole family?

He would remind her, too, that the accident hadn't been his fault. He hadn't meant for it to happen. Not really. He had gotten Zach to shore. He tried to make sure Lizzy didn't risk her own life, too. And he would have gone back for Marie. Of course he would have. Why didn't he just tell Lizzy that the first time? She hadn't given him a chance. Any father would've done what he did, and Marie, whose entire purpose was those two kids, would have expected no different. Lizzy would just have to grow up and understand.

"What do you mean Lizzy isn't here?" Daniel asked the principal. He had already been to Lizzy's homeroom, where her seven masked and distanced classmates shrugged at his question. He had checked on the twelfth graders, too, since half of Lizzy's classes seemed to be with them these days.

Biology Lab, Computer Science, followed by the classroom where both English and Bible were taught, and where posters of Revelations' Beasts flanked a whiteboard full of perfectly diagrammed sentences.

"Lizzy has two spares before lunch, and the Grade 12s are allowed to leave campus when they're on their breaks," Mr. Borthwaite explained, having set aside a stack of papers he'd been reviewing. He folded his hands atop his desk and offered Daniel a mask. He refused.

"Let me get this straight," Daniel said. "I pay thousands—thousands—of dollars, every year, for my children to attend this school, so I can know where they are and what they're being taught, and you're telling me you can't even suggest where I might find my sixteen-year-old daughter?"

"Like I said. The Grade 12s—"

"Lizzy," Daniel interrupted, "isn't in the twelfth grade. You people here do know that don't you?"

"Wait. Just a second. Lizzy turned in a work credit form a while back. Maybe that's where she's gone."

"Excuse me?"

"A work credit. We allow the high school kids to get credits for certain non-academic activities. Royal Conservatory music exams, lifeguarding lessons, after-school jobs—"

Daniel pounded his fist on the principal's desk. "I only know what I'm told."

"I see," said Mr. Borthwaite. "But I have a signature . . ." He got to his feet, slid open a black metal drawer and fished out a file.

"Here it is." He handed a sheet of paper to Daniel. "It looks like your signature, but it appears Lizzy forgot to write down where she's employed."

Daniel marched down the wing of the school that held the classrooms up to Grade 7. Zach's featured a pet tortoise and rabbit, which Daniel assumed had been chosen by the teacher as an object lesson. To his mind, *Uncle Arthur's Bedtime Stories*, an Adventist staple since the 1920s, had endured that long for a reason, and were a better choice for any life lesson than Aesop and his fables.

"Here is a very sad little story, and I hope you won't shed too many tears as you read it," Marie used to recite before putting the kids to bed.

"I need to take Zach out of class for the rest of the day," Daniel said when his son's teacher scurried to meet him at the door.

"Is everything okay?" she said. "Zach's mom, she hasn't—"

"Marie's fine," Daniel said, irritated.

"Maybe I should run and let Lizzy know you're taking him out of class," said the teacher. "She always wants to know everything about her brother."

"Lizzy doesn't seem to be here. Zach," Daniel said, speaking over the teacher's head, "get your things. We need to go."

Zach, who had set down his pencil when Daniel appeared, picked up his schoolbag and, with a barely noticeable glance at a boy to his left, got up and joined Daniel at the door.

Outside the school, Daniel put his hand on Zach's shoulder and pulled him close like he'd seen once in a commercial for soup. He was agitated about Lizzy, and while he had come here looking for her, it felt good to have his boy beside him, scrambling a little to keep up, the way a boy should stretch himself to lengthen into his father's footsteps.

"Do you know where your sister is?" Daniel said when he and Zach reached the gate. "I need to talk to her, but it turns out she's not here."

Zach stiffened for a moment and fell a step behind. Daniel stopped, knowing he had just discovered a lie. He picked up their pace. He himself had learned, around Zach's age, that it was difficult to spin a web of falsehoods while trying to catch one's breath.

"She has a job, I hear," Daniel said, letting out a little string, just like the tiny nooses he'd once been taught to tie and lay over gopher holes back home.

A cow could trip and break her ankle in that thing's hole, his father said when Daniel went to pieces over the strangled body of his first rodent. After that, he had made himself noose up a dozen or more gophers every day after school. Eventually, it had become as easy as tugging an overhead chain to turn off a light.

"She's not skipping classes," Zach said from two steps behind. "She's taken almost all of them already. She has . . . spares."

"I see. And why do you suppose I've been kept in the dark about all of this, Zach? Why is that?" This time, Zach was the one to stop.

Daniel returned to where Zach was rooted to a square of sidewalk. He crouched down until he was looking up into the face of his son.

"I don't want you to ever be afraid of telling me the truth, Zach."

MRS. WROBLEWSKI'S SPECIAL K ROAST

    4 cups cottage cheese
    1 cup finely chopped walnuts
    5 eggs, beaten
    1 packet onion soup mix
    1 cup water
    6 cups Special K cereal
    3 cups cooked rice

Combine all ingredients and transfer to a glass baking dish that's been greased with margarine. Bake 1 hour at 350°F.

SUNNY DAY PANCAKES

At work a few days later, Lizzy carried a tray of chicken breasts to restock the front showcase. She had butchered the birds from whole, and skinned the breasts herself, which was one of her favourite jobs. She enjoyed the way the fascia between the muscle and the skin peeled apart like plastic wrap.

"Someone will be with you in a minute," she called out when the bell on the front front door jingled.

"Is that so?"

The chicken remaining on Lizzy's tray slid to the floor. "Dad." Lizzy slipped off her nitrile gloves and dropped them in a garbage can by the till, suddenly aware of the blood and the spackle of rendered flesh that stained her apron. "I can explain."

"Can you? I'd like to hear you try. And what's that? Pork? Have you touched that?"

Lizzy looked over her shoulder as Janet, who usually worked in the front of the store, returned from the office.

"Can I help you?" said Janet, looking from Daniel to Lizzy.

"You can help by telling me what kind of place hires a teenage girl to muck around in guts without her father's consent."

"How long have you known?" Lizzy said.

"Long enough to pray and get an answer. Now take that filthy apron off and get your things. I've spoken to Director Schlant and they're making up rooms for us."

Lizzy stripped off her apron, folding it to conceal bloodied hand-prints on the front of the white cloth.

"When?" she said.

"When I say so."

Since that day, Lizzy had spent her morning spares in the biology lab.

Today, Miss Taylor was already there and waiting. "I'll lock the door," she said, slipping Lizzy a butcher paper-wrapped package from under a black and grey shawl she wore like a woollen signature. She dropped the package on a lab bench. "They'll just think I'm eating lunch. And see? It's true." From under her shawl, she pulled a sleeve of vegan Oreos from the ABC. Made with hydrogenated oil instead of lard.

Lizzy accepted a cookie and held it between her teeth as she sliced open the butcher bundle. "Fresh pig's feet!" Lizzy whisper-squealed, biting through the Noreo so that she had to catch it as it crumbled.

Brushing away a few crumbs, Lizzy opened a drawer and with-drew a roll of dissection tools, selected a scalpel, then put it down. She was getting ahead of herself and went to a nearby cupboard to fetch a dissection tray while Miss Taylor helped herself to another cookie.

Because the worst of Marie's injuries were to her left hand, Lizzy selected the left front trotter and placed it on the tray. It was too bulky to pin to the nearly half inch of white wax, so she left it loose and picked up the blade. She made an incision shaped like a T so she could peel the skin away from the pig's inner wrist.

"I can see you learned a lot at the butcher shop," Miss Taylor said as Lizzy retracted a flap and pinned that to the wax. "I'm so sorry it ended the way it did. But dissection, or surgery if you ever go that direction, is infinitely finer. You need to peel away the fascia next, and the ligaments and nerves will be underneath. What do we call it when we share structures in common with an animal?"

"Homologous," Lizzy said without having to think.

For the next half hour, Lizzy cut, snipped, scraped and tweezed away muscle and other connective tissues from around the structures she wanted to see, and when she had done that, she became certain of only two things: she didn't have any idea how to help her mother, and she didn't need to look inside the second foot.

"So, what are you going to do with it?" said Miss Taylor.

"I don't know. Cook and serve it to the Grade 9s for hot lunch?"

One week passed and collided into another. Even the Sabbath in between, from sundown Friday to sundown Saturday, wasn't so much a rest as a crumple zone that absorbed the impact. Christmas was only days away, when the academy would close, but like a few other Adventist families, Lizzy's didn't celebrate. Decorating trees was pagan, and children who expected presents, Daniel said, showed a lack of appreciation for what they already had.

"Here," Daniel said, and handed Lizzy an empty cantaloupe box from the grocery store. "We can't take everything, so other than your clothes, I suggest you fill this with what's most important from your room. Then pack up the rest to give away."

Lizzy took the box, which still smelled strongly of melon. One of them must have gone mouldy and leaked juice into the cardboard. "I could still tell Mom."

"You could. But I gave up my job because of you."

"Nice excuse, Dad."

"Put some things in that box, or I'll go into your room with garbage bags," Daniel said, his voice low and as even as a metronome. "Are you really so sure you know what happened that night?" He snatched her hand.

"I remember it just fine. You were going to let Mom—"

"Is that really the kind of man you think I am? That I'd drive my own family—"

"When you're mad at us? I don't think you even know what you might do."

Daniel tightened his grip until she could no longer tell whose pulse she felt beating inside her palm.

"It was icy and then when we went in the water," Daniel said. "We were all panicking, and I was desperate for you to come with me. That's all it was. I would've gone back for Mom after you and Zach were safe. That's what she would've wanted."

He sounded so sure. For a moment, Lizzy felt her memory begin to loosen.

"Here. Maybe this is a better box for you," Daniel said, letting go and handing her a box that was rank with the smell of old meat. "Put some things in here before you go to school." He walked away, then, leaving Lizzy alone, surrounded by the smell of grocery store cardboard, pork and yesterday's melons.

The first thing Lizzy packed was her mother's recipe box. With its cards written by her mother and grandmother, and the mysterious Aunt Toots, it was the closest thing they had to a family tree. She was sure the family photo albums, kept in an end table in the living room, would make the cut some other way, so she went to her room and opened her closet.

Hermione was there, reclaimed from Zach and stuffed with the envelopes of her mother's fentanyl stickers, along with prescription bottles she filled with cotton balls to keep them quiet. She settled the bear in a corner of the box, next to the recipes, followed by a few things that only a week ago she would not have thought to save.

There was a crib-sized quilt she used to carry everywhere from the time she could walk, whose edges were frayed from being dragged along every floor and sidewalk. She had lost it once when she was six, left it behind in the Zellers restaurant while out shopping with her mother on a Sunday. That night, realizing it was gone, she had cried and cried until she had managed to wake up her father.

He should have been angry. He usually was over something like that. Instead, he had dressed and picked up his keys from the front door table and driven out into the night. An hour later, maybe more, he returned. The store had already closed, he said. But there were cleaners inside. He'd gotten their attention and explained that he had an upset little girl at home. Eventually, they let him into the restaurant to look.

The blanket had slipped under a table, so he insisted that Marie wash it before giving it back to Lizzy, but that was all he said. Otherwise, he simply went back to bed for another hour of sleep before work.

Now Lizzy used the blanket to wrap up a set of laboratory slides she had set and stained herself. One was the thinnest of cross-sections from the tongue of a dead hummingbird she had found once, before putting the tiny creature in a small wooden box and burying it near the flowers it had loved.

The last items Lizzy added were a pair of library books she could not bear to return: Judy Blume and another about a young girl who got left alone on a Pacific island and had to forage for abalone by herself. These she hid under everything else, imagining how her name would forever bear a black mark with a fine against it at the place she loved most.

At school, the day before the Christmas holiday, Lizzy sat through a chemistry class, where they practiced a provincial exam she wouldn't be around to take in January. After that was family management, where they learned that dating, kissing and especially sex would weaken the glue that would eventually bond them to their spouses. For extra reading credit, Lizzy had selected a page-worn copy of

Erma Bombeck's *The Grass Is Always Greener Over the Septic Tank*. The date inside was from 1976.

When Lizzy finally slipped into the biology lab, she wrapped her arms around Miss Taylor and cried.

"Okay. Okay, Lizzy. I know you're upset. But what are you going to do about school once you're at Stillwater? Have you figured that out yet?" Miss Taylor held Lizzy for a moment longer, then wiped her tears with her shawl.

"I don't know. I just came here to cut something."

Miss Taylor pointed to a package on the lab table. "A kidney today. Just for fun."

Lizzy sniffled. "I guess I'll . . ." she said but had no way to finish the sentence.

"Okay. Well. I've been thinking about it. You can't let your education be interrupted. It's too important."

"Yeah, but they don't even have Grade 11 and I'm leaving at the end of the year."

"I had an idea," she said, handing Lizzy a key. "I drove up north and rented a post office box. I know you won't have access to a computer, but you can take classes through the mail. It's up to you, though. Lizzy, listen. You're an extraordinarily bright student. The answers you find, even here in a school like this, will never be enough."

Lizzy was still thinking about Miss Taylor's idea when the bell rang at 3:20, thirty minutes later than the surrounding public schools, so the students wouldn't mingle. She began the short walk home, with Zach trailing behind her by half a block. By the time she came within sight of their house, he had fallen even farther back.

Lizzy was the first to discover the family's bed frames and box springs set out on the house's front lawn. Dressers and nightstands stood next to them, loosely arranged according to the rooms from which they'd been taken.

On the other side of the willow tree that divided the yard was the living room furniture and kitchen table. The only large item that seemed to be missing was the piano.

So, this was it.

Lizzy crossed the yard and sat on the edge of her own box spring. Ordinarily, she would go inside, set out her homework and change out of her school uniform, hanging it up to let the day's wrinkles fall out. Before Zach could catch up, Lizzy left her school things on her bed and went into the house.

Inside, the walls had been stripped of pictures and even nails. Mattresses, still fitted with sheets and blankets, remained on the floors of the bedrooms, and behind where the frames had been, the wallpaper was perfectly preserved. Even the application of a pair of wall mops, left propped against an emptied bucket, had not been enough to blend in the areas exposed to so much family life. It was the same with the carpet, where a rented cleaner sat inside four square impressions left by the feet of the couch.

In the kitchen, only the chairs remained, shoved against the wall. Even the fridge, when Lizzy looked inside, had been emptied, scoured with Vim, with just a few ingredients left on a single shelf.

With her ears beginning to buzz, Lizzy startled at the sound of her father's voice.

"It's looking good, isn't it?" he said, opening a cabinet door, followed by another, to reveal nothing left inside but a mixing bowl, a pan and a few ingredients.

"You didn't say it was going to be today," Lizzy said. "I thought we had more time."

"There's no reason to stick around. We'll sleep here tonight, but they have beds for us and everything at Stillwater. We can make pancakes for supper," he said. "I had Mrs. W. leave you some ingredients."

"Couldn't we just go out to eat?"

"We don't need to waste money on restaurants. There's peanut butter to put on the pancakes, and I'll bet there's still a jar of apple-sauce somewhere."

"There isn't," Lizzy said. She knew, because she had eaten it all a week ago, along with their canned peaches and pears from the summer. That was the same night she had gone down to the basement, under the stairs, and rolled almost five hundred dollars' worth of coins into scraps of paper. All that was left there now were empty jars.

"Let's you and me drive up to Coopers and get some, then."

"We could. If we still had a car. Where's Mom?"

"Well, then I guess we can walk," Daniel said, ignoring Lizzy's question. "Or maybe we can take this." He reached into his pocket and handed Lizzy a key. "It's outside. The landlord came by with our damage deposit, and one of the men helping us today was selling his truck. How's that for a sign of good things?"

"Show it to Zach," she said. "He's probably wondering if we're going to sleep outside tonight."

Lizzy waited until her father was gone before she went to find her mother. "He bought a truck?" Lizzy said when she found Marie in the bathroom.

"He's happy. That's a good thing," Marie said, sitting fully dressed on the edge of the toilet seat.

"All of our stuff is on the front lawn."

"The ladies from the church have arranged a trailer to pick it all up for another family."

"What about your piano?"

"Your dad sold it. The money went toward the truck. The landlord will take it after we go. It's okay, though. I don't suppose I'll ever play again, and your father says if I do, they have one at Stillwater."

"There's something you should know," Lizzy said, and the words hung in the air for a moment.

"Your father already told me. Just before you came home," Marie said, her voice splitting like a reed. "Lizzy. I had no idea you helped him save me that night in the lake."

That evening, Lizzy mixed pancake batter in a salad bowl, using a plastic picnic fork from a bag of them left next to the fridge.

Sunny Day Pancakes was a recipe they usually only made after Vespers on Saturday nights. It felt wrong, somehow, on a Wednesday, to level off the cups of whole wheat flour and oat bran, the spoon of baking soda; to crack eggs and beat it all into a slurry with barely enough milk.

When she was finished turning the pancakes over, the family each took a chair. From her place next to Zach, Lizzy watched as her father carefully fed forkfuls of pancake, with peanut butter and applesauce, to Marie.

SUNNY DAY PANCAKES

2 cups oat flour
½ cup all-purpose flour
1 tbsp plus 1 tsp baking powder
½ tsp baking soda
1 ½ tsps cinnamon
¼ cup maple syrup
1 tsp vanilla extract
2 tbsps apple cider vinegar
2 cups almond milk
2 large eggs

Whisk together dry ingredients. In a separate bowl, whisk together wet ingredients, then mix both together with a fork. Set a griddle over medium-high heat and add a little oil. For each pancake, add about ⅓ cup of batter to hot skillet.

Cook until small bubbles appear on the surface of the pancakes. Flip and cook a few minutes more, until golden. Repeat.

Note: Cook pancakes immediately after making the batter, as the oat flour soaks up liquid and can over-thicken the batter.

Part Two

STILLWATER

WALNUT PATTIES

With no one to teach Grade 11 or 12 classes, Lizzy had been assigned to the greenhouse. An old building with crumbling paint and new glass, it appeared out of place no matter which way she looked at it.

It was April. More than three months since Lizzy and her family had arrived at Stillwater, bags and boxes scattered in the back of the truck. Three months since Joel, three years older than Lizzy, had begun to teach her how to think like a plant. So far, it wasn't working.

"In the winter and spring, the heat trapped in here by the glass lets us force things to grow ahead of their seasons," he said. Again.

"Almost like a greenhouse effect," Lizzy replied, the words dripping off her tongue. Sarcasm helped. Without it, she felt as wilted as the table full of mint she'd lately forgotten to water.

"Yes, Lizzy. Almost like that," Joel said, rolling his eyes. "We can even grow a few pineapples. I don't know if you saw them over there, but I think it's best if I take care of them. They take two years, so it's a lot of work to risk losing."

Although she pretended otherwise, Lizzy felt sorry for the plants under her care. Today, though, because the orchard just outside the glass was bursting with tiny white flowers that she ached to go outside and touch, her sympathies were limited.

"Cherries won't be ready until July," Joel said.

"June if we were in Osoyoos," Lizzy said. "My mom took us picking down south one year."

"Yeah, well, we're not quite as hot up here."

"What about the strawberries?" Lizzy said, increasingly concerned that Joel was able to read her mind.

"We can check on the ones in here once we're done. A few of them looked almost ready yesterday, and Mrs. Schlant always has some Cool Whip in the fridge."

"You know there's skim milk and sodium caseinate in that," Lizzy said. "It's not vegan."

Joel shrugged.

"Mrs. Schlant wouldn't use it if it has dairy."

Lizzy didn't bother to argue, and kept herself from saying what else she was thinking, that one of the other ingredients in Cool Whip was polysorbate: a major component in condom lube. She wasn't supposed to know things like that. But even in church school, kids went on TikTok.

Joel got up from his work stool, where he had been using electric shears to trim micro-lettuces to place in plastic clamshell containers. Coming up behind Lizzy, he rested his hand on her shoulder. His skin smelled softly green from the snatches of butterleaf that still clung to his fingers.

With a twitch, Lizzy dislodged Joel's hand and jammed a mustard seedling into a pot of fresh medium, accidentally cutting off its roots with fingernails Joel had been after her to trim.

The plant would die later unless mustard greens possessed an axolotl's powers of regeneration. Lizzy both adored and was jealous of axolotls. Pink-frilled amphibians from Mexico that always looked like they were smiling, they reached adulthood without going through metamorphosis and could regrow their limbs.

For now, because Joel hadn't seemed to notice she'd killed another plant, Lizzy braced its stem with a little extra soil and added it to her tally of plastic pots. Each transplant was meant to be included as a gift with today's salad orders and had to be pegged with a handmade card that read: *The Kingdom of Heaven Is Like a Mustard Seed.*

Lizzy pushed the stalk of a card into the soil and nicked her finger, which started to bleed.

"Here, give that to me," Joel said, taking Lizzy's hand and pressing on the wound as though she had hit an artery. He reached under the worktop for a first aid box. "You never know what's in soil. Anthrax comes from soil. And tetanus," he said, opening a tincture bottle of iodine with his teeth.

"A little water would be fine. It's not like it's chicken guts," Lizzy said, pulling toward the sink near the door. Joel was stronger, though, and droppered a tiny amount of the yellow-brown solution onto Lizzy's cut, which although small, suddenly burst into an explosion of pain.

"Ow," Lizzy said when Joel asked whether it hurt. "My dad used to put it on my canker sores."

Joel handed Lizzy a Band-aid and a latex glove. "You'll want to keep it clean. Dirt can kill you, too. And by the way, you wouldn't get so hot in here if you wore something other than that stupid turtleneck."

"Whatever." Almost finished with the mustard plants, Lizzy turned her attention back outside. She hoped they'd find ripe strawberries today, sun-hot and sweet and definitely ready to eat.

Lizzy's mind had drifted back to amphibians when she spotted a familiar shape nibbling around the roots of the nearest tree. Joel saw it, too.

"Director Schlant told me how you feel about animals," he said.

"I'm sure he did."

"He said you're only interested in their guts. That you'd sooner open one up with a knife than let it be."

"I don't kill animals." Lizzy jammed another scripture stick into one of the finished pots.

"Sure. But wanting them to die so you can cut them up is just as bad."

Lizzy counted to five. It didn't help. She had been in the greenhouse since early that morning, and if someone didn't come soon to announce lunch, she might just . . . Her train of thought, which had involved turning Joel into a bagful of fertilizer, was interrupted by the opening of the greenhouse door.

"Hey, sweet girl!" Joel said, putting down a trowel to shake the hand of nine-year-old Ruth. Behind her, in a loose formation, was Stillwater's little flock of orange-eyed children. Zach was among them, hanging back with a boy named Thomas. At least the whites of Zach's eyes hadn't yet turned.

"Mrs. Director says it's time for lunch," Ruth said, dispensing her duty with the good cheer of someone born to gather disciples wherever she went. "She says to bring some salad. We're having patties."

"Right, then," said Joel, as though taking down an order.

Lizzy felt the corners of her mouth twitch into an involuntary smile, which she quickly rearranged into something neutral.

Having dispensed with her task, Ruth waved to Lizzy and gathered up her flock, most of whom were older than she was. Soon they were halfway across the lawn, then disappearing through the side door into the house.

"She seems to like you," Lizzy said, brushing potting medium from her work surface.

"And that surprises you?"

"It does," she lied. Everyone seemed to like Joel. The men and women. The children. Lizzy's father, even, had come down from the house one day to say how much he appreciated Joel's patience with Lizzy. Although she suspected he was just there to check on things between them. Zach seemed to be the lone exception. Lizzy didn't know how to feel. Joel was patient and could be funny. But sometimes . . .

"By the way," Joel said. "Ruth and the other kids love that rabbit, so try not to kill it, okay?"

"I'll try," Lizzy said, brushing dirt onto the sides of her jeans. "Maybe if we go inside for lunch, I'll forget my murderous ways." She recounted her pots one more time before heading for the door.

"Wait," said Joel. "You forgot something."

"No. I finished my part of the orders." Lizzy went back and waved her hands over the pots and leaves. "One for every box."

"Yeah. The boxes."

"Jeez. Can't the men do anything themselves?" She began to stuff one mustard pot into each of the boxes Joel had already packed. They had to be complete before lunch, because afterward two or more of the men would come down from the house to drive the boxes into town for delivery to the various shops and restaurants that placed orders with Director Schlant.

Lizzy thought about this as she jammed her pots next to Joel's bags and bunches of perfectly arranged greens. She had thought about it every day since they arrived: how she might stow herself away in the back of the delivery van and slip out near the post office where Miss Taylor had set up a box for her. So far, Lizzy hadn't figured out how to actually get to town.

In the kitchen, the air was pungent with the smell of over-steamed broccoli. A pot of mushroom gravy bubbled next to it and, at Mrs. Schlant's direction, Lizzy washed her hands and poured it into a mismatched pair of gravy boats she set at either end of the table, coming back for another for the children. She retraced her steps a few more times with pitchers of carrot juice.

"So, what did you learn today, Lizzy?" said Mrs. Schlant, pulling Joel into a sideways hug like a hen trying to stuff an overgrown chick under her wing.

"I brought you some greens," Joel said, handing her a tray of neatly clipped arugula, endive and dandelion greens. "Did you make the dressing?"

"Green Goddess? Of course. Lizzy, the next time I get you in my kitchen for more than a meal, I'll teach you how to make it. It's his favourite."

"And these were ready." He reached into his pocket for a handful of strawberries. "First ones we've ever grown in the greenhouse."

Mrs. Schlant laughed and tucked Joel a little tighter into her side. "I'll tuck these away for after. I have some Cool Whip."

"If you still want to know, today I learned that strawberries are only ripe when Joel says they are," Lizzy said.

"Joel learned the hard way. He won't have told you, but when we first brought him here, he ate half a branchful of underripe cherries and was on the pot for half a week with the runs."

"That can happen with ripe cherries, too," Lizzy said. "My dad—"

"Your dad, what?"

The men, including Daniel, had begun to file into the room.

"Lizzy was just telling us how she likes cherries," Joel said seamlessly. "They're not ready, but in six weeks or so. I'll make sure to bring some in for everyone."

Daniel seemed pleased, and Lizzy, whose knees had jellied at nearly being caught telling a private story—all family stories were strictly private, especially her father's—picked up a glass baking dish full of patties, forgetting to use hot pads, and carried it to the table with fingertips that had begun to bake. The other women had been late coming in, but joined them now, taking care to seat Lizzy's mother at the table before hurrying to lift down dishes and load the table with food.

From end to end, Lizzy counted the people gathered around the table—Director and Mrs. Schlant; Ruth's parents, Mr. and Mrs. Albright; Jimena and Beatrice, who had become her mother's keepers. The Duncarins and Whites, too. Each of them had started off convinced that Lizzy's interest in animal biology would mean she'd take to plants just as well. Now it was no secret to anyone that Lizzy wasn't working out in her role as apprentice lettuce keeper. The Duncarins had begun to whisper that Lizzy's black thumb was intentional and an effort to get out of any work at all, while the Whites suggested she was receiving special treatment. They had begun to lobby for her removal from the greenhouse to the bread kitchen. Yeast, after all, was a less complicated organism, and if Lizzy could not be trusted with seedlings, it hardly seemed worth training her for work that could lead to calamity in the garden.

"How was your morning, Lizzy?" asked Beatrice, one of the black thumb theorists.

"It was fine." Lizzy picked up her fork and polished away an imaginary spot. "God is sovereign, so anything I kill, He can bring back to life if He wants to."

"Lizzy," Marie hissed under her breath.

"Plants don't have the breath of life, Lizzy. No soul. No resurrection," said Director Schlant, forking up a mouthful of patty.

"What about animals?" Every time she had ever failed to revive one, or had cut into a corpse, she hoped they, too, had a chance at a second life.

"No resurrection," the Director said again, putting his food where his certainty came from.

When lunch was finished, Lizzy and Joel both stayed back to help with the washing up. With the day's greenhouse orders done, and without classes to keep them busy, the two of them were expected to spend their afternoons either finding ways to learn from nature, or to discover what other departments might need extra help.

"Outside, the both of you," said Mrs. Schlant, shooing them like a pair of cats, while keeping the strawberries for herself. Lizzy started back toward the greenhouse for lack of a better idea, but Joel stopped her short of the door and pulled a pair of carrots from under his shirt. "The rabbit will still be in the orchard."

A few minutes later they knelt down together in the grass. "You shouldn't have said what you did at the table," Joel said. "The men argue about that kind of stuff all the time but they don't expect to hear it from a girl."

"Men never expect to hear from a girl at all," Lizzy said.

Joel broke one of the carrots in half and the rabbit hopped toward them.

"I think animals do have the breath of life," Lizzy said. "A soul."

"They do. But it's not the same."

Joel handed Lizzy a carrot, and the rabbit munched it from her hand, all the way down to its stem, which it nibbled through until it looked like it was wearing a green moustache. When it was done, the rabbit hopped away.

"Hey . . ." Lizzy said. She had a question, and it was burning a hole in her stomach.

"Look," Joel said as the silence stretched between them. "Either you're going to have to get over whatever it is you have against me, or you're just going to have to ask someone else."

"Ask someone else what?"

"Clearly, you have a problem you need help with," Joel said." And not just with your attitude." He tugged on the hem of her jeans. "Or your clothes."

Lizzy didn't respond. She'd been ignoring the long, frill-shouldered dresses she kept finding in the closet in the room she shared with Zach. A different dress each week, as though the seamstress ladies were trying to tempt her with their slightly shifting palate of drab.

"Okay, maybe another time," Joel said, standing up as Lizzy's father and Director Schlant came out of the house. "Looks like your dad's going to help with the deliveries. If you want, I can tell him you need help with something. I mean, that's who you'd ask, isn't it?"

Joel was mocking her and Lizzy hated it. Still, she didn't have any other ideas. She reached under her turtleneck, fumbled for a few seconds, and pulled out a thin silver chain, onto which was threaded a single small key.

"I really don't know who else to trust. Box 429," Lizzy said, dropping the key into Joel's hand. "Bring me what's inside and try not to be too happy about this."

MRS. SCHLANT'S WALNUT PATTIES

1 cup raw walnut pieces, coarsely ground
6 medium brown mushrooms, scrubbed and finely chopped
½ large onion, grated
1 white potato, cooked and grated
2 large cloves garlic, minced
2 tbsps soy sauce
1 tbsp Caf-Lib granules
1 tsp dried parsley
4 cups fresh breadcrumbs

Combine all ingredients and set aside for 30 minutes for the crumbs to moisten.

Shape into patties and fry in shallow oil over medium-high heat for about 5 minutes per side.

GLUTEN STEAKS

Marie was not used to Daniel being more than an imprint in their bed, a trench she fell into every so often, whenever she moved too far in the night. In the thirteen years since he had graduated from nursing school, he had almost always been on a graveyard shift at Cotton Glenn. In that time, she had forgotten how he barely seemed to breathe when he slept, and how, when they had first been married and she had woken up to silence, she'd held a tissue over his face and waited for it to flutter before she could persuade herself back to sleep.

Even then, she had dreamed of death coming in the night, unseen and unexpected. When the children had been born, she had set an hourly alarm in her mind, just to get up and check that they were alive. Sometimes, especially with Lizzy, Marie would wake her just so she could nurse, while Marie herself sipped a mug of warm milk with honey like her mother used to make.

Marie wanted to warm up a mug now, but Daniel's body kept her in place, while the light of a clock told her it was now five am. A thin gruel of morning had begun to spill between the curtains on the other side of the room.

"Why aren't you asleep?" Daniel asked, and at the surprise of his voice, a flash of current shocked its way through Marie's hands. The same thing happened at any surprise sound. A spoon clanging against a metal bowl. A sudden, sharp laugh. Her hands were now free of their pins, and the pain made them splay open in surrender.

"I can hear you thinking." Daniel's tone was soft. Soft like she always knew it could be. "If you can't sleep, we could talk about whatever's bothering you. If there is something." He rolled up onto one elbow, gently lowered Marie's arms to her chest, and looked at her in the almost-dark. "You're happy now that we're here, aren't you? I mean, I know you were unsure before. But you see now, right? You see how good this place is for us. These people."

Marie, who hovered her hands just above the quilt, moved one to cover her breath. "It's just that I'm still not used to us waking up together." She tried to turn onto her side to face Daniel. As she did, however, the mattress beneath them began to move.

Held together by nothing more than a king-sized sheet, their bed was actually two twins pushed together. Marie was caught in the hammock-y space in between as they slowly began to spread apart.

"I've got you," Daniel said, jumping up to scoop Marie under her arms like a farm cat. "There," he said, holding her almost close and laughing in a way that Marie remembered from a different time and place. "It's been a long while since we've had any adventures." He smiled shyly and kissed Marie on the apex of her forehead. "You should try to get some more sleep. If you've had any at all. Your two ladies will come for you soon enough."

Daniel guided Marie back round to her side of the beds and nudged them back together with his knee. Once he had settled her under the covers, he went over to a dresser beneath the window and took out a crisply folded shirt and pair of pants that the women had washed and pressed. He slipped into them and then out of the room, leaving Marie to replay the feeling of his arms wrapped around her.

Before the women came, Lizzy arrived. As had become their routine, she waited for Daniel to go downstairs, and then, from wherever it was that she kept Marie's prescriptions, she brought two pills—Dilaudid, the same as fentanyl but for swallowing, plus Ativan—and a cup of water from the bathroom. It wouldn't be time to change her fentanyl sticker until tomorrow.

"I know you think you need all of these, but they're still not supposed to be taken together," Lizzy said.

"I'm sure Dr. Vickers wouldn't have given me so much if there was anything to worry about. You're not the doctor, Lizzy."

"I'm not. But some doctors graduate at the bottom of their class, Mom. Or think rules don't apply to them."

"Well, maybe I won't even need them too much longer." Marie swallowed both both tablets at once and let Lizzy take back the cup. Before they left Kelowna, Dr. Vickers had given Marie enough of her scripts to last three months at double the dose, so they would last for six.

"At it again?" the pharmacist had said when Marie picked up as much as they could dispense from the safe. At the same time, Lizzy had seen that the remainders were transferred to a pharmacy close to Stillwater. Since then, Marie had managed to go on an outing with some of the women and made a stop at the Drug Mart carrying a purse full of Lizzy's cash.

Lizzy looked doubtful. "That would be good, but you can't go off them all at once, either. I looked it up at the library at home. You'll get really sick. And there's something called rebound pain."

"Fine, then. You can just keep me all drugged up," Marie said, accepting Lizzy's help to sit up against the headboard. The beds, Marie had been told, had belonged to a pair of old women who'd lived together all their lives. "Sometimes they pushed them together, too," Mrs. Schlant had said. "At that age, you can hardly blame them for needing a little warmth in the middle of the night. They were like sisters, the two of them."

Marie had known a pair of ladies back in her home village who had lived together, too. Marcy Froese, who never failed to have a cream cookie and a jar of milk for Marie if she dropped by after the school bus, and Lenore Rempel, who had taught Marie how to spot a good bull for breeding, how to pull the wings off a grasshopper and how to nurse a rejected kitten back to health with an eye dropper and a bowl of fresh, frothy milk.

There had been an unspoken something about the two of them, which everyone seemed to know but no one wanted to acknowledge. And Marie, who had sometimes watched them touch each other's hands while reaching into the cookie jar, now kept the same silence about the previous occupants of her and Daniel's room. "They died a week apart," Mrs. Schlant said. "It's too bad neither of them found husbands, but at least the old ducks had their friendship."

"I'll see you at noon," Lizzy said, getting to her feet.

"Have a good day. Make sure you listen to Joel. It's good he's teaching you so much," Marie said before Lizzy closed the door behind her.

Before she got out of bed, the warm weight of the Dilaudid began to press itself down on Marie's thoughts and on her chest, and she sank back into the mattress, which accepted her like a mother's lap. Before she could sleep, though, there was a knock at her door, and the two women Marie thought of as her charge nurses let themselves inside. Lately, she had begun to think of them as her captors.

"We have you for an hour before breakfast," said Jimena, who had moved to Stillwater with her orphaned grandson just before the Fischers. Thomas was a nice boy who had become friends with Zach.

"There's no better time for the body to heal than when it's hungry for its next meal. Gives it something to work towards, you know," Jimena said, with her musical way of speaking. From the tiny island of Bequia, the woman always had some kind of personal bromide to justify whatever she wanted Marie to do.

"If you ask me, the medicine we need is food itself, straight from

God's own table," muttered Beatrice, whose accent Marie had never been able to place.

For the next hour, which included an assisted visit to the bathroom and help getting out of her night clothes and into a dress, Marie did her best to stretch her fingers against a series of elastic bands, and contract them around a rubber ball. By the end of their session, she had sniffled back so many tears that her throat was raw from their salt.

Even at breakfast, for which the women came together after the others had already eaten and left for work or school, Jimena and Beatrice kept Marie under their watch. She was allowed to feed herself, but Beatrice was the one to cut up Marie's food into fork- or spoon-able bites. She was no longer permitted a straw.

Gathering a tumbler of apple juice toward herself and taking a sip, Marie thought about the old washing machines the commune kept in one of the outbuildings. Daniel was still excited about how, after a lifetime of laundry, they had been pressed into service as apple juicers. The idea of men's underwear being agitated in the same barrel made it difficult for Marie to swallow, and when she failed, she let the juice slide out of her mouth and back into the cup. There was no such thing as enough bleach.

When the dishes had been cleared, Marie accompanied her minders to the laundry. She was exhausted by her own efforts so far, and the idea of returning to her bed seemed so far off that she ached for it.

From a chair in a warm corner by the dryers, Marie watched as the women demonstrated for a future time, when they said Marie might be able to join them in their work there.

"Now that we have extra bodies in the house, we're going to need another hand in here," Jimena said, and Marie felt the sting of knowing she and her family were making extra work.

"See how we don't let the rinse water go down," said Beatrice, when the first of three washing machines clicked to a pause between cycles. "We use that for the next wash." She reached down through the open lid and pulled out a sopping wet pair of men's pants, wrung them with her hands, and switched on an antique wringer-washer, the make and model of which Marie recognized from one of the storage buildings on her parents' farm. The pants were fed between the rollers, ankle to waist, followed by item after item of other men's clothes. Once the washer was empty, a load of dresses was pushed down into the water left behind. Men's clothes were never washed together with women's. "And since we've no rain in the forecast, these all go outside on the lines. We'll use the dryers for everyone's underthings, though. No one likes to see those flapping around in the breeze."

Marie nodded with all the interest she could manage. Even at home in Kelowna, laundry had been the least favourite of her tasks. She had always preferred to be out in her little garden. She was good with soil, so it disappointed her to know that Lizzy was doing so poorly with the plants. As a child, she had spent all her time in her mother's garden plucking raspberries and peas into her mouth and ignoring the lessons about sun and soil. She knew instinctually how deep to plant the potato slices with their wandering eyes. She knew when to cover the corn so birds wouldn't line up behind her like widowed old men at a Sunday potluck.

Out by the laundry lines, Marie stood in the warm breeze as Jimena and Beatrice pinned clothes above their heads. She could see the greenhouse, and the figure of her daughter working away at whatever had been put before her.

Could I? Marie thought. After all, she had never been told that she couldn't go where she pleased. The ladies were just there to help, no matter how they might make it seem. She glanced back at the two women.

Both were engrossed in a debate about the merits of a little polyester in a blend, to help release wrinkles. Jimena was in favour, while Beatrice pointed out that blended fabrics were forbidden in the same book of the Bible as pork and fish without scales. They seemed to have forgotten Marie entirely.

Moments later, using a hanging bedsheet to hide her departure, Marie took her chance. Hurrying down to the greenhouse made her feel like Lucy discovering Narnia behind the winter coats—a book she'd read as a child herself, and then secretly shared with Lizzy. Except here, instead of everlasting winter, everything was alive and smelled of soil and green.

"Well, isn't this a nice place to spend the day?" Marie said, lifting the outside latch with her elbow to let herself inside. "I'd sure say the two of you are lucky to be in here instead of doing laundry."

When they'd first arrived, Marie had had certain concerns about Joel. Every time she saw him with Lizzy, though, he was a respectful distance away. Joel had taken Lizzy in like a brother, a teacher even, showing her about the greenhouse. Helping her fit in.

"What are you doing here, Mom?" Lizzy turned on her stool to face Marie, and Marie suddenly felt altogether out of place.

"Mrs. Fischer, it's so nice to see you down here," said Joel, who'd gotten up to greet her.

"Well, I wasn't helping much with the laundry, so I thought I'd let the ladies have a break from me." She laughed a little to cover up the half-truth, and stepped farther inside. "So what are the two of you up to today?"

"Just the usual," Lizzy said, giving Marie the sense that she wasn't very welcome. In fact, Marie thought maybe Lizzy had even pushed something out of sight the moment she'd heard her voice.

"Actually," said Joel, "Mrs. Schlant gave us her kumquat tree to clean up and transplant into a bigger pot." He steered her toward a sunny corner and Marie recognized the tree that usually sat in front of the large window in the eating area. "I'm going to wait a while, though. It's putting on some fruit, and that's the worst time to upset its roots." Joel reached round to the back of the tree and plucked a single small oval. He handed it to Marie, who instinctively put out her hand before remembering herself and pulling it back.

"Here," Joel said and bit the tiny orange fruit in half. The other half he popped into Marie's mouth, skin and all, before she could react. Sweet and floral, and a little sour, the glands behind Marie's jaw clenched painfully, delightfully, before giving way to a burst of pleasure.

"Well, isn't that something?" Marie said, catching a dribble of juice that threatened to spill down her chin.

"Not everyone gives plants a lot of notice, but none of us, not even the animals, could exist without them. Isn't that right, Lizzy?" he said.

Lizzy crossed her arms and rolled her eyes. That was something she seemed to do a lot more of these days. Marie made a mental note to talk to her about it in private later. It was the kind of thing other people must notice by now, too.

"Mom, do you need to be here?" Lizzy said. "It's just that I . . . we . . . have stuff we need to get done." Lizzy glanced at whatever it was she had hidden away. It looked like nothing more than a stack of paper and a couple of books.

If nothing else, Marie knew how to take a hint. She sniffed and turned to leave, and Joel accompanied her out the door.

"Sorry about that, Mrs. Fischer. I think Lizzy's just anxious about some things."

"Really? And what does she have to worry about?" Marie could list a number of things that might concern her daughter, but at this moment, on a sunny day in May, none of them seemed like much.

"Well, you'd know about girls her age better than I do," Joel said. "And really, it's a mother's prerogative to come check on her daughter, especially when she's working with someone you don't really know."

Marie smiled in agreement at the young man before her. She had heard the stories about how he'd come to be here. Clearly, though, Stillwater was having a good effect. "I think I'm starting to know you," she said. "And it's Marie. You can call me Marie. I'll leave you to your work."

As Marie made her way back toward the house, she could see Jimena and Beatrice. They were unpinning one of yesterday's bedsheets from a line and, in what could only be described as choreo-graphy, stepped together, matched each other's corners, folded, stepped back, and repeated until there was nothing but a plump rectangle of cotton between them. Marie knew they would undo all of those folds once inside. The two of them put an iron to every single item they laundered, including the ladies' bras. Those, of course, were also dried inside.

Instead of returning to the laundry lines, Marie changed direction toward the kitchen door where she could smell the aroma of Mrs. Schlant's gluten steaks frying on the stove. She wasn't ready yet, but if she ever was, she hoped that Mrs. Schlant would invite her and Lizzy both to work in the kitchen. Somehow or other, she would have to make the director's wife understand.

GLUTEN STEAKS

8 cups organic, unbleached flour
3 cups water
8 cups homemade vegetable stock

Add water to flour and combine. Knead until dough becomes elastic, and then form into a ball. Place ball in a large bowl and cover with water. Allow it to soften overnight.

To "wash" the flour, work the starch out of the dough by kneading it in the bowl of water while making sure to keep the dough together. It will become more elastic as you work. Discard the washing liquid.

Covering dough with water, let dough rest for about 30 minutes, and then wash it again in fresh water. Repeat washing and kneading until the water is almost entirely clear.

Bring vegetable stock to a rolling boil.

With clean kitchen scissors, snip steak-sized slices of the gluten meat into the stock. Boil gently for 30–35 minutes, until the steaks float to the top. Remove with tongs.

Coat the steaks in breading and fry in a little oil. Serve with mashed potatoes and well-cooked vegetables.

Note: Can also be ground up for burgers or spaghetti sauce.

VEGEMITE

A hundred times during the day, and even more often at night, Daniel thought about Lizzy and Joel, down there together in the greenhouse. The image of it cored away at his concentration. It gnawed at his ability to participate in the men's morning prayer meetings, and the decisions they made on behalf of the community. And it stole the satisfaction he should have felt at having shepherded his family to this place.

At first, Daniel had prayed about his feelings, hoping to make them go away. When he was unsuccessful, Director Schlant had prayed with him, and calmly insisted Joel was no more a threat than the rabbit the children had turned into a pet: a wild thing that had been tamed by God's grace.

"The Prophetess spoke to him, you know. Down in that church basement. Sometimes the Grand Lady's words lifted right off the page and arranged themselves in front of him like a vision."

"He told you that?" Daniel said, suffering a pang of jealous doubt. Ellen White, anointed more than a hundred years ago by God to bless His remnant church, made Daniel long for the voice of a wise woman. He himself had never met one.

Director Schlant nodded. "And do you know? On nights when Joel was too tired to keep his eyes open, the books read themselves out loud. Now," he said, holding up a hand when Daniel was about to speak, "I'm not saying it was Mrs. White herself. We all know she's asleep in Christ with the rest of the saints. But her prophetic voice was there with Joel, as a comfort, until it readied him to come and be with us. Do you believe that?"

It felt like a test, and in the end Daniel passed. He believed. He believed that the word of God could lift from the books that bound it. He believed in a voice that spoke in the night, even if he had never heard it. And he believed all that the director had told him, except the part about any young man being tame as a rabbit.

"How long was it you lived in the church, then?" Daniel said. He was driving his truck to town to pick up a few items for Mrs. Schlant, and while he had intended to bring Lizzy along for a talk, Joel had shown up carrying a satchel over his shoulder and invited himself along instead. Rather than Lizzy, then, Daniel had gone up to the homeschool and fetched Zach, because he, too, had a responsibility to know who was spending time with his sister.

"I'm not sure," Joel said, yawning and stretching his arms out in front of him. "I guess I lost track. A few months, maybe."

"And you read the entire Ellen White library while you were there? The whole thing?"

"And a bunch of other books, of course," Joel said offhandedly. "But nothing much holds up to Mrs. White." He began to quote. "Let the youth remember that here they are to build characters for eternity, and that God requires them to do their best. Let those older in experience watch over the younger ones; and when they see them tempted, take them aside, and pray with them and for them."

"I see," Daniel said, falling silent for a moment. "And what else did you learn from all that time?"

"Well, since the only food I had was what was whatever people left behind after potlucks, I learned that some casseroles go into the fridge untouched for a reason."

Zach was the one to snort, and Daniel, who glanced back at him through the rear-view mirror, knew they were both thinking of the same brown and grey matter, the shredded carrot-and-raisin-studded agar agar salads, the freezer-burnt offerings that even the people who brought them could no longer seem to identify. For that matter, Marie's food, even fresh from the oven, hadn't been much better. But at least with her, because he kept track of the receipts, he had always known what had or hadn't gone into it.

"So, what is it you need from town?" Daniel asked Joel, trying a different approach.

"Vegemite," Joel replied, and Daniel took note of how quick he always was with an answer. "I got a taste for it down in the church basement. The staff were always leaving jars behind, and Mrs. Schlant said she'd make me some next week—she has a recipe for every-thing—but the health food shop next to the post office has it, so I told her I'd get a jar for our toast. You can just drop me off there."

Once in town, Joel got out in front of the shop and leaned back into the truck before closing the door.

"We can wait," Daniel said. "If you're just getting Vegemite."

"You and Zach go ahead. I'll be here when you get back. Zach, should I go to the grocery store too and get some of those cherry candies Lizzy and your mom like?"

Once Joel disappeared inside the health food store, Zach climbed into the front seat and pulled the belt over his shoulder, adjusting it to fit snugly across his smaller waist.

"I suppose you like him," Daniel said, and Zach shrugged.

"He's all right. It's good for Lizzy to have a friend, I guess."

"And you think girls and boys can be friends?" Daniel said.

Zach shrugged again. "Mrs. Schlant goes down to check on them all the time. And she sends us. I mean all us kids. They're always just planting things when we show up. Mrs. Schlant says boys and girls need to be supervised for their own good. She says boys can't be expected to trust themselves because God made us that way."

"Okay, Zach. That's good to know," Daniel said. A few blocks down the road, however, he flicked on his signal and turned left into the parking lot at the back of the Seventh-day Adventist Church.

"Come on," he said to Zach, who trailed along behind him like a duck on a string. "You and I need to know everything we can about anyone who spends that much time with your sister."

They'd all been here, every Sabbath. A brown building, inside and out, the church's roof vaulted toward the back of the sanctuary. A sign out front, with changeable letters, listed the times for Sabbath School and Service, and proclaimed that *All Life Grows Better Under the Son*. Surrounded on three sides by an asphalt skirt, and on the fourth by a bed of green-blooming hydrangeas, it was easy to overlook.

Today, instead of the combined scents of fabric softener from ladies' fresh laundry, and the mothballs that filled certain men's pockets, it smelled of warm copy paper, freshly imprinted with ink. Pastor Emmons, a short man with a fluff of grey hair, a deep widow's peak and stacked heels, was busy sifting this week's newsletters and tithe envelopes into a bank of member mailboxes.

"Good afternoon, Pastor," Daniel said, putting out his hand. "If you don't mind, I've come to have a quick look around, and then I'd like a few minutes of your time."

Pastor Emmons, who had looked startled at first, appeared even more so as he shuffled his papers from one hand to the other to take Daniel's in an obligatory shake.

"Of course, of course. God's house is your house," he said. The two men had talked after most sermons. Daniel was in the habit of challenging preachers who took too much liberty in their interpretations of scripture, finding lively metaphors between every line. Pastor Emmons was no exception.

Daniel felt good about neither of them wearing masks. "It's nice to see a face," he said.

"Well, I wasn't expecting anyone. But yes. We do all miss that these days, don't we?"

The downstairs Fellowship Hall, a concrete bunker with tables festooned with plastic flowers, was currently occupied by the church secretary. Olivia Pender had taken up a table for eight and spread out a ream of papers, along with a plate of toast smothered in jam.

"I hope that's some of Stillwater's bread," Daniel said.

"In fact, it is," said Olivia, covering her mouth to speak. She swallowed hard and lowered her hand. "I tried to sprout some grain and make it myself at home, but nothing I did turned out the same."

Daniel recognized a slice of Stillwater's flax loaf and felt a warmth of pride. He took it as a good sign and helped himself to a chair across from her. He looked her in the face, and when she didn't look away, it seemed he could expect from her the sort of honesty he was looking for. Then again, a woman with an unashamed stare might be another kind of concern.

"You spend a lot of time here," Daniel said, "so you'd know. How is it, do you think, that that boy Joel lived inside this church for so long without being noticed?"

Olivia's smile was as bright as her jam. "Oh," she said, her voice filled with wonder. "We know God had something to do with that. But come look for yourself." She stood, inviting him to follow.

Daniel, who didn't like to be alone with a woman who was not his wife, motioned for Zach to follow them out of the Fellowship Hall and down a bunchy-carpeted hallway flanked by closed doors to various children's classrooms.

"We keep them shut to save on heat during the week. Here. This is the one," Olivia said. She reached for the doorknob.

"How did he come to be here at all?" Daniel asked before they stepped inside.

"We're not sure about that. Joel never said, unless he's spoken to your Mr. Schlant out there. But there was a man around here for a while with a camper truck. A blustery fellow. Red in the face. The elders tried to help, gave him food and prayer, and they say he mentioned a boy sometimes. When he finally moved on—and I must say a good many of us ladies were glad that he did—well, a couple of months later, we found Joel in here." She moved aside, revealing a storage room filled with church supplies.

At first, nothing looked out of the ordinary. Daniel began to pick his way through the warren of disused items and then there it was: a hollow, under a table, where what looked more like a nest than a bed had been made and surrounded by books.

"Blankets from ADRA donations," Olivia said. "We think he washed them in the laundry we keep for things that come in. And of course, there would've been clothes for him there, as well. He never once took from the lost and found, though. He wouldn't know it, but I keep a log of what's in there, so I don't have to come down and check every time someone calls about a missing glove."

Daniel crouched until he was sitting on his heels, his tendons stretching painfully to enable a better look. He reached into the nest of blankets and touched the flannel of a fitted sheet whose elastics had long since lost their resilience. A small stuffed animal peered out at him from behind a corner of fabric, a rabbit with glass eyes that seemed far too knowing for a toy.

As a boy, Daniel had kept a cache of bedding in the hayloft of his father's barn. The mice got to it between the times he hid himself away, nibbling at the quilted cotton to extract the batting inside. Every time Daniel had gone there, the blankets had been a little thinner. And every time he had awoken, he had found a mouse sitting nearby, or curled up with him along the edge of a tattered covering.

"So, he really lived here?" Zach said, bringing Daniel back to the storage room where, for the first time, he felt how cold this room must have been, especially at night.

"I keep meaning to clean it up," said Olivia, whom Daniel had almost forgotten. "But every time I come to take it all away, I feel like I'm intruding on something that shouldn't be disturbed."

"You should take it away," Daniel said. "There's nothing here that needs remembering."

Daniel and Zach left the church without talking to Pastor Emmons again. They got into the truck, drove to the grocery store, fulfilled Mrs. Schlant's list, and were about to return for Joel when Daniel pulled to the side of the road. He shifted the truck out of gear and set the parking brake. "We don't need to tell anyone where we've been today."

"Everyone already knows."

"Not the store. The church. No one needs to know we went asking about Joel. He deserves his privacy."

"Everybody already knows about that, too."

"Yes. But did you see how they're keeping it like a shrine? It's not right. He should be allowed to forget and have everyone else forget along with him. Do you understand?"

"No."

"Zach. If you can't put yourself in someone else's place, then just do as I say." He shifted back into gear and they soon pulled up alongside the health food store where Daniel motioned for Zach to give Joel the front seat.

Joel took a jar of Vegemite from his pocket and set it in the cup holder between them. Daniel was sure it was just for show, and that Joel had another reason for coming into town. But he no longer cared what it was.

"I've never tried Vegemite," he said. "What's it like?"

"Salty. Sticky. Kind of like spreading beef bouillon on toast. If you know what beef tastes like."

"Interesting. My mother used to roast our cow bones before simmering them for soup. I always thought it made the kitchen smell like burnt hair. But her soup, back before I found the church and learned a better way, was very good."

Zach leaned forward between the front seats and cleared his

throat. "I didn't know you used to eat cows," he said, inserting himself into the conversation. "Why can't I have a cheeseburger, then?"

"Because you have to kill them first. If you can kill one, you can eat one," Daniel said.

"Cool," Zach said. "Lizzy only ever got to cut them up." He coughed a little, then sat back in his seat.

Daniel could feel the weight of his own father's bolt gun in his hand. "Zach, I've never even seen you kill a flower."

"So, Lizzy really was a butcher?" Joel said after a while.

"I guess," Daniel said, surprised Lizzy had told anyone about her job. "She was more of butcher's assistant. She likes to know about the insides of things."

"I thought she was kidding," Joel said. "I didn't think she'd actually know where my spleen was when she said she'd stab it out for me."

"She wasn't kidding," Daniel said, half amused, half concerned. "Well, hopefully the part about taking out your spleen." He turned right off the highway and bumped along until they reached the laneway that took them back to the community.

"Thanks for the ride," Joel said, getting out. Daniel watched as the boy made his way back to the greenhouse. A few minutes later, when he emerged again, Daniel shooed Zach away and waited until Joel had crossed the lawn and disappeared into Mrs. Schlant's kitchen before heading to the greenhouse himself.

"Dad?" Lizzy said, coming out from the storage room at the back.

"Working hard?" Daniel said and heard his own father's voice. *Or hardly working?*

"I'm done, actually. Just putting some things away."

"I see. Well, that's good. I don't want to take you away from . . ." Daniel let his voice trail off. He knew Lizzy was not of much use here, but until the director decided to find a better fit, this is where she had to be. "How's it going here? With you, I mean." He walked alongside his daughter until they reached the front of the greenhouse, where he sat down on a potting stool and spun it a few degrees to face her. She did the same.

Lizzy reached out and dragged her hand along the upturned faces of edible flowers that were huddled together in a transplant tray. Even Daniel could see they seemed to cringe beneath her touch.

"It's nice in here," she said, then corrected herself. "I mean, it smells nice. It's pleasant and all that. But I'm not good at plants. Joel says they can tell I resent them."

"And Joel? Is he teaching you a lot?"

Lizzy shrugged.

"Does he do anything else?"

Lizzy drew her head back. "What do you mean?"

"I mean, does he ever make you feel uncomfortable? Does he, I don't know, watch you when you work, or get too close when he's showing you how to do something?" Daniel's heart had started to beat loud enough for him to hear and he was having a hard time getting enough breath to keep on speaking. "He's a young man, Lizzy, and I expect you to know what that means."

Lizzy stopped him. "I didn't like him the first time you brought us here. Not. One. Bit," she said, crossing and uncrossing her arms. "But everyone else seems to think he's just fine."

"And did I ever teach you to think like everyone else?" Daniel said. "Well?"

"Yes. Of course you taught me to think like everyone else. But only if you agree with them first." She muttered this last part, and Daniel slid his hands into his pockets to keep them from turning into fists. His mother had taught him to do that after he'd put a hole in her wall. They'd patched it together with a scrap of drywall, toothpaste instead of spackle, and a drizzle of old paint. He had had to fix the wall in Kelowna a few times, as well. For those times, he had gone to the hardware store to get proper spackle.

"I'm going to ignore that," Daniel said, after chewing on the words a few times. "Look. That young man, I can tell you, deserves every benefit of the doubt we can all give him. But I also know a thing or two about boys his age. I was one, and I don't trust them with a daughter of mine, and it doesn't matter what everyone or anyone else thinks, unless it's about you. If people start to get the wrong idea, you could end up with a real problem here."

"So, what do you expect me to do?" Lizzy said. "Are you going to have me moved from the greenhouse?"

Daniel pushed his fists deeper into his pockets and leaned back a little. He felt good about what he'd accomplished so far today. "I'm not going to do anything. I've told you what I think, and now it's up to you to make the best of things."

HOMEMADE VEGEMITE

1 litre Brewer's yeast
1 tsp kosher salt
1 onion, diced
2 medium carrots, diced (storage carrots are best)
1 medium turnip, diced
½ celery stick, diced

Place brewer's yeast and salt in a double boiler. Using a thermometer, keep warm on the stove at blood temperature for 10 hours or overnight. In the morning, increase heat and simmer the mixture at 50–60°C for 2 or 3 hours, then at 90° for 30 minutes more.

Filter mixture through cheesecloth and a sieve. Discard liquid. Allow to drip for a full day to further drain. Discard liquid.

Boil the vegetables until very soft. Strain, mash fine and incorporate into the yeast mixture. To turn into a paste, transfer mixture onto a large flat pan and place in a low oven to allow the moisture to evaporate. Be sure watch very closely, stirring often. Let the mixture reduce into a sticky paste. Transfer into jam jars and refrigerate.

CLOVE OIL TOOTHPASTE

During the night, even though it was almost summer, Lizzy's bed felt as damp and cold as a fish.

She had barely slept. And when she managed to at all, the cold only sunk deeper until, finally, she had touched two frozen fingers to the inside of her own wrist to find whether she could still detect a pulse.

With proof of life, a raw ache in her muscles and a pressure in her chest, Lizzy slid her feet to the floor and made her way to the bathroom. She had already tried warming herself with extra blankets. She had tried crawling into bed with Zach, who had kicked back at the touch of her icy feet without waking.

Back in Kelowna, she would have gotten into bed with Marie, but now her father had taken the place next to her mother, and Lizzy couldn't gather up the courage to attempt another few hours under her own icy quilt. Instead, she padded her way to the bathroom where, by the glow of a nightlight, she spun the bathtub faucet to hot and leaned into the resulting cloud of steam.

Her nose dripped and her mouth felt dry, as though it had been lined with cotton balls, and before she stripped off her pajamas she dipped her toothbrush into a jar of clove oil toothpaste, a personal jar with her name written on the side. With her tongue and gums numb from the spice, Lizzy wadded her pajamas onto the toilet seat as a layer of moisture from the bath settled over her in a fine mist.

The tub was always scrupulously clean here, but she still swished a few splashes of water up the sides before lowering the plug and allowing it to fill. The effort took too much energy, though, so she stepped into the water as it poured in, knelt and closed her eyes. At first, the water was almost too hot to bear, but the steam felt good in her lungs. After she was used to it, Lizzy slid back until she was half submerged. She silent-screamed when the heat scalded the ragged, still-pink scar on top of her thigh.

When the level reached the overflow drain, Lizzy turned off the faucet with her toes. She pinched her nose, closed her eyes and slipped her head underwater. It was the first time she had been completely submerged since the night in the lake, and she told herself it wasn't so bad. The air was right there, just centimeters away. And it was so wonderfully warm. When she surfaced, she reached for a fresh washcloth, dunked it, then used it to capture a bubble of air. Years ago, this had been the first science experiment she could remember having ever conducted as a child. It had fascinated her and taken several trips to the library before she formed a hypothesis about the role of hydrogen bonds in the surface tension of liquid, held in shape by the cotton. In childish notes scribbled into a specially lined notebook meant to record musical notes and rhythms, she had explained that the same force that trapped water molecules in a cloth also allowed a water strider to skim a pond. One hydrogen atom clung lightly to the oxygen in the next, holding together like hands held around a table for prayer.

Lizzy dragged the sopping cloth over her face. She leaned her head against the back rim of the tub and began to count silently. One, two three, she thought, using a small cup to pour more water over the cloth. Four, five, six. This, too, had been one of her childhood games, one she had used to train her breath for swim lessons, or one of her father's interrogations where breathing too much, like blinking, was taken as a sign of guilt. Holding her breath often served to calm her.

Thirteen, fourteen, fifteen, sixteen . . . By the time Lizzy reached her own age, she could feel a softening around the edges of her mind. But before it could sink any deeper, there was a single, sharp blow against the bathroom door. She gasped against the soaked washcloth, and it sealed itself over her mouth and nose. At the same time, she pushed against the end of the tub with her feet; a wave crested over the side and splashed to the floor. Lizzy sat up coughing as the cloth fell to her naked lap.

From the other side of the door, she heard her father's voice. "You aren't in bed," he said.

At once, Lizzy felt every inch of her own bare skin, including the scar no one but the doctor who had sewn it had ever seen. Even Dr. Vickers hadn't seen it; Lizzy had taken the stitches out herself.

"I was cold," Lizzy said, pulling a towel into the tub to cover herself. "I'm coming out right away." She gripped the edges of the tub and pushed her way to almost standing, stepping out onto a bathmat now swampy with bathwater. Her head began to go dark, and a moment later she fell to the floor.

Mrs. Schlant came in and draped the windows in Lizzy's shared room with heavy blankets. Every six hours, she smeared Lizzy's chest with a fresh mustard plaster that burned at her skin. Each time, she changed the onions in Lizzy's socks and fed her a spoonful of paste from a tube. "We're lucky there's a horse rancher nearby to give us this," she said to someone else in the room.

Coughing from morning to night and then through the darkness, Lizzy lost track of the days.

She wasn't the only one sick. She was aware enough to know that Zach was coughing, too, and from the snippets of conversation that filtered through Lizzy's waking dreams, she could tell there were others.

Marie's soothing voice and a cooling cloth on Lizzy's forehead.

Marie's voice and spoonfuls of broth tipped into Lizzy's mouth.

And then Zach's voice saying, "Dad's okay. Which is good because with Beatrice gone now, someone has to help out in the laundry."

"Gone?" Lizzy coughed out the word, which razored its way out of her lungs.

"Yeah. She hardly seemed sick at first, but when she didn't get out of bed yesterday, Jimena and Mom found her. She was still in bed and hardly breathing. The Lord took her before lunchtime."

"Mom?"

"You're really tired. Dad said to let you sleep."

When Lizzy was finally able to sit up and then stand on her own, the soles of her feet were blistered and smelled like soup. Her chest ached from the inside and burned on the outside. The air around her felt thick, as though she was breathing through a wrung-out cloth.

For the first time in weeks, Lizzy was able to bathe. She still needed help from Mrs. Schlant, who had sponged her through the worst of her illness.

"Lizzy, a few of us would like to talk with you now that you're feeling stronger," said the director's wife as she towelled Lizzy's hair.

Clean and dressed, Lizzy sat on the edge of the landing and slid down, stair by stair, to the bottom floor of the house.

"Thank you for coming," said Director Schlant when she reached the living room. It was the first time Lizzy had seen or heard him since the night her father broke down the bathroom door, wrapped her in towels and carried her to bed.

"Okay," Lizzy said, looking around to where the rest of the community was already seated.

"Here, sit over here with me, over by your dad and brother," said Mrs. Schlant, holding Lizzy's arm.

"What's going on?"

"I made you some nice tea," said Jimena. "Chamomile. Not too hot."

"Zach told me about Beatrice. I'm really sorry. She was a good friend to my mom," Lizzy said, although the last part was only sort of true. "Right, Dad?"

"That's right, honey."

"Where is Mom?"

"Lizzy."

"No, seriously. Where is Mom?" Lizzy began to gasp.

"Most of us didn't get sick at all, praise the Lord," said Director Schlant.

"Dad?"

"We prayed and prayed, Lizzy," said Mrs. Schlant. "But Marie needed a little more help than the rest of us. More than even your father could give her."

"Prayer only works if every one of us is doing our part," said one of the other women.

"Yes, and that's why we want to talk to you, Lizzy. Your mom is in the hospital in Kelowna. We won't stop praying for the tube to come out, but we learned something these last few weeks about you and your mother. We know about the drugs you were giving her. We found the rest and put them in the burning barrel this morning. And part of what we've discerned in prayer now is that there's something you need to do to bring your mother home."

Lizzy's spine felt watery, and she slid from her seat to the floor, where she tried to prop herself up with her hands. She'd divided up her mother's prescriptions as soon as they arrived, realizing that the director and her father would go through her things if they got a chance. But Daniel had never once thought to look inside Hermione for whatever Lizzy needed to keep hidden, so the last of Marie's sleeping pills, Ativan, fentanyl stickers and half a bottle of Dilaudid stuffed with cotton were likely still wadded up in her old teddy bear.

"Since you came to us, we've been letting you get away with some things," said Director Schlant. "Hoping that you would come to recognize them for yourself. It's time, now."

Lizzy could barely hear her own voice. "What are you talking about?"

Mrs. Schlant leaned forward and picked up something wrapped on the tea table in front of her. "We're trying to be delicate, Lizzy, but here. It's one of the dresses from your closet. It should be your decision, but we need you to put it on. I'll help. And then I'll bring down your old clothes for the burning barrel. There are some tights for you here, too."

"Dad," Lizzy said, struggling to her knees, her voice rising with her, before deflating again into a painful wheeze. "This is your fault. Mom would be vaccinated by now if we hadn't come here. She got her flu shot. But she wouldn't get this one. Because of you."

Lizzy slumped forward and held her throat with one hand. Her lungs felt full of glass. "How many times are you going to try to kill her?"

Marie was still in the hospital a month later, when Lizzy was well enough to return to the greenhouse.

"How is she?" Joel said.

"Same."

"But not worse?"

"No. She can't really get worse."

"Sorry. The dress looks good, though," he said. "A little loose."

Lizzy had no doubt the dress would have fit before she got sick. It clearly had room for the almost twenty pounds she'd sweated into her sheets. "Yeah, the dress is great."

"No, I mean, really. I like it."

"Well, then, you should wear it," Lizzy said and scooped up two handfuls of potting soil to cram into a new tray.

"Calm down. I'm just trying to give you a compliment. Do you really like going around looking like a boy? Or making it hard for the men here not to look at you?"

Lizzy clenched her muddied fists and found a pair of pockets to stuff them into.

"What I wear and whether I like it has nothing to do with you or . . . or . . ." Lizzy, fists still in her pockets, flapped the skirt of her dress and waved in the direction of the house. "Them."

"Ellen White would disagree. Have you read—"

"Oh my God. Just shut up about Ellen White. I don't want to hear it today."

"Hey," Joel said, grabbing Lizzy by the arm. "Questioning everyone around here is one thing. Flaunting your legs in pants is one thing. Being blasphemous about our prophet isn't something I'll accept. Not from anyone."

Lizzy dug her fingernails into the top of Joel's hand. "Let go of me, Joel."

"Say you're sorry."

"You're hurting me."

"Say it."

"I'm sorry," Lizzy said, and Joel let go.

"I forgive you, and so will God. Here, I picked this up yesterday," he said, reaching under his workbench for a padded envelope from Miss Taylor.

Lizzy ripped open the seal. Already, she could feel the impressions from Joel's fingers starting to bruise under her sleeve.

"You could just say thank you. I put your lesson packets in the cellar."

"Thank you," Lizzy said, not to Joel, but to the teacher who had graded her latest exam. "I'm going downstairs. Cover for me."

Down in the cellar at the back of the greenhouse, surrounded by shelves of gardening tools and empty canning jars, Lizzy spread out the textbooks she kept hidden behind a wall of vegetable sacks and opened her newest envelope. Buried as she was in this potato-scented gloom, she left the overhead hatch open to allow her eyes to adjust to the single bulb of light.

> June 3, 2021
> Dear Lizzy,
> You are dearly missed in class. Today I brought in a calf fetus for the Grade 12s to dissect—you could have shown them how it's done. You know how the church wants lots of doctors and nurses for the Lord, to testify in the End Times, so the school was happy to agree. A doctor came in and did a career day at the same time.
> Anyway, the fetus was given to me by a farmer I know in Armstrong and, while there, I thought about how close I was to Stillwater. I wondered about stopping by but didn't want to cause any trouble for you, if that's the kind of thing they consider trouble there.
> I think about you, though, pursuing your studies. I hope your father has come around and you're able to do so without having to hide. Either way, I'm proud of you, my clever girl. If you need anything at all, you know how to reach me.
> I've included a little gift, which I couldn't have given you when you were when you were an academy student. At the very least, it will help you better understand what you're studying now.
> All my best wishes,
> Miss Natalie Taylor
> PS They've opened up vaccines for your age group now, so if there's any way to get yourself to town, find a pharmacy. I pray all is well with your family.

Lizzy set the letter in the well of her lap and wept. When she was able to collect herself, she wiped her eyes and nose on the sprawling handkerchief of her skirt and opened her teacher's gift: Charles Darwin's *Origin of Species*. Inside the front cover, Miss Taylor had written, *Between God and Science, all truth can be known.*

Her eyes having adjusted, Lizzy climbed up the ladder and closed the hatch over her head. Returning to the dirt floor below, she sat, leaned against a sack of potatoes and began to read, grateful for the extra warmth of the jeans she'd kept back from the burn barrel. She wore them over her tights, rolled up to her knees beneath her dress.

No more than twenty minutes passed before Lizzy heard a squeak of floorboards and her father's voice.

"I need to see Lizzy. Why isn't she here?"

"I don't know," Joel said, and Lizzy heard him step directly onto the hatch. "She was pretty upset about about having to wear that dress."

"I see. But just so we understand each other, that's my concern and not yours. Right?" Daniel's voice was surprisingly soft. "Lizzy is not yours to worry about."

"Of course," Joel said. "And just so you know, I have a great deal of respect for you. And for Mrs. Fischer. I'm happy to keep an eye on Lizzy for you while she's away. You know how young girls are. They always have their minds on something and forget to think it all the way through."

By the time her father walked away, and she heard the sound of the greenhouse door swing shut out front, Lizzy could barely breathe.

Joel opened the hatch to the cellar and shone a light down. "Your dad's looking for you."

"I heard. Thanks for not telling," Lizzy said, a little sourly, climbing back into the greenhouse. This time, she meant it.

"What good would it do me to tell on you? Your dad already thinks I'm not good enough to be around you."

Lizzy hesitated. Something in Joel's voice had changed, and she felt the hair on her arms prickle in response.

"Actually, he likes you. He just thinks I'm too young to—"

"What? Have a friend? Have someone teach you things? Exactly what does he think is going on with us?"

It felt like an accusation. Part of Lizzy wanted to take a step toward Joel, while another wanted to take two steps back. With the hatch still open behind her, she stayed where she was. "He thinks . . . He thinks boys can't handle the sight of a girl in jeans," Lizzy said. "And you said as much yourself."

"Yeah, well, he might be right about that," Joel said and started to walk away.

"I meant he thinks we can't just be friends."

"Really?" Joel said and turned back. "And what do you think?"

Lizzy didn't know what she thought. In her time in the greenhouse, she had swung from suspicion to trust and back more than once. She would think he was a friend and then, moments later, he'd become someone she'd rather not know. She had been grateful to have at least one other person who was sort of her age, while also feeling she might be better off as the only one. Sometimes she looked for him at breakfast. Sometimes she hoped he wouldn't show up.

"I think you're a friend. But maybe you're not used to having one," Lizzy said, realizing the same thing could be said about her.

"Okay," Joel said, moving toward her. "But do *you* think we can just be friends?"

This time, Lizzy took an instinctive step back.

"Watch it!" Joel said, snatching her by the waist a moment before she would have fallen into the open cellar.

"My dad—" Lizzy said.

"Your dad isn't the problem. He's just the excuse you're using because you don't like me."

"I never said that."

"You don't have to." Joel let go of Lizzy and went around her to close the hatch.

"I like you just fine."

"Do you? You never want to spend any time with me unless it's here. And you don't have any choice about being here. So what am I supposed to think?"

"But we're here for hours almost every day. And my dad—"

"Stop using him as an excuse. I can handle him if I have to."

Lizzy froze. What, exactly, did he mean by that?

"I should go down and put my things away," she said. "I'll tell my dad I wasn't feeling well. He'll believe that. And maybe he's heard something about my mom and that's why he was here."

"Tired," Lizzy said, when her father found her climbing the stairs to her room. When it seemed like he was about to question her, she pressed her hands onto her low belly. "Cramps."

Daniel stopped her mid-climb. "I see. Did you ask Mrs. Schlant for supplies for that?"

"I have what I need," Lizzy said. "Maybe you could get me a hot water bottle."

"Your mother said the ladies make reusable items for themselves. Are you taking advantage of those?"

Lizzy made a face. "I still have some store-bought ones from home. I stocked up."

"It's a bit early in the month for you, isn't it?"

"Excuse me?"

"I mean, you were on your period three weeks ago. And now again?" Daniel narrowed his eyes.

"It happens sometimes," she said. "And if you're keeping track, then you'd know that."

Lizzy stomped up the rest of the stairs and disappeared, just for a minute, into the room she still shared with Zach. When she came back out, she was carrying a plastic-wrapped pad for effect.

"How are things with you and Joel?" Daniel said, having followed her up to the landing. He now stood outside the bathroom door, blocking her way.

"Just friends. Not even that."

"Having him cover for you seems like you're friends at the very least," Daniel said. "Maybe it's time to find you a different place to work. With Mrs. Schlant. Or Jimena needs help in the laundry. Or there's the bakery, you know. I'm sure the school could even use someone like you. Didn't you say you could teach every class?"

"You never said you wanted me to quit working with Joel."

"I shouldn't have to spell out everything for you. Not when you keep letting us all know how smart you are."

"Maybe I'm not so smart, after all. If I was, Mom might not be in the hospital with a tube down her throat."

When Daniel spoke, his voice had softened. "I'm only trying to protect you, Lizzy," he said. "All of you." He touched the side of her face with the back of his hand. It smelled of stale smoke, and Lizzy wondered where, among so many watchful eyes, he found a place to keep such a thing to himself.

"You're smoking again," she said, and Daniel tucked her hair behind her ear before lowering his hand.

"It's been a difficult few months," he said.

"You promised you wouldn't."

"I'll quit again. I promise. I'll do it right now. If you go see the director and talk about where else you might be able to serve."

"And if I don't, you'll keep smoking?"

"I don't want to put it that way."

"But that's the way it is?"

"Lizzy, listen to me. You should know this by now, but you can't trust boys. They're all the same in a certain way; they don't think the way girls do. Especially someone Joel's age. It's the way God made them. It's God's design for humans, but it means that it's up to you to make sure you aren't a problem."

"Are you done?" Lizzy said.

"If you've heard me, then yes. I'm done."

Lizzy was trembling now and didn't try to hide it. She pushed past her father and into the bathroom, but he caught the door before she could close it.

"I'll know if you've lied to me about anything," Daniel said, and shut the door himself.

Lizzy turned the lock and collapsed onto the toilet seat. She hated it here. She hated Joel, simply for existing. And most of all, she hated her father.

What, exactly, did he mean by knowing whether she was lying to him? Did he know about her classes? That Joel was getting her mail for her? That she had been right beneath his feet when he had come looking for her in the greenhouse? That she was not getting her period right now?

At least for the last part, Lizzy knew what she had to do. She got up, took a straight razor from inside the medicine cabinet behind the mirror above the sink, and rinsed it with a splash of yellow Listerine.

Lifting her dress and lowering her jeans, she ran a finger over her scar. Just a nick was all she needed, she told herself as she pinched the razor between her fingers and poised it over her thigh. Next to the scars she already had, a new one would blend right in.

Lizzy took a deep breath, and before she cut, reached for her toothbrush and bit it between her teeth. With the scent of cloves filling her nose, she made a short, shallow incision and soaked the flow of blood up into a pad. When it was enough, she wrapped the pad in toilet paper and placed it in the garbage before dressing her wound.

"Lizzy," Daniel said from just outside the door. "I meant to tell you. They're taking your mom off the vent."

CLOVE OIL TOOTHPASTE

>   3 ounces kosher salt
>   6 ounces baking soda
>   6 drops clove oil

Combine well and keep in a small jar. To use: dip toothbrush into mixture and brush as usual. Keep covered.

APRICOT PLATZ

Daniel replaced the cloth on Director Schlant's forehead. While the first of Stillwater's residents to become sick had mostly recovered, the director and some others had since taken their place.

It happened the day after Lizzy was finally well enough to return to the greenhouse. The director collapsed while out surveying the orchards. Hail had destroyed the fruit of other farmers in the region but passed over all but a few of Stillwater's trees. The greenhouse was unharmed, and only a few apricots were damaged. The women quickly came out with baskets to collect the spoils for baking and jam. Marie had an old farm recipe. One of the only ones that Daniel had ever liked. Maybe if he could find that, Mrs. Schlant would agree to make it for dessert tonight.

Daniel pressed his stethoscope—a gold-plated gift marking his tenth anniversary at Cotton Glenn—to the director's chest and listened to the crackles of breath deep under his skin. Crepitations. Profound enough that Daniel could feel them beneath his hand. If he could procure an x-ray, the lung tissue would look like the frosted glass of a shower door.

And yet, Director Schlant refused to be seen by a doctor. "If the Lord decides to take me, there's nothing that can add an hour to my life," he had managed to say between fits of coughs, only the day before last. He had grasped Daniel's hand. "This virus is a test, brother. A test of believers."

Daniel had tried to make him save his breath, but the director waved him back.

"This," he said, struggling to take in enough air to go on, "this is a trial run. We who keep the Sabbath Day holy will be persecuted at the appointed time. Those who choose Sunday—the devil's counterfeit—will come for us. This is just the same. Accepting a vaccine over faith. A tube down the throat. Just the same."

And then the director had prayed. He prayed that Daniel would stand fast, and God would forgive his lapse in seeking treatment for Marie.

Before he left the room, Daniel opened the director's mouth and slipped three children's aspirin from Marie's purse under his tongue. Afterwards, he made his rounds to the others who had succumbed to this second round of illness, changed their sheets where necessary and carried the laundry downstairs.

Without Beatrice to help, the volume of laundry was getting on top of Jimena. "You need to scrub out the vomit before it goes in my machine," she said. "And filth from the other end, too."

Daniel, who had only suffered a sore throat that had quickly passed, draped himself in a heavy, oilcloth apron covered in flowers and pulled on a pair of yellow rubber gloves before getting to work in the utility sink.

He was glad to have something to do. And before long, he and Jimena were outside, pinning sheets and pajamas to the line, where the heat from the sun dried the first items before they could hang up the last.

"I'll go up and check on the director again," Daniel said, leaving Jimena to start another cycle of wash on her own.

Upstairs, Mrs. Schlant sat rocking in a chair across from the bed where her husband wheezed and sputtered in his sleep. "It's good you're here with us," she said.

"I can only do so much. He really should see a doctor. There are at least three in the church in town. I'm sure any of them would come."

"And they'd be wrong," said Mrs. Schlant, threading a needle through a frame of embroidery in her lap. "You know what the director said. If God's remnant people don't pass this test, He won't bring on the Sabbath test for generations yet. God told him. It's just like in World War II, you know. That Hitler started with the Jews over in Europe, and he would have come for Adventists next, if he'd gotten as far as our shores."

"I don't think—" Daniel said.

"The Nazis were after the Sabbath-keepers. It's terrible to say, but if we had let him have his way, this old world could have passed and been made new already. Instead, it's up to us. We have the Ivermectin that the Lord provided through the horse people down the road. And we have prayer. No one can hope for any more than that."

Daniel leaned over the director for another listen to his lungs. "Hopefully tomorrow will turn things around," he said and left the room.

Within a week, the director began to breathe more easily, and Daniel, along with the others at Stillwater, couldn't help but think it was a miracle.

APRICOT PLATZ

2 ¼ cups flour
¾ cup sugar
¾ cup cold margarine
½ tsp baking powder
½ tsp baking soda
¾ cup plus 2 tbsps nut milk
1 egg substitute*
2 pounds frozen pitted apricots
⅓ cup brown sugar

Place apricots in a large saucepan over medium-low heat. Add a couple of tbsps water and close the lid. When thawed, add brown sugar and continue cooking until fruit is thoroughly heated and the juice bubbles and begins to thicken. Set aside. Grease and flour an 8 x 11 ½ x 2-inch glass baking dish. Set aside.

In a large bowl, whisk together flour and sugar. Using a pastry blender, cut in margarine until mixture is coarse and crumbly. Set aside 1 cup of the crumbs for the topping.

Into remaining crumbs, blend in baking powder and baking soda. Make a well in the centre and pour in nut milk and egg substitute. Using a fork, pull crumbs into the liquid in the centre, mixing just to combine. Spread ⅔ of the batter over the bottom and half-way up sides of the prepared dish. Using a slotted spoon to leave behind some of the fruit juices, spoon fruit over the batter. By spoonfuls, drop remaining batter evenly over top of fruit. Cover with set-aside crumbs and bake at 350°F for 40 minutes, or until a tester inserted in centre comes out clean. Let cool on a baking rack for 20 minutes before serving. Simmer the remaining juice over med-low heat, reducing it to a sauce to be drizzled over the cake.

*egg substitute: combine 1 tbsp ground flax with 3 tsps warm water. Let sit 5 minutes.

SPROUTED WHEAT BREAD

Marie sat back on the edge of her side of the bed and pressed her hands lightly over the ache in her chest. It had been three weeks since she'd come home from the hospital, but dressing herself had left her breathless again, and she could feel her heart knocking against the insides of her ribs as though death itself was still at her door.

"Mrs. Schlant has a surprise for you this morning," Daniel said. He climbed onto the bed behind Marie and brushed her hair into a bun. She could do it herself if she caught her breath. But since it seemed to be the one way Daniel had thought of to help settle her back into Stillwater, she was grateful for the attention.

"Where's Lizzy?" Marie asked. "She usually comes to say good morning."

"Probably over at the greenhouse even though I told her she should try something else. Are you sweating?"

"It's hot," Marie snapped. "Don't you sweat when it's hot?"

"Not like this. Do you feel okay? Is this still the fever?"

"Just take me to Mrs. Schlant if you aren't going to tell me what's going on."

"Have you seen Lizzy?" Marie asked after Daniel had dropped her off in the kitchen.

"I have," said Mrs. Schlant. "She grabbed a piece of toast and headed down to the greenhouse. She had on that new dress we made for her. Or, well, you picked out the fabric. She looked very pleasant in it. Fits her better."

Marie had come home from the hospital weaned off the medications. For four days, she hadn't approached Lizzy. The pills and patches would all be gone, anyway, she thought. Surely the director and Daniel had made sure. But on the fifth day, Marie had gone into Lizzy and Zach's room and fumbled through all of Lizzy's drawers and under her pillow.

Lizzy found her and had stuffed a partial bottle of Dilaudid into Marie's pocket, saying, "Don't ask again because that's all there is."

After the first week, Marie had tried to taper herself down again. Next she reasoned that she could go off all at once. It would be easier that way, because there wouldn't be any more temptation. Now, though, she was all out of pills and, after twelve hours with nothing but the last of the children's aspirin from her purse, she could feel a familiar crack of pain, deep in the knitted splinters of her bones. And, as Daniel had noticed, she had started to sweat as though it was already high summer.

Marie's head felt light, and she had to steady herself with the back of a chair.

"Lizzy can wait," said Mrs. Schlant. "Now, Marie. Do you know the reason I asked Daniel to bring you down? I think it's time you and I work on a little therapy together."

"Therapy?" Marie said, her heart striking striking hard against the inside wall of her chest.

"I don't know if you know this, but the director and I see you working in the bakery one day." She paused. "Of course, that's too much to ask of you now. But the other night in our prayers before bed, we talked with the Lord about your poor hands, and all you've been through, and it came to me. What you need is for your tissues to remember something they used to do. Something familiar."

"Okay," Marie said, lifting her hands from the chair to hold them close. "But I don't really see how I'll ever be of much use."

Mrs. Schlant pressed Marie with her warmest smile. "Never mind being useful. Today all you need to do is try to handle a little dough, because you and I are going to bake some bread together. What do you think of that?"

Marie knew exactly what she thought. "Oh, I don't know about that. I do want to," she said. "But Lizzy, or Daniel even, still have to help me cut my food."

"Yes. But you'll you'll see." Mrs Schlant took Marie's hands in her own, as softly as she spoke. "The Lord wouldn't have told me if it wasn't the right idea." She began to gather up bowls and directed Marie to wash her hands at the kitchen sink.

Marie started by lightly rubbing her skin with a small scoop of soap granules, before rinsing them under a stream of cool water.

As she dried her hands with a fresh tea towel, Mrs. Schlant handed her a wooden toothpick. "For under your nails," she said, and Marie did her best to pinch the splinter she had been given, digging away a few imaginary half-moons of dirt.

"As you know, the bread we make here is with sprouted grains. It might be a little different than you're used to, but when it's time to knead, I want you to get your hands in the dough. The way I'm sure you did when you were a girl. Your mother taught you, didn't she? I'm sure she must have."

Marie nodded. "*Zwieback*," she said, recalling the soft white milk buns they had always made at home. Instead of flour and milk, however, Mrs. Schlant set down a bowl of wheat berries that had been left to soak until each kernel had sprouted. Once drained, these went into an enormous food processor, together with proofed yeast, honey and salt.

For several minutes, the wheat whirred about in the machine's blades until it came together into a ball that Mrs. Schlant scooped out and dropped onto the counter in front of Marie. "It just needs a little kneading," she said. "Now, I know your hands remember how to do that."

Marie looked at the mound of yeasty-smelling mash in front of her.

"*Oba,* I don't know," Marie said.

Back in her mother's kitchen, not only had Marie's hands been strong and fit, but the dough in front of her had been sweet and soft. The smell of that morning's bacon and eggs would still grease the air with the aroma of ingredients—chickens and pigs—they had raised on scraps from their own table.

Marie touched, just lightly, the centre of the mass before her. It was warm and, she had to admit, felt comforting under her hands. As she began to push at the dough a little with the heels of her hands, she did find that her fingers and palms, too, began to remember how to work. Maybe she didn't need Lizzy, after all.

Slowly, carefully, and with sweat trickling down her back and into the dress shields under her arms, Marie kneaded the way her mother had always done, until she became less tentative, and the mass became more like a dough. Rougher. Abrasive, even. Like loofah, as Zach had said.

Mrs. Schlant was right. The dough felt good under her hands. Together with the sour smell of the yeast, it soon had Marie thinking of better times.

There was the day, early in her courtship with Daniel, that he had driven out to her family's farm to introduce himself. She had spent that morning shaping loaves into pans and had been proud to put out her best one, alongside her sister's slices of luncheon meats and marbled cheddar. Daniel, who had been vegetarian for most of two years, had eaten almost half of the bread himself, with cold pats of butter and most of the cheese, refusing the meats.

Years before that, there had been those days Marie had spent alongside her mother, spreading sheets of risen and punched-down, rolled-out dough, covered with softened butter and piled high with cinnamon and sugar before they rolled them up, then sliced and arranged the rolls into pans to rise one more time before going into the oven.

"Very nice," said Mrs. Schlant, giving the dough a squeeze. "How does it feel?"

Until that moment, Marie had forgotten to be afraid. She had forgotten about the jagged surgical scars that crisscrossed one another on the backs of her hands, where the surgeon's scalpel had cut across shreds made when her finger bones had pierced through her skin from the inside. She had forgotten about waking up in hospital to hands held together with hardware. And she had forgotten the bone-deep pain that had been with her every moment of every waking day since then. She had even forgotten about waking up in the hospital again, this time to a tube being pulled out of her lungs.

"I . . ." Marie said, and her hands began to tremble, even as she gathered up the dough one last time and pushed down. "I . . ." Marie said again, turning to face Mrs. Schlant. Seeing a look of concern dawning across the older woman's face, Marie's newfound confidence began to crumble. "I . . . I have to go," Marie managed to say, before she turned on her heel and stumbled out of the kitchen.

Marie reached the middle steps on her way upstairs before a sudden crack of pain and nausea dropped her to her knees. The kneading had been too much. She needed more pills. Or stickers. Lizzy must have them somewhere.

Marie pressed her forehead into one carpeted tread. She gasped, hiccupping before her breath started to come in shallow breaths that began to darken the edges of her sight. "Lizzy," Marie said, a sob that turned into a remnant cough. "Someone needs to get Lizzy."

"There, there," said Mrs. Schlant, her voice soft as flannel as she sat next to Marie on the step. "Lizzy isn't what you need, is it? You need what she brings you. She kept some, did she? But that won't give any lasting comfort. Only God is able. Do you know that?"

Marie tried to speak but choked on her own breath. Finally, she was able to inhale, and with her lungs bursting, a scream wrung its way out from her throat and into the carpet.

Before long, Jimena joined them at the bottom of the stairs, asking if she could be of any use.

"All we can do right now is bear witness," said Mrs. Schlant, whose hand Marie felt cup her shoulder. "We can let our sweet sister know we will carry this with her."

"Lizzy," Marie sobbed, one syllable at a time, just before she began to heave.

"That vase will do," said Mrs. Schlant.

Marie felt her chin being gently lifted and a cylinder of cool ceramic held beneath her face. She came halfway up to kneeling, pulled the container into an embrace and emptied herself into it.

Sweat poured over her skin. Not like before. Nor like after a day's canning in the kitchen on the farm, or in the heat of an Okanagan afternoon, picking cherries. A flood of salt sprung into a river that ran down Marie's spine. The sweat from under her breasts soaked her bra. Her scalp drenched the roots of her hair. And sweat sluiced from the folds behind her knees. Even the cotton of her underwear held sweat against her skin like an unforgivable sin. Another round of vomiting threatened to come, but before it did, Marie shuddered so hard that her spine felt as though it would break.

"Well," said Mrs. Schlant, gathering several slips of Marie's hair that had escaped its bun. "Now we both know why the good Lord told me what He did. This is a burden you've been carrying too long now. You and Lizzy both."

SPROUTED WHEAT BREAD

5 cups wheat berries, soaked overnight in cold water
1 tbsp plus 1 tsp dry yeast
¼ cup lukewarm water
¼ cup plus 1 tsp honey
1 tbsp plus 1 tsp kosher salt

Drain the wheat berries and allow the berries to rest for 24–36 hours, until there are signs of germination.

Dissolve yeast in warm water, along with 1 tsp of the honey.

Place half of wheat berries in a food processor. Add half of the dissolved yeast, 2 tbsps honey and 2 tsps of salt and process several minutes until the mixture pulls away from sides of the bowl. Continue processing until a loose ball forms. Remove and repeat with second half of ingredients.

Knead both batches together into a large ball and place in a large bowl. Cover and allow to rise in a warm place for 3 hours.

Divide dough in two and place in two greased loaf pans. Cover with plastic wrap and allow to rise in pans for another hour until taller than the sides of the pans.

Bake at 350°F for 45–50 minutes.

When bread is cool enough to be handled, remove from pans and finish cooling on a wire rack. Do not eat until fully cooled as there may still be alcohol from the yeast.

GREEN GODDESS

Lizzy tucked the creation science textbook she'd been given under her arm.

"Do you really have to be our teacher?" Zach said as Lizzy bent down and rolled up her jeans so they wouldn't stick out from under her dress.

"It was Dad's idea. You'd have to take it up with him and the director."

"But everyone will treat me like I'm teacher's pet."

"Not if I'm mean to you. I could do that all day if you want." Lizzy smiled, and Zach did too.

"Maybe just a little. To let the other kids know I'm not special."

"Not special?" Lizzy said, making a face by pulling on the corners of her eyes and mouth and sticking out her tongue. "But you're the most special person I know."

Zach laughed. "Stop that. And don't do anything to embarrass me when we get to the school. Or in front of Thomas."

Lizzy put down the book and began to flail her arms like a cartoon ape, and soon Zach dissolved into giggles, pinching his nose to keep from being too loud.

"That, and don't say things like the science books here aren't real science books."

"But they're not," Lizzy said, sitting on the edge of her bed. "I mean, even the academy had real textbooks, even if they didn't like everything in them. This . . ." Lizzy held out the book. "I don't even know what to call this."

"Yeah, well. Just do what you're told, and you won't get into trouble again."

"I didn't mean for Mom . . ." Lizzy said. "She was in pain. I thought if I just helped her a little . . . Anyway, don't worry. I have something planned for science class today that doesn't involve opening a single page."

"Teaching will be good for you. You'll see," Daniel said as Lizzy and Zach came out of their bedroom.

"I'm sure," Lizzy said.

"After what happened with your mother. And, well, you know you were getting too close to Joel."

"He's in my class, you know," Lizzy said. "He's going to the greenhouse early to get everything done just so he can come to science."

"Well, that doesn't bother me so much. You can't get up to anything you shouldn't with a classroom full of kids."

The schoolhouse was an older model trailer home located across the yard. Lizzy hopped up to sit on the kitchen counter and faced her students. Including her brother, she had seven, from two in kindergarten to Joel, who had decided to return to school and Grade 11.

"Can you tell me a little about your science classes up until now?"

Joel was the first to put up his hand. "Are you actually qualified to teach anyone?" he said. His voice sounded brittle, much like when she told him she had to leave the greenhouse. At the time, just a few days ago now, she'd thought it would be best for him to hear it from her. "Or are you going to be just as bad at this as you were at growing plants?" Now, Lizzy was almost sure, he was trying to make a joke.

"I am absolutely not qualified. Just like everyone else around here. Does anyone else have a question?"

Ruth's hand was next in the air.

"Is your mom going to be okay?" she said, and suddenly the other children stopped fidgeting and offered Lizzy their full attention.

Lizzy looked down at her lap and twisted the heels of her hands against each other, hard. "I don't know," she said. "I mean, she'll stop feeling so sick pretty soon, I think."

"My grandmother says you gave her drugs. She says you're just as bad as a drug dealer and she doesn't want you teaching me anything," said Thomas.

Lizzy decided that question period was over and slid off the countertop, back to her feet. "I've decided that we'll spend our first class together outside."

Fetching down some old Tupperware bowls and a larger plastic tub she'd spotted earlier earlier, Lizzy paired off her students, taking the littlest girl, Anita, into her own care, and assigning Joel to look after the youngest boy, Timothy.

Handing each pair a bowl and a lid, she said, "We're going on a scavenger hunt." Her tone was more enthusiastic than she suddenly felt.

"What are we looking for?" Anita said, slipping her hand into Lizzy's.

"Well, we'll look for a lot of things, and some of them we'll write down in these journals," Lizzy said, distributing four scrap paper notebooks she had stapled together, along with a bouquet of freshly sharpened pencils. "I want you to write down all the birds and mammals you see. And in the bowls, I want you to collect things like worms and droppings and, if you're lucky enough to find some, old animal bones or owl pellets we can dissect later."

"Isn't that unclean?" Ruth asked.

"We'll wash our hands when we're finished," Lizzy said. "But it's okay to touch, just not eat. Otherwise, we'd never be able to pet a cat or a dog, right?"

Ruth, together with her partner Meagan, replied to Lizzy with a harmonious "Ew."

"You know we girls use these bowls in culinary science, don't you?" Meagan said.

Seriously? thought Lizzy. At their age, she would have trampled over the other students in her class to go out on a nature hunt.

"We'll use bleach on them," Lizzy said before sending the kids out the door. "And one more thing. Ruth and Meagan, if you can manage it, try to get just a little bit dirty. It's good for your immune system." *But not as good as vaccines.*

This time, it was Meagan who shot up her hand.

"Yes," Lizzy said. "You will be graded on it."

Both Ruth and Meagan frowned, but it was Ruth who went back to the schoolhouse kitchen and returned with a pair of tongs.

"Okay, Anita, what do you think we'll find today?" Lizzy asked the six-year-old who'd finally let go of her hand. Instead, she slipped two fingers through the fabric tie around Lizzy's waist.

Anita crouched down, pulling Lizzy with her, and picked up a wriggling centipede. She offered it to Lizzy, and as she did, her shy face let Lizzy in on a secret.

Lizzy opened their bowl and Anita dropped the angry creature inside, adding a scattering of dry pine needles and other debris. "To help it hide," Anita said simply, and Lizzy closed the lid.

Before long, Anita had catalogued a pale green scrap of lichen, an enormous dead hummingbird moth with only one wing, and a slimy lobster mushroom. "We still need some poop or an owl pellet," Anita said. She had let go of Lizzy some time ago, and now dashed into the forest as though she knew exactly where to look.

With Anita still in sight, Lizzy went around to check on the other pairs.

Thomas, who was Zach's partner, opened their Tupperware to

reveal a swarm of ants he had scooped into the bowl by using it like a shovel. "A multitude of ants," he said, clearly as pleased by his word choice as the swarm marching up the sides of the bowl. He snapped down the lid.

"Zach, have you found anything?" Lizzy said. Zach shrugged. He was looking in the direction of the little boy that Joel was supposed to mind.

"Don't worry, we're keeping an eye on Timothy," Thomas said, brushing away a few ants that had crawled out onto his arm.

"What do you mean?" Lizzy said.

"Joel's not always nice to the little ones," Thomas said simply. "He gets impatient. But he'll behave with Zach and me watching him."

"I see," Lizzy said. "Thank you for that. I need to go check on the others and keep my eye on Anita. Would you mind sticking a little closer to Timothy? I should have taken both of the little ones myself."

Ruth and Meagan surprised Lizzy with half a bowlful of dried poop, much of it held together by fur or feathers. And Timothy, when Lizzy caught up with the three boys, handed Lizzy a bowl with the nearly fresh, jam-like droppings of a bear.

It was then that everyone heard Anita scream.

Lizzy dropped the bowl and froze.

"It's probably just a garter snake," Ruth said, but Lizzy had already found her feet and started running. Anita was only about twenty meters away, but Lizzy could see she was down on her knees. Had she eaten a mushroom? Had she been bitten by something? Had she slipped and hurt herself?

Half tripping over a tree root, Lizzy dropped to Anita's side, ready to scoop her into a hug for whatever had hurt or frightened her but she stopped at the sight of a dark and spreading stain on the front of the girl's dress. Cradled in her skirt lay the lifeless and blood-matted body of the children's pet rabbit. The animal's mouth hung open, and Lizzy, in a futile effort, tried to close it. In the end, she was only able to shut its eyes.

"Do—do you think—a—a coyote—" Anita gulped, petting the rabbit's long ears.

Lizzy touched the limp body. Already, she could see that there weren't any of the bite marks or saliva stains she had found on animals back in Kelowna over the years, who had clearly been caught in a vice of teeth and tongue. Rather, Lizzy felt the familiar sensation of bone grinding against bone beneath her fingers.

Maybe it had been hit by a car. But there were no cars up here in the forest, and the ones from here were all down by the house or bakery. None of them had left yet today, and the rabbit was still warm and floppy. She didn't think it could have been here any longer than an hour or two.

By now, the other students had gathered around. Joel was last to arrive. His lips were pinched together, as though suppressing something. A smile?

Meagan started to cry.

The next sniffle came from Thomas, and Zach, as though it was the most natural thing he had ever done, reached for his friend's hand and held it tight.

Lizzy lifted the rabbit from Anita's skirt, accepted Ruth's offering of the apron she'd been wearing, and wrapped the small, broken body in its folds.

"What are you going to do with it?" Joel said. "I mean, for a biologist like you, it's practically a gift."

"Zach and Thomas, if you could take the kids back to the house, that would help a lot."

"We want to stay," Zach said, and Thomas, whose eyes had dried a little, agreed with a nod.

"Okay. Joel, could you please take the others. Meagan and Ruth, please see to Timothy and Anita, okay? Mrs. Schlant will know what to do when you get there."

Joel scowled at the suggestion. "Fine. Have it your way," he said, and soon had the other children, Anita included, trailing miserably in the direction of the house.

"What *are* you going to do with it?" said Zach. He had let go of Thomas' hand, but the two of them were still huddled close to one another. Thomas looked down at his own shuffling feet.

They could bury the rabbit, just like this, right now, over by the cherry tree next to the greenhouse. Something, though, made Lizzy uneasy. It was possible, she supposed, that one of the men had taken out a vehicle early in the morning. They could've struck the rabbit and carried it into the forest where the children would be unlikely to find it.

Except they didn't take it nearly far enough. Even if she hadn't taken her class outside, the children spent hours in the woods after school, playing tag and making games. Everyone knew that.

"I think I need to take a closer look," Lizzy said. "I'm really sorry. Neither of you has to be around for this."

This time, it was Thomas who slid his arm through Zach's.

"Really," Lizzy said. "You should both go to the house. I'm sure Mrs. Schlant will put on some soup or something to help everyone feel better."

"The bunny was our friend," Thomas said. "Someone who knew him should be there."

Lizzy sighed, a deep, unsteady breath. "We'll take him to the greenhouse."

Wrapping her arm around her brother's shoulder, Lizzy led the two boys down to the greenhouse, the only place that had lately felt anything like home. The only place with a table where Lizzy could work without being interrupted.

Zach was trembling, and Lizzy was reminded how gentle he

could be; how he had cried when Lizzy, nine years old to his five, had taken a salt shaker to the snails that kept getting underfoot on their front walk back home. Really, she had just wanted their shells. But when they started to bleed, it was Zach who went running for the hose to pour water over them, and Zach who had mercifully crushed them with a rock from the garden when water wasn't enough to save them.

"Okay, you two stay to the side and look away if it's too much. Okay?"

Receiving two nods, Lizzy unwrapped the rabbit and set it on what used to be her workstation. She pushed aside a tray of basil sprouts that were intended, she was certain, for Mrs. Schlant's Green Goddess Dressing, which she remembered was Joel's favourite.

With the herbs scenting the air, Lizzy ran her hands over the rabbit's soft, bloodied fur, before pressing more firmly to feel along its spine and legs.

There were several obvious bone breaks, and mushy spots, where soft tissue had been crushed. But what Lizzy needed to see most was the rabbit's skin, and for that, she reached under the counter where some of her schoolbooks and supplies might still be hidden. Joel had left them there, and a shiver scrambled down her back at the thought. Ignoring it, she took out her pencil case.

From inside, Lizzy selected a razor blade taped between two pieces of cardboard, which she had sometimes used to take dissection slices to put on slides. "I'm going to have to shave some of his fur," Lizzy said, unwrapping the razor. "I need to see underneath."

Again, two nods, and this time Lizzy, angling the blade, began to shear away a flank of thick brown fur.

Almost immediately, Lizzy saw what had happened. A bruise, the size and point of a garden spade, had purpled and broken the skin. From the colour and intensity, Lizzy knew that it had happened while the rabbit was alive. It had also happened some amount of time before it died, which meant it had probably managed to get away, before dying where Anita had found it in the woods.

What was it that Joel had said? *For a biologist like you, it's practically a gift.* Lizzy's ears began to ring. She had told him her plan for the class at the same time she explained that she was leaving the greenhouse. Confiding in him was the only way she could think to calm him down. He was the only one who knew about the scavenger hunt. And yet, Joel couldn't have known that's where the rabbit would end up.

"What happened to him?" Zach said.

"Someone killed him."

"But," Thomas said. "Who would do that?"

Lizzy turned toward Thomas, who burst into hiccupping sobs.

Lizzy wiped her hands on the front of her dress, leaving a smear of blood and fur on her bodice. She emptied a small paper lunch bag of the tulip bulbs it contained and held it out to Thomas.

"Breathe into this," she said, her voice a near whisper. "Zach, cover the rabbit back up with the apron, okay? We're done."

Zach had just finished when the door to the greenhouse swung open. Director Schlant came inside, followed by Lizzy's father and Jimena, Thomas' grandmother.

"What the hell is going on in here?" Daniel said, seeming to grow to twice his usual size. However, at a flick behind his ear from Jimena, which Lizzy took to be a reproof for his language, he quickly shrank back.

"Joel said we'd find you here," said Director Schlant, who glared at Lizzy and looked nowhere else. "Why are you always in the middle of all the trouble around here?"

"Someone killed our rabbit," Zach said. "It wasn't a car, either. Someone hit it with a shovel. Lizzy figured it out."

By now, a few more of the adults had squeezed in through the door. Mrs. Schlant was among them, the front of her apron twisted up in her hands.

At any other time, Lizzy would have been impressed with Zach's assessment. She hadn't offered much in the way of commentary, but the shovel-shaped bruise had been telling.

"I see," said Director Schlant. "And where is this rabbit of yours now?"

Draped in the apron, Lizzy was all that stood between the dead creature and the crowd now pressing toward it.

"We should give it a burial," Lizzy said, moving closer to Director Schlant so she could speak just to him. "But I think you should know, my brother's right. Someone killed it, and it was on purpose."

"So you say," he said. "As I understand things, you've been quite dejected ever since you stopped having animals to cut up at school and at that job you had. Isn't that correct? Is that what you were about to do here? Have a little science lab?"

"Director, no," Daniel said, and Lizzy's surprise caught like a fish-hook in her throat. "If there is one thing I can tell you about my daughter, it's that she would never harm a living creature. Dead, yes. She'll cut those up to figure out how they worked. Living, absolutely not."

Daniel guided Lizzy by the wrist to stand in front of him, facing everyone who had gathered. "She has peculiar interests, I'll give all of you that. And Marie and I have never been able to understand why she needs to cut open everything she finds. But I know, and I can tell you, there's another explanation and that's all there is to it."

Lizzy was stunned.

"I'd like to hear what my grandson has to say," said Jimena, who had dragged Thomas toward her. She pushed him out in front of her now and waited along with everyone else.

Blinking rapidly, Thomas looked ready to be swallowed up by the wooden floor. But he did as his grandmother asked.

"She shaved off its fur," Thomas said. "It was bloody and now some of it is on the plants and we won't be able to eat them. It was dead when we found it."

"Thank you, Thomas," said Director Schlant. Having given the boy his full attention, he turned back to face Lizzy.

"Elizabeth," he said, "it may be that we'll never have an answer about what happened to our little friend here." He stepped toward the apron and lifted up a corner to see underneath. "But what all of the children witnessed today is down to you. You didn't have permission to take your class outdoors. You certainly didn't have permission to bring an animal, especially an unclean one, in here, bleeding, where we grow food. And then to terrorize these two boys."

"I didn't terrorize anyone."

"Maybe we can salvage some of the seedlings for the garden, but I can tell you, no one here wants the blood of a dead rabbit, or even the idea of it, on their salad tonight. And we certainly won't be able to sell any of this in town now."

"Zach, can I ask you something?" Lizzy said to her brother later, when they were supposed to be asleep.

Zach turned toward her, his face shadowed in the nightlight that trickled in from the hall.

"Promise me you won't be upset with me?" Lizzy said.

"Okay."

"Do you have a crush on Thomas?"

Zach pulled his blanket over his head, then lowered it again to speak. "Why are you asking me that?"

"I see you. I see the way you look at him. And the way he looks at you, too. It's dangerous. Maybe not everywhere. But definitely here."

"But maybe . . ."

"Zach. Listen to me. Maybe somewhere else, and with a different boy." Hot tears slipped down the slopes of Lizzy's cheeks. "But not with the director and Dad and the others around all the time. Not with Jimena's grandson. You know this. I know you do. Because you and I don't belong here."

GREEN GODDESS DRESSING

    2 avocados, seeded and skinned
    ¼ cup chopped chives
    ¼ cup chopped parsley
    1 tbsp lemon juice
    2 large cloves garlic, minced
    1 cup egg-free Miracle Whip*
    ⅓ cup cashew milk
    salt to taste

Blend the first five ingredients in a blender. Add Miracle Whip and cashew milk and blend until smooth. Salt to taste.

*EGG-FREE MIRACLE WHIP

    ½ cup plus 4 tbsps liquid drained from canned chickpeas (aquafaba)
    1 tbsp plus 1 tsp lemon juice
    Pinch salt
    1 tbsp grainy mustard
    1 cup plus 2 tbsps vegetable oil

Using a hand blender, whip together the aquafaba, lemon juice, salt and mustard for about 1 minute, until creamy.

Continue blending and add in oil in a very thin, consistent stream, until all of the oil is incorporated and the consistency of Miracle Whip is achieved. Store in fridge.

CHICKPEA MERINGUE

"Daniel," Marie said, sitting up and pushing her feet into her yellow-and-brown crochet slippers. Daniel was over by the closet, where he stepped one leg, and then the other, into a pair of weekday pants. "Daniel," she said again as she shushed across the carpet toward him. "Daniel," touching and sending a spark from her fingertips to his arm, so that they both, if just for a moment, jumped away from one another.

"You and Lizzy have made a mess of things, haven't you?" he said.

Marie, already tired just from getting dressed, sat down on the edge of their unmade bed.

"I . . . I don't think it's all that bad. We've each made some mistakes. But aren't we right where you wanted us all to be?"

"We are. Look at us, though. At me. They invited me, along with my family, and I brought them an addict who lied to all of us. And Lizzy."

"Dr. Vickers prescribed those," Marie said. "He thought—"

"That man should have his license run through a blender."

"We're all flawed, Daniel. Even you. But don't forget how much you helped when everyone was sick. They might have had to bury more than just Beatrice, or send more to the hospital than me, if not for you."

"My family has always been my weakness. You and the kids."

Marie bristled. "Maybe it's time you stop using us as your excuse."

Now, in the kitchen, it was well after breakfast, and although Marie still sometimes broke out in a slick of sweat, or was overcome by a wave of nausea, she had been made responsible for overseeing a trial run of a special dessert, something she'd had once at a wedding reception in their Kelowna church. This time, the dessert would be for Lizzy's baptism.

Marie wanted it to be perfect. It was her way of offering an olive branch to the whole community. And maybe she and Lizzy both had a little bit of that to do for one another, too.

"If this works out," said Mrs. Schlant, as she turned an industrial-sized can of chickpeas with a can opener, "I could see five different uses for it right now." With the can open, she tipped the contents over a colander, set aside the chickpeas to use for supper, and brought Marie a bowlful of the brine.

"Do you want to do the honours? After all, it is your Lizzy we'll be celebrating in a few days' time."

From across the kitchen, Marie heard Jimena clear her throat in a way that sounded like commentary. Nevertheless, she had joined them today to practice her part in the dessert.

"It's been a long time since I made one of these," said Jimena. "But I suppose it'll come back to me. If you think your Lizzy will actually go into the waters."

Back when they were first married, key lime pie had been a favourite of Daniel's, and Marie had made it every Sabbath until the kids came along. She had no idea, though, how to reproduce the filling without eggs. Or butter. That's where Jimena came in. Jimena, who had grown up in a citrus-growing part of the world, liked to suck on those same little limes here when they could be found, with a sprinkling of sugar.

With Mrs. Schlant's crust already cooling, and Jimena's blended cashew-lime filling ready for the blender, it was Marie's turn to whip up the meringue using Mrs. Schlant's sturdy stand mixer.

Meanwhile, Mrs. Schlant checked on a pot of beet juice reducing on the stove. That would be the final ingredient, turning the meringue a celebratory shade of pink.

The pink, which had been Marie's mother's way of brightening up the frosting for her cream cookies, had been Marie's idea, and she smiled at the thought of it as she added a measure of cream of tartar to the liquid from the chickpeas. A few minutes later, it began to froth and then stiffen softly into peaks. She tasted the meringue with the tip of her finger, added sugar, and remembered how she used to lick the velvety-coated tines of the beaters in her mother's kitchen whenever the two of them were baking.

When Lizzy came in from teaching her morning class—English, now, because what harm could come from grammar?—Marie saw her chance. "Want the beater? It's meringue," she said, pointing to the mixer. "For you. For this weekend."

Lizzy hesitated but removed the whisk attachment. "It tastes like beans," she said, and dropped the beater into the sink.

"She'll come around," said Mrs. Schlant, after Lizzy went upstairs. "Here." She took three spoons from the cutlery drawer and dipped each one into the bowl. Marie and Jimena each accepted one, and the three of them tasted what Marie had made.

Marie watched as two smiles spread in front of her, although Jimena's seemed at least a little against her will.

"It's good," said Mrs. Schlant, which sounded like the truth. Marie, though, could only taste the beans, and after she set her spoon in the sink, next to Lizzy's beater, she excused herself and went to find her daughter.

Lizzy was in her room, sitting on her bed with her back pressed up against the wall, reading one of her books. By the look of it, it wasn't one that the director was likely to approve.

"I'm surprised they didn't collect that when they went through here."

"It's not what they were looking for," Lizzy said without looking up. Ever since the incidents, first Marie's collapse and then that poor rabbit, Lizzy had become increasingly sullen. "But don't worry," she added. "I'm sure they'll be back soon to take whatever they missed."

Until then, it had been Marie's intention to try to draw her daughter out. To find out what else might be bothering her so much. "I'll tell you what," she said instead. "I didn't agree with your father at first, mostly because of how you felt, but I think this is exactly where you need to be."

Lizzy closed her book and set it down. "Really?" she said. "Exactly what is it that's been good so far? No school? Weird food? A guy who kills rabbits and leaves them for me to find?"

"Joel promised he had nothing to do with that," Marie said.

"Right. Because it was me? Is that what you think? And if it was, and I only turned into a murderer after we got here, then exactly how is this place so good for me?"

Marie was about to reach for Lizzy when she stopped herself. "Well, what about Zach? Your brother likes it here. He has that friend of his. He and Thomas are practically inseparable."

"And one of these days," Lizzy said, "Everyone here is going to decide that's a bad thing, too."

CHICKPEA MERINGUE

    1 15-ounce can chickpeas
    ¼ tsp cream of tartar
    granulated sugar
    1 tsp vanilla extract

Drain chickpeas, reserving the liquid and setting aside the beans for another use. Place liquid in the bowl of a stand mixer fitted with the whisk attachment. Add cream of tartar and whip for 3–6 minutes to get to semi-firm peaks. Add vanilla and sugar, a little at a time, until desired sweetness is achieved.

NUT BARS

"You've wrinkled your new dress," Daniel said, and Lizzy looked down to find that he was right. She hadn't been careful to arrange the pleats of her skirt so that they lay neatly across her lap. Instead, when she'd climbed into the passenger seat of her father's truck, she had plunked herself down and balled up a fistful of fabric in each hand.

"I'll be wearing a robe over it when I go in the water," she said, trying to smooth out the creases. And Mom's bringing a different dress for me to change into after. No one's going to see this one."

"God will see it," Daniel said. He took his hands off the steering wheel and began to steer with one knee so he could light a cigarette. "You don't know how to take anything seriously, do you?"

Until he replaced one hand on the wheel, Lizzy was unable to speak. "I am. I am taking this seriously," she finally said, breathing in a cloud of smoke before it was sucked outside through a crack in the driver's side window. "I took all the classes. I read the book."

The book, *What Adventists Believe*, was a heavy yellow hardcover edition that itemized and explained each tenet of the Adventist faith. Any applicant for baptism was expected to read it, cover to cover, and be able to affirm they agreed with every point, no matter how dryly written, or challenging it was to stay awake.

"Tell me about the Investigative Judgement," Daniel said and took another puff.

Lizzy, who had plunged in and out of sleep all last night, and whose mind felt as gritty as her eyes, flipped through the pages in her mind until she came to the one she was looking for.

"The Investigative Judgement is the second part of Christ's atonement," she said, paraphrasing. "The first was His work on the cross. And then, on October 22, 1844, He moved from the first part of the heavenly sanctuary into the Holy of Holies, where He's been going over the naughty and nice list ever since."

It was the wrong thing to say. Of course it was. Lizzy, however, felt as bunched up on the inside as her dress was on the outside. Baptism was her last chance. It had been presented to her as an atonement of her own: for the sins she had committed against her mother, the community, the children's rabbit and the salad greens she had soiled by bringing the animal into the greenhouse.

"We believe it will help curb your ideas," Director Schlant had said, having called Lizzy into his office the day after what everyone now referred to as the incident.

"We've waited, Lizzy. We've waited and waited for you to make some right choices for yourself. Now we're making one for you."

"What do we know about the state of the dead?" Daniel quizzed, bringing Lizzy's mind back to the truck.

Lizzy cleared her throat. She had known all this before. Eleven years of religious classes at the academy had made sure of that.

"The dead are asleep," Lizzy recited. "No one has gone to heaven yet, and immortality is conditional. There is no hell, and the wicked will be destroyed. We call this Annihilationism." She brightened for a moment. "Annihilationism is an excellent word if you ask me. It's not often you get to use seven syllables all at once. Unless you're speaking Latin."

Annihilationism was also Lizzy's favourite doctrine. It came from the books of Ecclesiastes and Thessalonians and meant that if she was judged and found wanting when her name came up, she would simply be burned up in the lake of fire and cease to exist at the end of days. And her mother wouldn't have to worry about her going to hell.

"Ellen G. White . . ." Daniel prompted.

" . . . is the spirit of prophecy. Her writings are authoritative as a source of truth. They provide us with guidance, correction and comfort. They are a lesser light shining toward the greater light of the Bible." Lizzy paused and nearly swallowed her next words. "Which, if you ask me, doesn't make any sense, because a larger light will eclipse a smaller one and you won't even know the smaller one is on."

Daniel didn't reply.

"Also, the Archangel Michael and Jesus are the same," Lizzy added, tacking on a bonus point. "Which, incidentally, is why Principal Borthwaithe said that the two Michaels in the Academy should use their middle names."

With that, the quiz was over and Daniel pushed the stub of his cigarette out the window.

Lizzy hadn't been able to eat breakfast that morning, but now, with the church and her dunking imminent, she pulled a nut bar wrapped in beeswaxed cotton from one of the deep pockets Jimena had sewn into her baptism dress.

"Want a bite?" Lizzy offered. The sticky bar of cashews, almonds and pecans was one of Mrs. Schlant's best recipes, and Lizzy had secretly added it to her Ziploc bag collection. She kept it in front of the recipe for Nuteena, which, along with all the others, was slightly warped from lake water that had managed to seep in.

When Daniel refused the nut bar, she bit into it herself, tasting honey and cinnamon, large flakes of coconut and the tiny pops of extra sweetness provided by the scoopful of dried currants from Mrs. Schlant's own bushes next to the house.

Bits of nuts were stuck between Lizzy's teeth when the church came into view. Daniel pulled into the parking lot and backed into a space along the fence that had lately been put up by one of the congregation's neighbours to keep church people off his lawn. Daniel shifted the truck into neutral but didn't turn off the ignition. Lizzy understood that she had not been given permission to go.

"I have something for you," Daniel said, but didn't, at first, reach for whatever it might be. "It's the same copy someone gave me when I was young and new to the church. Just a little older than you are now.

Lizzy accepted the book-sized object, wrapped in fancy paper and tied with a bow. She could tell that her father had done the job himself: the paper was crooked, and the bow double-knotted, the same way he had long since taught her to tie her shoes. "Thank you," Lizzy said, certain what she would find. Mrs. Schlant had already given her one.

"All of us ladies can be proud God chose a woman to be His voice," Mrs. Schlant had said when she'd given Lizzy her first copy of *Messages to Young People*. "Not once did He do that in all of the Old or New Testaments. Not even when the stories were about women. Why don't you read me something?"

"The trials of life are God's workmen," Lizzy had read, remembering a sermon instead of opening the book itself.

She turned to her father. "Should I open it?" Unlike *What Seventh-day Adventists Believe*, *Messages* was not required reading before baptism.

"If you want to."

The book fell open to an underlined passage. "While you remain in listless indifference, how can you tell what is the will of God concerning you? and how do you expect to be saved . . ." Lizzy read, quoting Ellen G. White. She closed the cover and felt every bit as listless as the prophet had predicted. She was still hungry, and while God's word was supposed to be the bread of life, reading it now did nothing to fill her up.

Lizzy could still smell the heavily salted aroma of Stripples from breakfast on her father's breath. She herself had asked for white bread toast and was given a vegan version of her mother's milk buns, instead. Stillwater didn't bake white bread.

Lizzy touched a thumb to the back of one of her earlobes, followed by the other. Earlier that morning, after getting dressed, she had gone into the bathroom with a children's marker she'd stolen from the schoolhouse. It was red and smelled of raspberries, and with it, Lizzy had pressed two ruby dots—earrings—into the hidden side of her ears. Ruby for her seventeenth birthday, which her parents had recently forgotten. And earrings, not just because Adventists didn't wear jewellery, but because her father said that earrings made girls look like they wanted to be whores.

"There's hardly anyone here," she said.

It was true. Between the early hour and concerns about the virus, there was only a handful of other cars and trucks in the lot. Enough, though, to indicate the church was unlocked and she could, if her father would let her, go inside.

"I wanted us to be early," Daniel said. "I want you to be able to take the time to be truly present today, in what you are about to do in there." He gestured toward the church, where an elderly man guided his bent-over wife through the door. "Too often, these kinds of moments pass by us too quickly, and we don't remember them well enough. When you're up there, Lizzy, I want you to do something. I want you to look out into the front row, where your mother and I will be, and then behind us, where you'll see everyone else who's brought you to this moment. I want you to listen to the pastor's words and be mindful when you agree to our statements of faith. And when you go under the water, I want you to think about how you're dying to your old self today, the one you are right now, and coming back to life a whole new creation."

"Is that all?"

"Yes," Daniel said, and then did something Lizzy could never have expected. He leaned over and folded her into a hug.

Lizzy made her way behind the sanctuary. There was a bridal room there where she could wait until the service. First, though, she climbed the short flight of stairs that led up to the dais, and then a few more that were tucked out of the way, until she reached the tank of water set into the back wall. With its clear, acrylic pane for viewing when the curtains were drawn back, it had always reminded Lizzy of an execution chamber she had seen once at a friend's house, on American TV.

Up until now, Lizzy had always been one of the spectators, looking on. Today, though, as her father said, it was her turn to drown and come back to life. Just like her mother in the lake.

Except Lizzy didn't want to die. Not even symbolically. Not even for a moment. *Let the youth remember that here they are to build characters for eternity, and that God requires them to do their best,* Ellen G. White reminded Lizzy as she knelt at the water's edge and leaned over to touch its surface. It was cold. Much colder than she had expected, and a shiver raced across her skin in response.

"Did they forget to turn on the heater again?" came a voice from behind, nearly causing Lizzy to fall face first into the tank.

Steadying herself, Lizzy swivelled on her knees until she was face to face with Joel, standing at the bottom of the stairs.

"What are you doing here?"

"I knew where you'd be," he said. "Same place I was when it was my turn."

"You probably wanted to do it, though."

"You're going to love it," Joel said. "Not getting wet, necessarily. But afterward, that's when the folks at Stillwater really knew I was serious. They'll trust you after this. Probably. Although you will still be a girl."

"Is everyone here already?" Lizzy asked, trying to look around Joel for any sign they weren't as alone as they seemed.

"No, just me. I took one of the work vans." To illustrate, he jangled a set of keys before closing his fingers back around them. "I figured you might need a friend."

"Well, I don't." Lizzy got to her feet and began to climb down the stairs.

Joel, however, didn't make room for her to pass. "I know this isn't what you want. None of it. But you should change your mind. One day, you and I—"

"Maybe they'll postpone because the water's cold," Lizzy interrupted, suddenly not wanting to know how that sentence was supposed to end.

"No. They've gone ahead with it before. It's nicer if it's warm, but the cold is good, too, if what you're looking for is a more grave-like experience." He laughed a little. "I wish you'd let me support you. You just have to ask."

"I don't need anything from you," Lizzy said, "But—wait. Why didn't you tell me you could drive?"

Joel, who had already turned to go, turned back and said, "You ask too many questions."

"It's time, Lizzy," said a deaconess whose job it was to make sure Lizzy was robed and ready. She knocked at the door a second time. "Pastor Emmons is ready for you."

Lizzy stepped out of the bridal room and slowly returned to the stairs that led to the tank.

There, the pastor was already in the water, which lapped lightly around his waist. "Today we welcome Elizabeth Fischer into the family of God and His remnant church." He held out his hand and Lizzy took the first step down, followed by another, until she was soaked to her knees. Her robe had weights sewn into the hem, helping it to sink down under the water. One more step, and Lizzy was submerged past her own waist. Although she could reach the pastor's hand now, she waded the rest of the way into place on her own.

Shivering, Lizzy tried to listen, as her father had said. Unable to concentrate, she remembered to look out into the sanctuary, where both of her parents and Zach smiled up at her from the very front pew. Arranged behind them was the entire Stillwater community.

"Lizzy," said Pastor Emmons, holding his right hand over her head. "Do you believe there is one God: Father, Son and Holy Spirit, and that They form a unity of three coeternal Persons?"

Lizzy, hearing her name but little else, said, "I do."

"Lizzy, do you accept the death of Jesus Christ on the cross as the atoning sacrifice for your sins, that He has forgiven your sins, and do you renounce the sinful ways of the world?"

"I do," Lizzy repeated as the water seemed to rise up around her.

"Do you accept faith in Christ, your Intercessor in the heavenly sanctuary . . ."

"I do."

Lizzy was shaking now, so hard she thought she might slip on the blue-painted floor below. She could hardly speak to answer question after question.

"And Lizzy, is it your intention to keep God's law, including the fourth commandment, which requires observance of the seventh day of the week as the Sabbath of the Lord and as a remembrance of His Creation?"

Lizzy felt as though her bones were about to crack from trembling. Her shaking caused small waves to crash against the acrylic, rebounding and intensifying as she shook. Although the pastor remained still, they rocked at her body, threatening to pull her under.

"I do," she said, a squeak of a sound that agitated the microphone that dangled from the ceiling and caused a squeal to reverberate through the sanctuary.

"And although I can see that you're cold, do you, Lizzy, believe your body is the temple of the Holy Spirit? Will you honour God by caring for it . . ."

They were getting close to the end and, seeming to understand that Lizzy's body no longer obeyed her, Pastor Emmons offered his arm. She would need to take it for him to lower her all of the way under, and she grabbed at it now.

"I do."

"Do you believe that the Seventh-day Adventist Church is God's remnant church, as prophesied in the Bible, and do you desire to become a member of this congregation and the world church?"

It was the thirteenth and final question, but as Pastor Emmons lifted her own hand toward her face so she could pinch her nose, the smell of lake water filled her senses. The room began to spin around her and turn dark. "I have to . . " Lizzy said, and and lunged, half swimming, in the direction of the stairs.

Lizzy's robes sluiced water as she made her way down to the bridal room, holding onto the wall for support.

The dress she was supposed to change into was there, dangling from its shoulders by a hanger.

"What happened?" said Zach, rushing into the room behind her. "Mom's crying, and Dad—he's practically apoplectic."

Lizzy covered her mouth with a wet sleeve to hide an almost laugh as the room came into focus and stopped seeming to move. Thomas, who loved words more than just about anything else in the world, was clearly having an effect on her brother.

"Excellent use of vocabulary," Lizzy said, then pointed to the hanging dress. "Did Mom bring this?"

"What? The dress? No, I did."

"Thank you."

Lizzy unzipped her robe and let the heavy, sodden fabric puddle at her feet. She stepped out of its burgundy circle but couldn't make her hands work to unzip herself out of the pleated dress that clung to her like one of those beeswax wraps.

"I can do that," Zach said and tugged the zipper. He handed Lizzy a towel, which she held against her, still shivering, as he peeled the fabric from her shoulders. "Can you dry yourself?"

Lizzy nodded and wrapped herself in the towel before accepting a second one for her head. She had tripped before reaching the stairs and gone under. "I don't even know if I'm baptized now," she said.

"I don't think so. You missed the last of the vows. And he didn't get to say 'In the name of the Father, the Son and the Holy Spirit.'"

Lizzy started to cry. "But I went all the way under," she said. "And it felt like I died."

NUT BARS

Bottom layer:
1 ½ cups almond flour
¼ cup plus 3 tbsps coconut oil, melted
1 tbsp maple syrup
Pinch salt

Top layer:
½ cup raw almonds
½ cup raw cashews
½ cup raw macadamia nuts
½ cup unsweetened coconut flakes
½ cup cacao nibs
3 tbsps honey
3 tbsps coconut oil
¼ tsp ground cinnamon

Combine the ingredients for the bottom layer and press into the bottom of an 8x8-inch, parchment paper-lined baking pan.

Warm the honey and coconut oil in a small pot over medium heat until melted, stirring frequently. Remove from heat and add cinnamon.

Add nuts, coconut and cacao nibs to the coconut oil/honey mixture and stir together until fully coated. Refrigerate mixture for 10 minutes. Stir. Refrigerate 10 minutes more.

Spread nut mixture evenly over the bottom layer and bake at 350°F for 20 minutes or until nuts start to turn brown around the edges.

Set pan to cool on a wire rack and then refrigerate until set.

FRICHIK BUNS

The following Sabbath, Lizzy was was told to stay home from church.

"No one needs to be reminded so soon of what happened," Director Schlant said, leaving Lizzy to stand alone on the doorstep while everyone else got into the cars and drove away. Everyone but Joel, who at the last minute said he felt called to stay home and pray.

"Did you get your dad's keys?" he said when everyone was gone.

Lizzy nodded. Her father's truck wasn't needed to get people to church, and he had already left with Marie and Zach.

"Good. Get in. I brought us a little picnic." He held up a bag, and Lizzy could smell the Wham and homemade Miracle Whip sandwiches inside.

At first, Lizzy went for the passenger door, but quickly corrected herself. She would be the driver today.

Back home in Kelowna, when Lizzy had taken an interest in learning to drive, she had borrowed her father's keys just to see what it felt like to sit behind the wheel. After that, he had sprinkled a little flour on the driver's side front tire, every day for the next month to make sure she wasn't tempted to roll down the driveway and onto the street. Lizzy checked for flour now, and when she didn't find any, climbed up behind the wheel.

"Have you ever driven stick?" Joel asked, seating himself beside her.

"I've never driven anything."

"Good. A driving virgin. No bad habits for me to break."

Lizzy then learned how to stay stuck in a single spot.

"The emergency brake," Joel said, and Lizzy, after some confusion, figured out how to release it.

"You have to feather the gas as you let go of the clutch. Slowly. Slowly let off the clutch."

Lizzy let go and the truck stalled. "Dammit," she said and tried again, until she managed, finally, to pull forward and turn in a sweeping arc. Soon, they were pointed down the lane.

"Okay, you've got this now. Shift into second."

Lizzy plunged the clutch to the floor once again and found the gear she was looking for. She liked being in second gear, and soon they made it as far as the forest road that, if she turned to the left, would take them to the highway.

"Go right. You're not ready for other cars," Joel said, and Lizzy flicked on her signal and turned the way he said.

Hemmed in by trees, Lizzy felt the gravel crunch like knuckle bones beneath her wheels, and because being in the driver's seat let her feel everything in a different way, she experienced every sensation for the first time.

"What if a logging truck comes toward us?" Lizzy said.

"It's the weekend. There won't be anything. Those guys are union."

Like other Adventists, Joel spat out the word "union" as though it was a sour taste in his mouth. Just another blasphemy, according to Ellen G. White.

"Watch where you're going," Joel said, reaching for the wheel and correcting Lizzy's angle. "You can't have your head in the clouds when you drive. You have to be one hundred percent focused on what you're doing." He leaned closer to Lizzy and placed his hand lightly on the wheel, four o'clock to Lizzy's nine and three. "You're doing well. You can speed up a little more. Try third gear now, and then we'll go up to fourth. You'll need to be in at least fourth for any highway driving."

Lizzy stepped on the clutch and tried to force her way into third. When it made a noise, she let go. The truck lurched and the power went out of the engine.

"Okay, stop. You heard that, right? Third is a little tricky in this truck, so you'll have to find her sweet spot. Start out again."

Lizzy found first and second gear.

"Like this." Joel indicated for Lizzy to step on the clutch, and when she did, he slipped the truck out of second, and then smoothly into third. "See. It's in the wrist, just a little careful coaxing, and she's right there with you."

Lizzy felt blood rush to her ears. Nevertheless, she persisted until she finally shifted noiselessly out of second and into third. And then into fourth. Stealing a glance into the side mirror, Lizzy saw that she was kicking up a trail of dust in her wake.

"There's a side road to the right in a bit. Slow down and let's go see what's there. We can have our picnic," Joel said.

For the next few minutes, Lizzy learned how to make the truck slow by shifting down. "I think I prefer using the brakes," Lizzy said when she lurched into second going too fast, just short of of where she was meant to turn.

"That's how you wear them out," Joel said as Lizzy, signalling to no one, turned the truck toward a clear-cut area in the forest.

With an expansive bramble of severed roots and left-behind limbs, the forest here looked savaged. As though a war against trees had been waged, and the trees had lost. "It's awful," Lizzy said.

"It's life. We need houses and barns and toothpicks and things like that. Besides, trees can be replanted. We really only borrow from nature when we cut them down. They grow back."

"In a hundred years." Lizzy watched as a squirrel hopped up

onto a leftover log and began to forage around in its bark. Finding nothing, it scampered back to the edge of the clear cut and into the still-standing trees.

Suddenly, Lizzy felt that she and Joel were much too alone. She wished the squirrel would come back. Or a bobcat. Anything. Even a bear. She looked in her side mirror, hoping for the dust plume of another truck, wondering how, on this too-tight lane, she would ever be able to turn herself back around.

"Let's get out," Joel said and soon they sat down together on the log the squirrel had abandoned.

"Maybe we should get back. My dad . . ."

Joel looked at his watch. "No. We have plenty of time. Here." He handed Lizzy a sandwich.

"I'm not really hungry," she said, and tried to give it back.

Joel took a bite of his own sandwich and refused to take Lizzy's. "Eat it, anyway."

Lizzy nibbled at the crust.

"Oh for crying out loud," Joel said and reached back into the paper bag. "Try this." He gave her a foil-wrapped bun stuffed with FriChik instead. It was the last one from last night's supper, and because it had been baked, felt hard as a stone in her hands.

"You know, you won't be able to be so fussy when we're—"

Lizzy's chest began to tighten. "When we're what?"

Joel finished chewing and swallowed. "The Schlants don't have children, you know."

"Yeah."

"Well, you don't think I just want to take orders around here for the rest of my life. And I'm sure you don't want to become one of the spinsters like Beatrice was, or those two others from before you came."

"I don't want to be here at all," Lizzy said, measuring her tone, if not her words.

"Look," Joel said. "I know you still think—"

"I know you did it," Lizzy said, and for once immediately regretted running her mouth.

For a long moment, Joel stared off into the edge of the clearing, and Lizzy could see he was biting down on the insides of his mouth.

"Well, since you seem so sure, could you blame me if I did? I mean, you took off, you decided to leave me, to leave the greenhouse. As though our friendship didn't matter."

He swallowed, took another bite, and a splodge of bright pink filling landed on his lap. He scooped it up with his fingers and popped it into his mouth.

Lizzy felt sick. The bites she'd taken of the FriChik bun, with its chunks of unmeltable soy cheese and olives, had been hard to swallow.

"You didn't have to do that," she said.

"And you could have said thank you."

FRICHIK BUNS

12.5 oz can FriChik
1 cup finely chopped celery
¼ cup finely chopped onion
½ cup diced soy cheddar
½ cup chopped black olives
¼ cup egg-free Miracle Whip*
1 tsp chicken seasoning
Salt to taste
10 burger buns

Combine filling ingredients. Divide between buns. Wrap each in aluminum foil. Heat at 350°F for 15–20 minutes until hot all the way through.

HAYSTACKS

Two Sabbaths and two secret driving lessons later, Lizzy was expected to return to church.

"We'll go practice when everyone's napping later," Joel said. Eating and then sleeping after church was threaded into their culture, along with weird vegemeats and believing Adventists were God's True Church.

Lunch was haystacks, an Adventist staple. A some-assembly-required meal, haystacks started with a base of taco chips, beans and rice, which were then layered precariously high with lettuce, tomatoes, cucumbers, pickles, olives and dressings. Whether it was here or for school lunches back at the academy, it was almost always everyone's favourite meal.

"Don't let yours get so big this time," scolded Mrs. Schlant, which started the director laughing.

"It's not my fault. I start off small, and then something happens."

"It's the devil in you," she said, almost under her breath. She was teasing, though, which she hardly ever did.

"I was thinking, Lizzy," said the director when he sat down at the head of the table. His bowl had taken on the dimensions of a medium volcano, while Lizzy was still topping her haystack with the extra-mild salsa that Mrs. Schlant made with their own tomatoes.

Lizzy didn't take the bait.

"I was thinking I could invite Pastor Emmons up here to finish your baptism. We have an old paddling pool in one of the outbuildings. It's a good two feet deep, and we can fill it up with warm water this time." He dug his fork into his food like a trowel and shovelled it into his mouth. Even the extra-mild salsa was too much for him, though, and he reached for a glass of his wife's fresh cashew milk, even before she finished pouring.

"Thanks," Lizzy said. "But no. I'm going to stick to showers from now on."

After lunch, while the women stayed to clean the kitchen, the men of Stillwater wandered off to their various rooms, nearly as faithful as sea turtles returning to their home beach.

Dishes done, some of the women followed, while a few stayed behind in the living room to chat about the week.

"Now," Joel hissed at Lizzy, flashing a set of keys. Outside, he led her to an old farm truck. "Jump in the box. I told the director I needed to go for a drive on my own. Find a place to pray."

"Or a burning bush to talk to," Lizzy said before climbing over the tailgate.

Joel didn't laugh. Instead, he got into the cab and sped off down the lane, braking hard when they reached the road.

"I don't like that kind of humour," he said, leaning out the window and shouting so Lizzy could hear.

Lizzy, who had been thrown against the cab when he stopped, curled her forehead to her knees and hugged herself around her legs.

"Get up here," Joel said. "There's an old road that goes all the way around the property. Time to learn how to put the truck into four-by-four."

Lizzy was about to say she wouldn't need to know that for what she had planned but remembered she hadn't said a word about that to anyone. Better if Joel just thought they were having fun.

Hopping down from the truck box, she thought about walking back to the house. Zach was there. She could join him and Thomas for an afternoon of UNO. They'd found a jar of pennies tucked behind the detergent in the laundry room. And since pennies were no longer legal money, they could bet with them without actually gambling.

Still, they only ever did it when no one was watching.

"Move over," Lizzy said, seeing Joel's face tighten before he climbed over the centre console into the passenger seat.

"Up that way," Joel said, pointing at a road, the entrance of which was nearly concealed by growth.

Lizzy drove, shifting from first to second and third, and back down anytime the road became too potholed to go any faster. She learned to set the truck into four-by-four to crawl up and down gravelly slopes.

"Women don't really need to drive, you know," Joel said as Lizzy ground her way down into second gear. "In fact, they shouldn't even learn unless their husbands say it's okay."

Lizzy's foot twitched on the gas pedal, which she quickly overcorrected, stalling the engine.

"Excuse me?" she said, turning the key in the ignition again and making her way to the top of another hill.

"Look. Women have men to drive them around. Doing it for themselves makes women feel independent, like they don't need us around. And women are supposed to be dependent on their husbands. That's how families stay together."

Lizzy tried to laugh, but the sound came out half-strangled.

"And what if I don't want to marry anyone?"

Joel shrugged, and his shoulders got stuck halfway to his ears.

"Then maybe you're already too independent-minded. Look. I'm trying to do you a favour, here, because I wouldn't mind coming to certain agreements one day. You're different. God gave you a brighter mind than most other girls, so I get that you'll need a bit of freedom. That's what these lessons are about, right?"

"I can see the house from here," Lizzy said without answering. She stopped, turned off the truck and set the parking brake. When she got out, Joel came to stand next to her near the crumbling shoulder of the road. They were elevated here, just enough for a panoramic view of the entire grounds below. It wasn't far, not more than a hundred meters. But from down there, Lizzy would never have known this trail was here.

"Nice, isn't it?" said Joel.

"Yeah. But we should get back. Look, there's my dad, smoking behind the bakery. Don't tell anyone. And there's the boys, sneaking out of the house. Zach probably stole the leftover chips."

It felt good to laugh. Soon, though, Lizzy watched as Zach and Thomas walked down behind the greenhouse. When they stopped, Zach leaned in for a kiss. Just the lightest of touches, and she could almost feel him blush. Then, across the lawn, she saw Jimena step out of the house.

Lizzy suddenly remembered who she was with. "You can't tell anyone. I'll make sure it doesn't happen again." Lizzy looked at Joel, who looked as though he'd been dipped in beets, then took off running down the hill toward the greenhouse.

Lizzy was too late.

"I suppose it's not enough that we let an addict and a child-butcher into our midst. Now we have this. A little degenerate, corrupting my grandson. I won't have it. I won't."

When Lizzy caught up, Jimena shouting, dragging each boy toward the house by an ear.

"Jimena. Stop."

"Enough out of you."

Already, the front door to the house was opening and closing as people piled outside. The director and Mrs. Schlant, him pulling a pair of suspenders back over his shoulders, and her patting at escaped strands of her hair.

"What's this, then?" the director insisted, as Lizzy's parents joined them on the porch.

"I'll tell you in your office, Director," said Jimena. "It's not a thing everyone should have to hear."

Outside the office, Lizzy sat next to her brother. They listened to the adults talk, shout and pray about what to do. " . . . abomination . . . Satan . . ." " . . . intercessory prayer . . ." " . . . a stiff belt and a month of fasting . . ."

Lizzy reached over and squeezed her brother's hand.

"I'm sorry," she said.

"It's not your fault. You're not the one they hate this time." Zach's knees were bouncing uncontrollably. "What are they going to do to me?"

Lizzy bowed her head toward her lap.

"Nothing. Because I'm not going to let them. I've been getting ready to leave. I was going to go on my own, but I want you to come with me."

Zach took his hand back and hugged himself by his shoulders.

"I knew you were up to something. I saw you go off the other week, and when you came back, you smelled like diesel. Dad spilled some when he was filling the truck and got it on the driver's seat. Joel's teaching you to drive, isn't he?"

Lizzy nodded.

Zach took a shuddery breath and tried to sit up straight but ended up slumped back where he started. "I don't want to leave Thomas. He'll be all alone if I go."

"I know. But listen to them in there. They're not just going to let this go. You won't be safe here, and Thomas will be safer without you."

Zach inhaled sharply, and Lizzy could almost feel the air scrape over the delicate tissues inside his nose.

"What about Mom?" Zach said.

"I don't think she wants to leave, Zach. But she's okay here, I think. Maybe."

"You're wrong. She's not okay here. At least she wouldn't be if both of her kids abandoned her. Remember a few years ago, when you got mad about something and said you wished she wasn't our mom? You ran off to Mrs. W, but I stayed home while Mom cried. She told me that if she wasn't our mother, she wouldn't have anything to live for. I don't know what the director and the others are planning to do to me, Lizzy, but we can't leave without Mom."

After that, the two of them stopped talking and listened through the door. Even before the end of the conversation, before Daniel flung open the door and grabbed Zach by the shoulder, Lizzy knew what she had to do.

Late that night, clutching the last of Hermione's stash, Lizzy slipped down to the kitchen. On her way down, she cringed when she stepped on the squeaky side of a single stair. Her father would be asleep, but her mother, she knew, would be on her knees in prayer. Lizzy had hoped for a few minutes downstairs on her own to get things ready.

"Are you okay?" Marie asked, peering out of her door.

"I thought I'd make some warm milk and honey. It's been a long day. Zach's already downstairs."

In the kitchen, Zach stood over a pot of cashew milk on the stove, stirring silently.

"My, but it's been a long time since the three of us have done this," Marie said, pulling out a chair.

"We thought it would be nice," Lizzy said. She joined Zach by the stove, where she crushed her mother's old sleeping pills under the flat side of a butter knife and added a generous dollop of honey to Zach's pot to disguise the taste.

The pot came to a simmer, and when it did, Lizzy poured the sweet milk into three mugs and carried them to the table. "This one's for you," she said, setting down Marie's favourite mug in front of her.

Together, the three of them sipped in silence.

HAYSTACKS

    2 cans brown beans in tomato sauce
    1 can kidney beans, drained, rinsed
    1 packet taco seasoning
    1 head iceberg lettuce, chopped
    3 large tomatoes, chopped
    2 cucumbers, chopped
    1 cup chopped dill pickles
    1 cup chopped black olives
    1 cup shredded soy cheddar
    1 bag tortilla chips
    Salsa and dairy-free Ranch dressing
    *optional: cooked brown rice

In a large pot over medium heat, stir beans together with taco seasoning. When hot, let each person crush chips into their own dish and top with beans, rice (optional), lettuce and other veggies. Finish with cheese, salsa and dressing.

Part 3

MAPLE CREEK

FIG POPS

"I don't think Mom's alive back there," Zach said, twisting in his seat to face the back of the truck while Lizzy stared straight ahead at the lines on the road. With headlights coming toward them in the dark, it was taking all her concentration to keep between them.

"Poke her. I can't take my hands off the wheel," Lizzy said, and Zach unclicked his seatbelt. "Not like that." But Zach hopped up onto his knees and reached to where Marie lay unconscious behind them.

"Put your seatbelt back on. Now."

Driving on the highway was nothing like driving on backroads with Joel. Lizzy's hands, slippery with sweat, held the wheel while her legs shook so badly that she couldn't keep up a steady flow of gas to the engine. It was starting to make her feel seasick.

"Yeah, okay, she's breathing," Zach said.

"Great. Seatbelt," Lizzy said and took *Killed Mom* off the running list of offences she had committed in the last month.

Botched Baptism. Lizzy put a star next to that one in her head, because it was the one that had started them all.

Stole Dad's truck for driving lessons.
Drugged Mom.
Stole Dad's truck. Again.
Kidnapped Mom.

Lizzy blew out her breath, thinking she was done, then added, out loud, "Driving without a license."

"I already know that," said Zach. "Why are you telling me?"

With Zach buckled in, Lizzy was able to steer better again, but found that the truck had started to sound funny and there was a string of other vehicles waiting for a chance to get around them.

"You're going too slow. You either have to speed up or shift down," Zach said.

"How do you know?"

"Dad taught me. Ever since I was little, he's been telling me things when we were driving around in the car."

"Of course he did."

"But I don't actually know how for real," Zach added. "So don't try to make me."

Lizzy sped up as much as she dared, anxious to put more distance between them and Stillwater. So far, they had been travelling for less than two hours and were just coming to the town of Sicamous. The three of them still had a long way to go.

"Look! Ice cream," Zach said as they approached a shop along the side of the road. In her headlights, along with lights on the shop and barn, Lizzy could see that *D Dutchmen Dairy* had its own dairy cows, along with a small zoo that included a camel.

"It's gonna be closed for hours. Reach under the seat."

Zach did as he was told and retrieved a small paper bag with something Lizzy had taken from the kitchen before they left.

"Mrs. Schlant's fig pops," she said. "Just a couple. They were supposed to be for Vespers tonight. I was going to save them until we're at the motel but we can eat them now if you want. It should get us through until we find some place to eat along the way. I'll buy whatever you want." Among the few things Lizzy had taken with them was her bank card, which she had kept taped to the underside of her box spring these last months. In her account was all the money she had made from the butcher shop, along with the jars of change she had rolled and deposited at the bank.

Altogether, she had just more than a thousand dollars. A thousand dollars, some fresh underwear for each of them and, for reasons she did not understand, the Ziploc bag of recipes she had continued to add to ever since the accident at the lake.

"Do you think that's what the farm we're going to will be like?" Zach said after they passed by the dairy.

"I doubt it. I mean, I think they have cows. But not every farm will have an ice cream shop. Or a camel."

"But if they have cream, we could make ice cream, right?"

"I suppose. If Aunt Toots will let us. I don't know anything about her, though. Or Uncle Henry. Okay, now be quiet, I need to concentrate."

Lizzy had never met their aunt and uncle. She knew Marie had other siblings, too, but Toots was the sister Marie talked about the most, even though she said little and, it seemed, half against her will: "Toots could cater a wedding for a hundred out of our little kitchen, and not be bothered one bit," Marie would say, cheeks flushed, while she herself was struggling to bring together a Sabbath lunch for four extra people. Or: "Toots could always do all the things the women were supposed to do, but she could kill a pig just like a man." Which seemed like a compliment, except for the way Marie actually made it sound.

Toots and Henry lived on the family farm near Maple Creek, two provinces over in Saskatchewan. It was the place where all of Marie's stories took place: Driving the big combine seated on her father's lap, standing in the back of the grain truck while the combine filled it with wheat and assorted grasshopper parts, reaching under chickens to steal their eggs . . .

"How's Mom doing now? But leave your seatbelt on this time,"

Lizzy said when Zach went to click himself free. So he pulled the belt loose around his lap and twisted as best he could to face behind them.

"Um. She's looking at me. No, wait. She's asleep again."

Lizzy, whose heart had thumped at the thought her mother might be conscious, let out a shaky, relieved breath. She was counting on getting through the mountains before having to answer Marie's questions, and according to the last highway sign she'd read, they had a few hundred kilometers until the Alberta border. Even then, they would still be in the mountains and have a ways to go before reaching Canmore, where, she hoped, they might be able to stop and sleep.

After Sicamous, and a series of bends and twists in the road that left Lizzy's hands and arms feeling as though they'd been drained of blood, came Revelstoke. By now, it felt like a thousand cars and other trucks, motorbikes, semis and oversized RVs had pulled out and passed them, with nearly every driver turning their head for a better look at the person they'd been stuck behind. When Lizzy finally turned into a truck stop, it was with the hope that every single vehicle still behind them might go past and leave the road wide open just for her.

"Here, go in and buy some things. Get ice cream. I'll watch Mom," Lizzy said, handing Zach her bank card and making him recite back her PIN.

Alone in the front seat with the ignition off, Lizzy listened to the dry, measured snores of her mother who shifted in the backseat, moaned, said a few words Lizzy couldn't make out and went back to sleep.

Lizzy closed her eyes and shook out her hands. Her face also felt numb, and the the calcium and collagen of her bones seemed to have been replaced by jelly, the kind they'd made in a vat at the back of the butcher shop.

When Zach returned from the gas station store, it was with two overstuffed plastic bags dangling from his wrists.

"What on earth did you get?" Lizzy said when he hopped back up into the cab.

"Sandwiches. For us and one for Mom in case she wakes up. And a bunch of chips and things. We should start with these." Zach pulled out two fat ice cream sandwiches. He handed one to Lizzy.

"You can have mine," Lizzy said as Zach lined up a row of chocolate bars on the dashboard, along with several other bags and boxes of sweet or salty snacks. When he had finished both ice creams, he took out two actual sandwiches.

"It's all they had," he said. "Do you think God will forgive us? Or Dad?"

Lizzy picked up one of the plastic, triangle boxes, which Zach had set on the seat between them. Ham and cheese.

"I don't know," Zach said, stuffing his hands up his opposite sleeves. "I really don't. I mean, it wouldn't be like accidentally eating a bacon bit. This would be on purpose. What if we get in an accident, and haven't asked for forgiveness yet?"

"We'll ask forgiveness after we eat, before we drive," Lizzy said. "Besides, we've already broken a lot of rules today, and I need something real to eat or I'm going to be sick. I should have taken more than just fig pops from Mrs. Schlant's kitchen."

Lizzy tore the plastic cover away from her sandwich, wriggled out one of the two halves of bright white bread, and took a bite. The meat, thin and pink, was sweet in her mouth. Along with a thick smear of cold butter and a ribbon of unnaturally orange cheese, she felt as though she was eating something closer to another dessert. She felt sick. "I'm going to save the rest for later. We should get going."

Zach spoke through a mouthful of sandwich. "Do we need gas? I can pump it if you want."

Lizzy hadn't looked at the fuel gauge once since they left. When she started the engine, the needle was hovering dangerously on empty. "Which side is it on?" she asked.

"Mine," Zach said, and Lizzy carefully pulled alongside a pump. She had to readjust a few times, and by the time she was lined up well enough for the nozzle to reach, she could feel every other driver, every actual driver, looking at her with either concern or contempt.

Zach, still holding onto Lizzy's bank card, swallowed the last of his sandwich, slipped out of the truck, jammed the card into a slot, and lifted the middle nozzle. "Mid-grade is better for the engine," he called through the window.

Lizzy didn't care about the truck. Today she didn't care about the money, either. A few extra dollars on gas would not bankrupt her today. At the next stop, though, she'd make Zach teach her how to fill, and choose the cheapest kind of gas.

"Dad taught you this, too, I suppose," Lizzy said when Zach got back in the truck.

"Yeah." His mood had changed and Lizzy wondered if it was on account of the ham.

"Here, sanitize. Do you want to pray now?" When Zach didn't reply right away, she started the ignition. "Okay, but could you put away all the food? I can't drive with stuff in front of the windshield." Lizzy slowly pulled out of the lot.

"Do you think Thomas will be okay?" Zach said after Lizzy navigated a tricky left turn back onto the highway at a traffic light. The sun was rising now, alternately making the road easier and more difficult to see.

"What do you mean?" Lizzy said, blinking hard against sudden sunspots in her eyes.

"Without me there. I—What if he thinks I don't care about him anymore? I didn't get to say goodbye. He'll think I hate him and left him alone to get punished." He paused. "Lizzy, what are they going to do to him? What would they do to me?"

"I don't know, exactly, Zach," Lizzy said, and risked taking one hand off the wheel for a second to touch her brother's arm. "I think they'll try to fix him."

Zach flinched and Lizzy nearly steered them into the oncoming lane. Lizzy replaced her hand on the wheel and stared straight ahead. "I'm sorry," she said. "I know neither of you needs fixing."

FIG POPS

1 ½ cups dried figs, stemmed and halved
1 cup chopped dates
1 cup chopped dried cherries
1 cup pecans
½ cup almonds
¼ cup cacao nibs
½ cup cacao powder
½ tsp cinnamon
Pinch salt
2 tbsps maple syrup
1 tsp vanilla extract

Soak figs in hot water for 5–10 minutes. Drain and squeeze out some of the excess water.

Working in batches, pulse nuts in a food processor, to a coarse meal. Add cacao powder and nibs, cinnamon, salt, syrup and vanilla. Add dried fruit and pulse to form a moist, crumbly dough. Form into small balls and roll in cacao powder.

WAFFLES WITH MILK SAUCE

All the rest of the night, through the mountains, around every hairpin that Lizzy took so slowly she nearly stalled the truck, and along every sheer drop that opened up to swallow them along the sides of the road, Lizzy thought about Canmore. When she finally pulled up in front of a motel, she opened the driver's side door, leaned out over the parking lot, and threw up into a sunny summer morning.

"I'll need my bank card," she said, and Zach, half asleep, handed it to her without a word.

By now, Marie was sitting, but only just. She'd slept all the way to Banff and, in the hour since, had looked confused whenever Lizzy snatched a glance at her in the rear-view mirror.

"Watch Mom," Lizzy said to Zach, wiping her face on her sleeve to wake up her cheeks. Hoping her mask would help disguise her age, she tried to imagine herself as twenty-something. Someone in grad school who might be on summer break and travelling through the mountains for fun.

"I forgot my driver's license. Could I just pay now instead of when we leave?" Lizzy said when the middle-aged woman at the counter asked for ID. "My mother's in the truck. She isn't feeling well."

The woman leaned over the counter and looked out into the lot, where Marie was now standing outside the truck, with Zach holding her up.

"It's been a long drive. She needs to rest." Moments later, Lizzy gratefully accepted a key.

"Living in fear, eh?" said a stranger as Lizzy made her way back to the truck. He came close, flicked her mask with his fingers and spat on the ground.

Moments later, Lizzy turned the lock to their room and fell onto the bed closest to the door.

"Who's sleeping where?" Zach said.

"I don't care. Just don't make me move."

"I'll sleep with Mom. You smell like barf."

"When's your father getting here?" Marie said. "Why didn't he drive with us?" Until now, Lizzy hadn't even noticed that Marie was wearing her yellow and brown banana slippers.

She dragged herself up to sitting and felt another wave of ham working its way up. "He's not coming. The three of us are taking a trip together."

Unsteady on her feet, Marie made her way to the window and drew back the curtains. Outside was a panorama of Rocky Mountains.

"Where are we?"

"Can we talk about that later?" Lizzy said, pulling a pillow out from under the bed cover and lowering her head to meet it. It was cool against her skin.

Marie sat on the second bed, facing Lizzy, and lowered her hands into the hammock of her dress. She seemed to be waiting.

Zach finally replied. "We're going to Maple Creek to meet Aunt Toots and Uncle Henry,.

As though he had yanked the strings on a marionette, Marie stood up. "We are not."

"It's the only place, Mom. Where else would we go?" Lizzy said. Sick, anxious tears slipped from her eyes, travelling across the bridge of her nose before wicking into the pillow.

"Your father will come for us," Marie said and looked around until Lizzy saw her spot the phone on a night table between the two beds. "Zach, help me dial." She held up her hands, but Zach didn't move.

"Fine. I'll do it myself." Marie picked up the receiver and Lizzy watched as her mother tried and failed to press down on the buttons. Zach took the phone from her and set it back in its cradle.

"Do you even know the number for Stillwater?" Lizzy said.

When Lizzy woke, it was after noon and Marie was sitting in a chair. Zach, with a pizza box on his lap, had turned on the TV and found a Disney movie. Ariel was giving up her voice in exchange for a pair of legs.

"Is there any left?" Lizzy said.

Zach tossed the pizza box across the divide, onto Lizzy's bed.

"Zach. We'll find out about Thomas somehow, okay?" Lizzy whispered across the space between them.

For answer, Zach swiped at a tear and then quickly nodded.

Inside the pizza box, Lizzy found half a cheese and pineapple pizza and gratefully ate a few bites. Cheese and pineapple was Lizzy's favourite. Still, she only managed to eat a single slice, and wondered whether her mother had eaten anything at all. After months of Mrs. Schlant's vegan cooking, her stomach cramped a little, even at the sight of so much cheese.

"Mom. We're going to need Aunt Toots' phone number. We should call her and Uncle Henry so they know we're coming."

There was silence between them for a while. Lizzy could almost read her mother's thoughts as they scrolled across her mind.

"Well," Marie finally said. "I can't call your father and you can't call my sister. So I guess we both have a problem."

"Because you don't know the number?"

"Of course I know it. The house has had the same number since the days of party lines. We used to share it with Jacob and Anna Janzen down the road."

"Okay, Mom. Why don't you try to get some rest. We still have a long way to go tomorrow."

"I think I've had plenty of rest already, thanks to you," Marie said, but she lay down on the bed nevertheless. Soon she was asleep—or at least pretending.

Lizzy spent the rest of the day awake, not wanting to drive again before night. The TV channel Zach had chosen earlier was playing back-to-back Disney, and by five o'clock that afternoon, when Snow White was biting into a red, red apple at the house of the dwarfs, she couldn't take it anymore. Not one more princess. She decided it was time.

"C'mon, let's get going," she said, going round to Zach's side of the other bed.

"You can't be serious. Aren't we spending the night?" he said.

"We can go down to the restaurant first. They have omelettes all day."

"As soon as this is done," Zach said, pointing to the movie.

Lizzy went outside where, for the next hour, she sat in the truck and practiced shifting with the engine turned off. After eight hours behind the wheel, which should have been five, her hand knew where all the gears were now. Even without gas, though, her left foot still shook when she let out the clutch.

"God," Lizzy said, letting her hands fall to her lap, palms up and fingers stuck in a curl the same shape as the wheel. "Thank you that we didn't die yesterday. That's a start and I appreciate it. And the roads should be straighter today. And Zach and I are both sorry about the ham. But I have to get through Calgary. I don't know if I can drive through a city. There's going to be so much traffic, and lights, and I don't know what I'm doing. What am I doing? Please help. That's all. I mean, Amen."

Waiting for a response she knew wouldn't come, Lizzy went into the restaurant where she placed a take-out order. When it was ready, she carried it back to the room for her brother and mother.

"Why couldn't we eat in the restaurant?" Zach said.

"Inside is only for people who are vaccinated."

"Your father would have something to say about that," Marie said.

"Then it's a good thing he's not here."

While Zach ate hash browns and eggs folded over mushrooms and cheddar, and Marie refused her plate with crossed arms, Lizzy nibbled on a corner of toast with strawberry jam.

"Have you ever driven through a city as big as Calgary, Mom?" Lizzy asked, attempting a sip of orange juice to wash down crumbs caught in her throat.

"I imagine it's the same as driving in any other place. I'm sure you can stop at red lights as well as anyone."

"I thought you might want to do the driving tonight," Lizzy said.

"I don't need you to think for me. And besides." Marie held up her hands. "Do you really think I can drive with these?"

"I guess not," Lizzy said. "Mom. I know you're really mad at me. But couldn't you forgive me? Tonight's going to be hard again. I don't know if I can drive and think about you hating me so much right now."

"Well, now you know a little bit about what it's like being a parent." Marie got up and smoothed out the house coat she'd put on last night before following Lizzy down to the kitchen. "Did you bring me a toothbrush, at least?"

Lizzy reached into the brown paper bag their food had come in for the three new toothbrushes and toothpaste she'd purchased from the front office, along with a few other things: some more wet wipes, deodorant and a bottle of aspirin.

"I'd still like to call Aunt Toots," Lizzy said. When Marie snorted and disappeared into the bathroom, she turned to Zach instead.

"I'm going to need you to get Mom settled in the truck and keep her company for a few minutes before we go."

"Why?" Zach dragged his last bit of omelette through a puddle of ketchup.

"Just because. Can you do that?"

"I've been doing that since we left."

"The number for Jacob and Anna Janzen in Maple Creek," Lizzy said to the operator as soon as she was alone. "No. Sorry. Not in Maple Creek. It's a farm. Near Maple Creek." She wrote the number she was given on a pad of motel stationery, hung up and dialled again. After talking to the Janzens, she typed in the number for her aunt.

By nine o'clock that morning, they had reached the outside edge of Calgary, and Lizzy was so nervous she sat straight up in her seat. Being unable to lean back and properly plant her foot into the clutch made it more difficult than ever to shift.

"You're gonna stall it again," Zach said, banging the heels of his hands against his forehead.

They were approaching the third traffic light, behind an enormous black pickup truck with a Canadian flag and a *Fuck Trudeau* window sticker, when Lizzy's vision began to blur.

"Just pull over," Zach said. "Pull over!"

Lizzy turned onto a wide shoulder at the side of the road, as drivers honked out a chorus of obscenities. Once stopped, she let her foot off the clutch and the truck lurched forward a foot or two before it came to a stop.

"You're in a merge lane," Zach said.

As a string of cars and other trucks pulled out and around them, honking and gesturing, Lizzy dropped her head to the steering wheel and onto the horn, which let out a short, terrible sound. "I can't do this!"

"Lizzy. Lizzy." It was Marie this time. She had managed to click out of her seatbelt and shuffle forward on the seat. "Zach, get out and trade places with me. I need to sit next to your sister."

Without protest, Zach got out of the truck and helped Marie into his place.

"Okay. My dad, your grandfather, taught me how to do this when I was a girl—younger than you—and now I'm going to teach you exactly what he taught me. Are you ready?"

Lizzy sniffled but nodded.

"You've got to do everything smoothly, just like when you're cutting a pig's throat."

Lizzy, who'd been lifting her hands back to the wheel, stopped in mid-air. She turned to face her mother, whose expression was, at first, deadly serious. At the corners of her mouth, though, Lizzy was almost certain she saw the tug of a smile.

"Are you listening?" Marie said.

"Yes."

"You can't let the pig know you're afraid, or it will be afraid, and then it's all over and you have to call the slaughter man to do it for you. Now, you've only cut things that are already dead, but I'll bet you know what I mean a little bit, don't you?"

Lizzy closed her eyes and leaned back in her seat. She imagined a scalpel in her hand, or one of the yellow-handled butcher knives she had used at the shop. She pictured holding a knife over a whole rib roast and smoothly lowering it down. As she did, she stepped down on the clutch, put the truck in first, let off the brake and slipped back into a break in the traffic.

"Okay," Marie said. "But next time, look where you're going and use your signal."

On the other side of Calgary, Lizzy was jolted by a shudder of relief. "Thank you, Mom," she said, as a road sign told them they were now only 250 kilometers from a place called Medicine Hat. If she could drive the speed limit, and they only stopped for a little bit to pee, they could end up in Maple Creek in just over four hours.

"I called Aunt Toots," Lizzy said. "I got her number from the Janzens. I thought you should know."

Lizzy drove in silence as oncoming signs continued to tick down the distance. She could almost feel her mother's pulse stall and then quicken at each new number, biting at the skin around her nails with the little slurping sounds that always made Lizzy's father either swat her hands away from her mouth or get up and leave the room.

After a while, Marie covered her eyes.

"Mom, are you okay? We can stop. I bought some aspirin. And Zach still has chocolate."

Zach opened and passed a Mars bar over the seat. Marie took a bite.

"They'll make little Mennonites of you two very easily," she said as she chewed.

"Is that a bad thing?"

"Being Mennonite? No. I just . . . For me . . . There were things that happened in that house. And your aunt. It was all so easy for her. And I never knew how."

"I'm sorry, Mom," Lizzy said. "I'm really really sorry. I know Grandma and Grandpa died there. We could—"

"What? Go back? Tell your dad we just went out for a little drive and lost track of time? And how would that go over for you?"

Marie turned toward the passenger window and didn't say another word for the rest of the trip.

"Come on in, come on in. Your aunt has been busy with the waffles," said Uncle Henry. It was after midnight when he greeted them in the floodlit driveway, along with a large black dog who had a white cross of fur on its chest.

Dressed in well-worn flannel dress pants and a matching vest over a white button-down shirt, Uncle Henry wore silver-coloured armbands to hold up its sleeves. He smelled sweetly of milk and hay, as though he'd just been to the barn. He was also older than Lizzy had imagined, maybe by as much as twenty years.

"Sit. I'm sure you missed more than a little lunch by now."

Following her uncle through what was both an enclosed porch and a kitchen that no one was using, Lizzy stepped up into the main house and another kitchen.

"There you are," said a clearly pleased Aunt Toots, who looked almost the same age as Henry. She wrung her hands into her apron, wiped the fabric smooth, and took a pot off a burner before coming over to greet them.

Lizzy was prepared for a hug but put out her hand when one was offered to her instead. Far from business-like, though, the handshake was as warm as Toots' skin was rough. It involved both of Toots' hands, wrapped around Lizzy's one, and a face beaming at her as though Lizzy was just who she had always hoped to find at her door.

"All these years," Toots said, and before she could finish, her eyes settled on Zach. "And you must be Zachary. Look, Henry. Look at what a fine boy we have here. Okay. Let's get you settled at the table. You must be hungry as geese after your long trip."

Lizzy sat down. She'd noticed that not a word had passed between the two sisters. As though to remedy that, Toots served Marie first: a waffle of small, joined hearts that together made a plate-sized flower; and a soup bowl filled with steaming, white sauce that smelled warmly of sugar and milk.

Following her mother's lead, Lizzy tore away a single, soft heart, folded it in half and dipped it in the cream.

MENNONITE WAFFLES WITH MILK SAUCE

2 cups flour
2 tsps baking powder
¼ tsp salt
2 cups milk
3 eggs
¼ cup melted salted butter

For the milk sauce:
4 cups milk
¾ cup sugar
¼ cup cornstarch
1 tbsp butter
1 tbsp vanilla

For the waffles: Whisk together dry ingredients. In a separate bowl, whisk wet ingredients. Combine wet with dry. Pour a scoop of batter into a greased, hot waffle iron and cook for 3 minutes.

For the milk sauce: Heat 3 cups of milk, stirring constantly, until it boils. Stir in ½ cup sugar.

Mix the cornstarch with the remaining 1 cup of cold milk and ¼ cup sugar. Add gradually to the hot milk mixture, stirring until it thickens. Stir in butter and vanilla.

Serve over waffles (or dip the waffles into the sauce like Mennonite kids do).

CRACKLINGS

Marie woke late the next morning, in a bedroom that opened onto her mother's kitchen. Her mouth was once again filled with the taste of dirty pennies from the sleeping pills Lizzy had given her, and her nose with the smell of pork cracklings being fried in their own lard. She could hear them as well, as though the sow they had come from was squealing from deep inside the cast iron pan.

I should get that pan for Lizzy. Toots would be using the good one, the one that had belonged to their mother and grandmother, and maybe their grandmother's mother before that. Instead of slipping her feet to the floor, though, Marie turned over in bed and tried to find her way back under the cover of sleep. It was no good.

Cracklings had been her father's favourite dish. And with the aroma of salted grease reaching underneath her door, she could almost feel him on the other side, taking his usual seat at the table, where he would flap out a folded tea towel and set it on his lap in anticipation of *lunsch*.

Marie needed to see for herself that he wasn't there, and instead of her father, she found both of her children, seated in her parents' places, digging into two bowls of spaghetti covered in *schmaunt fat* and Roger's syrup.

The cream gravy, no doubt, was left over from a recent night of *varenyky*, both cottage cheese- and Saskatoon berry-filled: a dish that Mennonites ate as though getting enough heavy cream in one's diet was an eleventh commandment.

"There's plenty left," said Toots, before Marie could disappear again.

"Just cereal," said Marie, stepping all the way into the kitchen.

"For lunch?"

"I just woke up."

"Cow's milk okay? The kids say you usually drink nuts."

"Fine," Marie said, then added, "For today."

With a bowl of Corn Flakes on the table in front of her, seated in the chair that had always been hers as a child, Marie picked up her mother's old sugar shaker with both hands and poured a white, crystalline mound over top of the flakes. She accepted Lizzy's offer to pour on the milk from a glass bottle that swirled with a generous skim of cream.

"What do you want to do today?" said Zach, and Marie closed her eyes.

"We've already played some games, but Uncle Henry said he'd show us the barn and other buildings," Lizzy said. "We played Crokinole."

Marie shifted in her seat. "You can go to the barn. I've seen it before."

"Aunt Toots said she'd show me how to make noodles," Zach said. "What did you call them?"

"*Kielke.*"

"For the love of God, Toots. They're already eating noodles."

"Those are from a box. They don't count."

Already exhausted from the effort of lifting spoon to mouth, Marie returned to her room. She tripped more than fell into sleep and, on her way down through layers of consciousness, felt as though she had taken a step off a tall bridge. In her dream, when she reached the bottom, she found she was still in her parents' farmhouse. Now, though, everyone was there. Her mother and father, Toots and Henry. Director and Mrs. Schlant, Joel and Jimena and

Beatrice and all the others. Daniel and Lizzy and Zach. Daniel's folks, even, whom Marie had only ever met once.

She could hear voices buzzing everywhere around her. The women were playing Crokinole in the kitchen while the men cracked nuts in the living room. Wanting to go to them, Marie first needed to get dressed and, without realizing it, pulled up a pair of double-layered underwear filled with bees. Against her skin, the bees hummed as tunelessly as a Mennonite hymn as they stung at her through clean white cotton.

The bees and the people were still buzzing in Marie's ears when she woke for the second time that day. The house was quiet now.

Slipping into the bathroom with a change of clothes and a towel, both of which Toots had left on the seat of a dressing chair, Marie locked herself inside and spun the tap on the bath, sitting on the toilet as the space around her began to fill with steam.

When she could no longer be tempted to look at herself in the mirror, Marie stripped down to her skin, adjusted the faucet to the shower, and stepped behind a flower-patterned curtain of blue and white fabric that she recognized, leftover from a dress her mother used to wear.

The water, when it hit Marie's hands, stung for a few minutes, after which Marie washed her hair with a bar of her sister's hand-made shampoo and conditioner. She sluiced the excess under her armpits and between her legs using a washcloth and then rinsed.

Towelled dry, Marie cleared a circle of mirror, dragged a comb through her hair, and twisted it as best as she could into a soggy bun at the back of her neck. She dressed and opened the door, letting out the cloud of steam.

When it cleared, Marie found that she was still alone. "Lizzy?" she called out, not too loud. "Lizzy? Zach?" She went around a corner.

"Toots or Henry?"

Silence. And stillness, except for a cat leaping onto the outside windowsill above the kitchen sink.

"Pusspuss-pusspuss," Marie trilled, her own voice sounding so much like her mother's that she had to take a seat and lower her head between her knees to still a sudden spin of the room. Maybe it was just the heat from the steam.

When Marie was able to sit up straight, she held her head for a few more moments. The room wasn't quite still yet, but she soon forgot when her fingers touched the soft coil of cord that draped down low from the old wall phone. It had been more her father's than her mother's. Before private lines came through the village, he always said it provided more news than the television. There was even a picture of him in an album, holding Marie, while he listened in. "That way, I don't have to pay attention later when the ladies talk to me," he'd say with a smile.

Marie sobbed, once, at the memory of his voice, and pressed her palms into her chest to make it stop.

After her parents had died, Marie made sure to never come home from school unless she knew Toots or Henry were there. Even though that had meant spending too much time with Toots.

"I can't always be here. Sometimes I have to go into town before you come home," Toots had scolded.

"But you could pick me up and take me with you," Marie would cry, not on purpose. Because the last time she had been in the house by herself was the night her parents died.

It had only taken a day for Toots and Henry to drive from Winnipeg.

Marie needed to hear Daniel's voice. With her fingers, she followed the cord up the wall to the receiver and lifted it down.

Just yesterday, Lizzy had given her the idea.

"The number for Stillwater Commune near Enderby, British

Columbia, please," she said to the operator, after dialling zero with the help of a pen gripped in her fist.

There was no such number.

"For a—" Marie stopped mid-request, having realized just then that she didn't know the director's first name. "For a Mr. Schlant."

"I'm sorry, but there's no number listed for that name. Is there another one you'd like to try?"

Marie hung up, although she would have preferred to talk to the woman a little longer and ask her about her day. Anything to hear another person's voice. But there was a crunch of gravel outside so she hung up the phone.

A few minutes later, having knocked at the same time as she let herself in, the village bonesetter greeted Marie. Minuscule in stature but not presence, Ina Krahn had been straightening the spines of the local children and medium livestock for longer than Marie could remember. It was a skill she had inherited from both her mother and her grandmother.

"It's nice to see you, Marie."

"I suppose Toots told you I was here?"

"We may not have party lines anymore, but it still doesn't take long for news of a prodigal daughter to go from house to house."

Marie knew this to be true. A single village baker, carrying excess cream cookies from door to door, would be all that was needed. Still, as Mrs. Krahn tilted her head and ran an evaluating gaze up and down, Marie had the feeling that her sister had everything to do with this.

"Let's have a closer look, then," said Mrs. Krahn who, smelling strongly of the liniment she used to lubricate her clients, closed the distance between them.

Marie pulled back her hands but needn't have. Mrs. Krahn spun her round, like a dressmaker's dummy, and began to feel up and down her spine, pausing here and there in a way that seemed to ask, then answer, a question.

"I didn't hurt my back," Marie said.

"Everything has to do with the back," said Mrs. Krahn. "Remember when you were this high?" She came round to show Marie a height that was about equal to the woman herself. "That cow stepped on your foot. Broke it. Six weeks with me, and it was like nothing."

Marie wanted to point out that she had also spent those six weeks in a cast. She willed Lizzy to come in from wherever she was and put an end to this with some scientific fact or another. When she didn't, Marie felt her soul slouch inside her skin, taking her neck and shoulders with it.

The instant that happened, Mrs. Krahn reached high, pushed the heel of her hand between Marie's shoulder blades and forced her back to straighten the same way she had offered Sunday school corrections when any of her students coloured outside certain lines. Or when Toots had called her after deciding Marie's grief had gone on too long. Mrs. Krahn had come with some liniment and a few unhelpful words, then, too. *Your Mama and Papa's bodies were nothing but the same fleshy tents we all live in. They're with the Lord now and that's better, you see.*

Now, though, she asked, "That husband of yours isn't with you?"

Marie slouched and was straightened, again. "The kids and I are just here for a visit."

"Like last time, when the girl was just—"

Before Mrs. Krahn could finish, Marie turned and bent low to face her.

"Lizzy has no idea about that—neither of them do—and they never will. Do you understand me?"

"Well—"

"Go. Get out and take your old lady witchcraft with you."

"Marie!" said Toots, coming into the house with an armful of vegetables from the garden.

Marie turned to look at her sister, and Toots sighed, as though Marie were still a child who needed another nap. "Don't mind my sister. She's been through an ordeal these last months."

"She could have helped you, you know," Toots said after Mrs. Krahn left to continue her rounds.

"Helped Mom with what?" said Lizzy, coming into the house two minutes too late.

"Nothing. Just a woman who thinks she can heal people," Marie said, feeling as though someone had pulled the plug from her drain. "She's like a chiropractor. Sort of. But without a license."

"Oh," Lizzy said. "Chiropractors are nonsense, you know. Pseudoscience."

That night, while Toots and Henry ate cracklings on warm milk buns, with potatoes fried in lard, Marie and the kids ate buns with cheese and jam, and potatoes fried in oil. Tomorrow. Tomorrow she would go back to eating like she did at Stillwater.

"That chiropractor woman," Lizzy said, between bites of food.

Marie bristled. "What about her?"

"On her way out, she said it was nice to see me again, but I've never been here. Did she visit us in Kelowna?"

"No. She probably mistook you for someone else."

Marie, her mouth still full of bun and cheese, got up and went into the bathroom. "Codeine," read a prescription bottle Marie had seen there earlier. And because it had long ago expired, she was sure no one would notice it missing.

MENNONITE CRACKLINGS (GRIEVA)

2 cup container of cracklings from the lard-making process (or get from the butcher)

If cracklings are frozen, thaw and then add them to a pot. Place pot over medium heat and cook until all of the fat has melted and is boiling.

Pour cracklings through a sieve, draining the fat into a container for other uses. Use a wooden spoon to press out as much fat as possible from the meat left in the strainer.

Return cracklings to the pan and add salt to taste. Add about 3 tbsps of water and continue frying while stirring constantly.

Once the cracklings start to darken in colour, remove from heat.

NÜDEL ZUPP

THWOK! Lizzy was surprised at how easily a head could come off a chicken, leaving its feet running through the air.

"Toots said to get one for the pot," Henry had told her, not ten minutes earlier. "And I remember how you always liked to look around inside things with your hands."

Lizzy thought she must have heard him wrong. "You remember?" she'd said. Henry had shrugged and said something about English and Low German getting mixed up in his mind. He had then opened the door to the henhouse, leaving Blackie the dog to sit outside.

Before Lizzy could think about it too much, Henry showed her how to reach under each of the hens to look for eggs, giving her one to hold. He then chose a bird who had not laid.

"Five days she hasn't," he said, and together, with Henry cuddling the chicken under his arm and stroking it like a pet. They had taken it behind the henhouse. There, the stump of a tree was stained with the blood of previous soups and suppers.

It was so quick. One moment, the chicken was alive, eyelids drooping with content. Then, even though its body didn't know it yet, its mind was unplugged like a lamp.

Leaving the head behind for Blackie, who had happily followed them round the back, Henry and Lizzy carried the headless chicken to the Quonset, an enormous silver building like an airplane hangar, where Henry hung the body by its feet from a hook made from a clothes hanger attached to a table. Neck down, the chicken continued to bleed into a bucket on the floor.

Leaving the bird to drain, Henry crossed the enormous indoor space, half full at the front with farm machinery, to a small fridge against the wall. He opened its door and returned with two bottles of Coke and two Buster Bars in Dairy Queen paper wraps.

"Now you're a Mennonite," he said, as Lizzy bit into the chocolate crackle, down to the ice cream, where she found a layer of peanuts and fudge. It wasn't D Dutchmen Dairy, but it was better than a truck stop. And she also didn't have her mother unconscious in the back seat of a stolen truck. The truck that was right now parked alongside yet another summer kitchen.

"We'll do some canning in that kitchen soon," Toots had said, and already enough chokecherries were ripening on their bushes that Lizzy feared she would soon have to spend an entire day in the little outbuilding, boiling up jars of syrup and jam.

"I've never had a Coke before," Lizzy said, before taking a sip that fizzed on her tongue.

"*Oba* no," Henry said, as gravely as though Lizzy had confessed to murder.

"Mom put 7-Up in the juice for Sabbath lunch. But only once."

Lizzy took a second sip of the Coke, tasting sugar and caramel flavouring alongside the acid of the bubbles. More than anything, she liked how grown-up it made her feel.

"Okay, then," Henry said when they were finished with their treats. From under the table, he produced a set of knives.

"Feathers first," he said, and pulled a stool out for himself. He sat and crossed his arms, along with one ankle over his opposite knee, and his entire face smiled, as though he knew what to expect.

With the chicken still dangling from its hook, Lizzy gathered up the used ice cream papers and empty Coke bottles and took them to a garbage can by the fridge. She set the bottles next to the garbage and said, "To recycle." There was a sink and a stove there, as well, and she filled a stock pot full of water and set it over a high flame.

"Doesn't Aunt Toots do this in one of the summer kitchens?" Lizzy said, marvelling that any two people would have appliances anywhere they felt like having them.

"She likes when I do it for her."

Lizzy leaned against the table and took a deep breath. She was waiting for the water in the stock pot to boil.

"Your papa, he doesn't like us killing the chickens," Henry said, and Lizzy stood up straight.

"I guess you met him before he and Mom got married. What was he like then?" She wasn't sure she really wanted to know.

Henry unfolded his hands and rubbed the inside of one with the opposite thumb, as though it had suddenly started to ache. "He was unhappy."

"Even when they first met? When they were dating? Wasn't he happy when he came to see her?"

"He tried to be happy. I don't think anyone taught him how. And then he wanted us all to go to church on his Saturday. Your Mama went with him."

"Did you ever go?"

"No. Your papa opened his Bible to try to convince us. But it's the same one as ours."

Across the room, the water began to hiss, before finally agitating its way into a boil. When it did, Lizzy lifted the hen by its feet. The blood had begun to clot from the wound at the stub of its neck.

Dunking it in the water, Lizzy swished the chicken back and forth for a minute, before pulling it out of its boiling bath and letting water fall from its feathers to the floor. It smelled of hot skin and cooked keratin, but after so much formaldehyde in science lab, it didn't bother her. She returned the chicken to the table and started pulling feathers at the chicken's tail, ripping across the grain in concentric circles as she turned the hen on its horizontal axis. Once the outer feathers were out, and in a heap on the floor, she started on the pin feathers, until the entire surface of the skin was bald and fleshed out with bumps.

"How did you know how?" Henry asked, shaking his head a little, as though he had just witnessed a thing of wonder.

"I'm good with things like this. I worked in a butcher shop at home. I didn't get to pluck or gut anything, though. I like to learn from books, too, but sometimes I need to, like you said, look around inside things with my hands."

"Do you read lots?"

"Some people think I read too much," Lizzy said, remembering the time her father had cut up her library card. He didn't seem to realize she could just get another.

"You should read. A girl needs to always be learning. How many grades do you have now?"

"I was in Grade 11, doing some Grade 12 by mail while we were at Stillwater. That's the place we came from. I left a bunch of my stuff behind. There's probably more at the post office there for me, but now I can't get it." She thought of Joel. He still had the key to her box. She should have given him money to forward her mail. If he didn't hate her now for leaving.

"You and me, we'll go to town tomorrow and have that sent to our box."

"I don't think that will work. The box is in my teacher's name. She's back in Kelowna."

Henry tented his hands in front of his mouth and nodded. "You'll call your teacher, then. They can send you new books. I'll pay."

By the time Lizzy and Henry returned to the house with the chicken—Lizzy carrying the bird and Henry two ice cream pails, one of which contained the heart, liver and gizzard—Toots and

Zach were ready with a cutting board full of chopped vegetables and a stock pot on the stove that simmered with broth.

"Look!" Zach said, holding up a small brown item that looked like a flower. "Star anise. It smells like licorice. Here. Mennonites put it in their chicken soup." He thrust the anise under Lizzy's nose.

The star anise did smell like licorice, and Lizzy wondered how that could possibly be a good idea for a soup.

"We have some eggs, too," Lizzy said.

Henry emptied his pockets of eggs from the henhouse and also presented the pail that contained a series of shell-less ones, like a string of pearls, that had been inside the hen. "I guess that hen wasn't done laying," he said with regret. "Or maybe one of the others has been on her nest, saving her own skin. But you should have seen. The *mejalas* here did it all herself."

"Well, I didn't kill it," Lizzy said, guessing that *mejalas* meant girl or niece. She handed the bird to Toots by its feet.

"Next time. You can choose the chicken."

Marie, who Lizzy hadn't noticed at the table, cleared her throat. "So, you fit right in," she said. "That's nice." She licked a fingertip and used it to turn the page of a magazine she didn't seem to be reading.

Toots traded the chicken, already in rigor, for one in the fridge, breaking its legs to make the feet fit below the surface of the broth. "Marie, let the *dotter* enjoy herself."

"*My* daughter," Marie corrected.

"Mom, it's okay. I plucked it. I don't have to eat it," Lizzy said.

"Next time we'll do a pig, you and me. You haven't learned sausages yet from the butcher shop?" Henry added the eggs from his pockets to a carton in the fridge.

"Henry," Toots said with a note of warning.

"Come sit with me, Lizzy," Marie said, the tone of her voice nearly forcing her into a chair.

Lizzy stuffed her hands in her pockets and felt an egg Henry had given her. She turned it over now, feeling the roughness where too much calcium had built up around an area of shell, like the mineralization at the site of a broken bone. The way Lizzy imagined the bones inside her mother's hands. She wondered whether eggshells could heal if they were somehow cracked before being laid.

Lizzy looked at her mother, whose hands settled in an uneasy rest on the surface of the table. Would they ever be normal again? Would they ever stop hurting her? She removed the egg from her pocket and slipped it under the trembling tent of her mother's purple-streaked fingers. "It's still warm," she said as, for a moment, Marie's hand curled around the shape.

"And its mother is dead," Marie replied. "Do you know what we do on the farm with eggs that have no one to sit on them?" She got up and carried the egg to the kitchen counter, where she cracked it against the edge and dropped it, its yolk catching on an edge of shell and stretching into a yellow ribbon, into Toots' cast iron pan.

That night, Lizzy waited until her mother was asleep and snoring in the bedroom next to hers and Zach's. She wanted to talk to Uncle Henry, whose room with Toots was at the top of the stairs. When Lizzy climbed toward it, she saw him sitting on the edge of his bed, holding a large black Bible in his lap.

She was going to wait until he was finished reading or praying, and was about to take a seat on the stairs when Henry slowly drew the book back alongside his ear, took aim, and threw it against the wall. It fell to the carpet with a thump. "Mouse," he said, turning to Lizzy, whose head must have appeared just above the landing. "I've told it to get out and go live somewhere else, but he likes it here."

Lizzy climbed the rest of the way up and Henry cleared off his dressing chair for her to sit.

"I like it here, too," Lizzy said. "I mean. I'm not a mouse. And we just got here. But . . ."

Henry patted Lizzy twice on the knee with a cupped hand before retrieving his Bible.

"It's like I've been here before. But I haven't. I guess it's just that you and Toots are family, so I guess maybe that's why you feel familiar."

"Your papa, he didn't like you being here," Henry said.

"You say that like I've been here before. But I haven't. And he doesn't know I'm here now."

"He'll come," Henry said. "Now I have something for you." He got to his feet and went round the foot of the bed, where he opened a closet door and got down on his knees. "What do you think the numbers are?"

Lizzy stepped closer and saw a large, heavy-looking safe taking up most of the floor.

"I wouldn't know," she said. "Maybe your anniversary?"

Henry began to turn the dial, and Lizzy soon recognized her own birthday, which had come and gone just before her almost-baptism. The safe clicked and Henry pulled the door open, revealing a shelf full of papers, and three mason jars full of coins underneath.

"Coppers," he said, taking out a jar full of pennies. He turned it over, causing the coins inside to slip and crackle against the inside of the glass. He opened the lid and spilled a handful of coins out onto the bed.

As Lizzy knelt to examine them, she found that all the dates were the same. Her birth year, 2004. "What are those?" she asked, pointing at the spines of two colourful books.

Henry drew one out and opened it, revealing not a book, but rolls of butterscotch Lifesavers candy. He handed it to Lizzy. "You can share, but keep most of them for yourself," he said. "They're for you. All of them. I've been saving them since you were just higher than my knee." He got to his feet and pointed to the shelf above the hanging rod, where more candy books were pressed together, cover to cover, by a pair of heavy-looking bookends. There were fourteen in all.

Lizzy unwrapped and crunched on a single butterscotch, tasting its soft sweetness before fingering a second candy from the roll. "I used to save money in jars, too," she said. "Back at home. In Kelowna. I had five hundred dollars that I took to the bank before we left. Some old pennies, too, but they couldn't take those anymore."

Henry selected another of the books of candy from the shelf above his head. "Cherry. They were always your mama's favourite."

"She likes the hard raspberries that get stuck together in her purse."

Henry piled the cherry book on top of the butterscotch one.

"Did my dad have a favourite kind?"

"Winter Mint. He didn't like things to taste too sweet," Henry said.

When Lizzy looked up, she didn't see a single book of those. "Do you have any for Zach?"

"Until you came here yesterday, I had no idea what flavour he might like. I think he's cherry.'"

"He wouldn't have anything for your dad, Lizzy. Not even the time of day. You should know that if you want to be here so badly."

Lizzy had come back downstairs to find her mother now awake and in the kitchen, sitting with Toots.

"It's just candy, Mom," she said.

"That's what you think. But if you listen a little longer, Henry will have you hating your own father."

"Nobody's going to—"

"No? Why don't you ask him just what—"

"Marie," said Toots. "You are a guest in my—"

"Home?" Marie interrupted, seeming to grow instead of shrink, the way she usually did. "It was supposed to be my home. You went off to have your own life. I was always the one who was going to stay."

"You were too young to be here on your own, Marie."

Lizzy was the one to shrink back, trying to become invisible.

"Yes, but I grew up, didn't I? And yet you're the one who's still here."

"Lizzy, I'm sorry, why don't you go and put some milk on the stove. There's honey in the pantry."

"Oh, yes, that will solve everything, won't it?"

"Mom, it's okay. I don't mind," Lizzy said, moving toward the fridge, but unable to get past Marie. "Aunt Toots, we should all just go to bed. It's my fault. I shouldn't have said anything."

"And that's the first sensible thing I've heard out of you in days," Marie said. "Get your father's keys. We're going back to Stillwater. Now."

Lizzy stiffened. "Really, Mom? Because it was so awesome there?"

"They took care of us."

"They did not. They just tried to control us. I didn't ask to be baptized. And Zach—"

Marie reached out and quickly slapped a hand over Lizzy's mouth, but Lizzy pushed it away.

"Yeah. I know. You don't want to hear anything. But while we're at it, why does it feel like I've been here before? You've barely told me about this place, but I know things I shouldn't. Why don't we talk about that?"

Lizzy caught a look that passed between her mother and aunt like a ring slipping down the length of a thread.

"I thought so," Lizzy said and pushed past her mother toward her room, where she saw that Zach had been listening to everything they said.

NÜDEL ZUPP

    1 roasting chicken, 3 or 4 pounds, gutted and skinned
    8 cups homemade chicken broth
    2 bay leaves
    Pinch peppercorns
    1 cinnamon stick
    3 whole star anise
    4 tbsps butter

Fit the chicken and broth in a large stock pot, along with anise, bay leaves, peppercorns and cinnamon stick.

Simmer for 2–2½ hours, occasionally skimming off foam. Add butter and simmer for another 30 minutes. Remove the chicken from pot and take meat off the bones. Remove whole spices from pot, skim off any remaining fat, and return meat.

MENNONITE EGG NOODLES (KIELKE)

    5 cups flour
    ½ tsp salt
    6 eggs
    ½ cup milk

Add all ingredients to the bowl of a stand mixer. Mix on low speed until the dough forms and is slightly sticky.

Transfer dough to a floured surface and add between ¼-½ cups more flour on top of dough. Knead by hand until all of the flour is incorporated. Roll out into a long loaf shape and slice into 1½-inch wide sections. Flatten each section and flour both sides.

Set your pasta machine to the thickest setting, and roll each section through, sprinkling flour on it before stacking the next flattened piece on top. Roll each piece out again on a thinner setting, and progressively thinner until desired thickness. Continue sprinkling flour on as you go to prevent sticking.

Cut rolled dough into noodles, sprinkling with more flour to prevent clumping together. Once the noodles are all cut and ready, place them in a pot of boiling water in batches, stirring frequently so they don't clump together, and boil for about 3 minutes. When done, strain your noodles and rinse with cold water to stop the cooking process. Add noodles to bowls and cover with hot soup.

ROLLKUCHEN

Marie had always hated the barn. As a child, learning to milk her father's cows, she'd resented the way their shit-crusted tails would swish in her face and leave a single fleck in the pail to spoil the entire batch. She hated the smell of soured milk from the separating room. The manure, mixed with hay. Cobwebs and dust motes and the stanchions that one of her cousins had locked her head into when she was ten.

The only part of the barn Marie had ever cared for at all was the hayloft, with its quiet, its sweet clean hay bales and the kittens sometimes tucked away between them by their mouse-hunting moms. She stood at the bottom of its ladder now and looked up. If she was going to get to the top, she was going to need the old strength in her hands. Or a plan.

Trying her fingers first, Marie found that her right hand was able to grip just enough. And with her left elbow jammed above and behind each rung, she began to climb until, at the top, she dragged herself up onto the floor like a seal from one of Lizzy's nature books, hauling itself onto the ice. Breathing hard and seeing a few dark spots pass in front of her eyes, she lay there for a bit, blinking until the blotches in her vision mostly disappeared. Reaching into a pocket, she took out the bottle of codeine and, using just the heels of her hands, opened the lid and shook out a single tablet.

Won't they know we're up here? Daniel's voice came to her from the last time she was here, when they had snuck up this same ladder together to get away from Henry and Toots.

What do I care?

That's when they had heard them, Toots and Henry, bringing the day's offerings of stale bread soaked in creamy milk and fork-beaten eggs for the barn cats, who meowed loudly for the bowls to be set down.

"He won't be good for her," Toots had said. Or maybe the word she'd used had been "to."

"There's a good boy somewhere inside. But his own papa, I meet him sometimes in town, you know. He didn't want his boys to be good. I think he never knew how."

"Well, I certainly don't think this one wants us to teach him anything new. I wish Marie would just catch the eye of that nice Neufeld from over in Swift Current. You know him. He owns that truck lot, and Marie wouldn't make much of a farmer's wife, anyway."

"But which one of them will cook?"

There was no laughter. It wasn't a joke.

The barn had gone quiet then, and when Marie looked at Daniel, tears were slipping over the edges of his eyes onto his cheeks. It was the first and last time she had seen any man cry, unless they had just hit themselves in the thumb with a hammer.

Now, alone in the hay, crushing the codeine tablet between her back teeth, Marie worked her way up to kneeling. She almost started to pray, but when words failed, she stood instead and began to make her way between the bales, which seemed closer together than when she'd been here last.

Near the door that led to a one-storey drop to the grass and concrete below, through which bales were tossed down to feed the cows, Marie found an old rug, rolled up and set against a corner. It looked as though it had not been touched since that same day, when she and Daniel had spread it out for a picnic of *zwieback* and a little cheese and jam, overlooking the whole of the farm.

"This could all be ours, you know," Marie had told him.

"I don't know anything about running a farm," he'd said.

"I could teach you."

Daniel had laughed. A rare enough sound, even then. "You don't know anything about running a farm, either," he'd said and touched Marie's cheek before he kissed her, long and deep, as though she was the water to everything that had ever burned him.

For the first time since her parents' deaths, Marie felt safe. "I feel like nothing bad can happen when you're with me."

Daniel touched Marie's face. "Bad things can always happen if God chooses to allow it. Like putting silver in a fire to refine what's precious. But Marie, if a man and his wife follow God's commandments together, in agreement with His ways, then they're already pure in the eyes of God. There's no stronger protection."

Marie pressed her lips together as Daniel reached into his pocket and withdrew a silver and gold engagement watch.

"Will you?" he said and slipped the watch onto Marie's wrist. She had been seventeen; Daniel almost twenty.

Marie left the rug rolled up. She didn't want to sit on it without Daniel. Nor did she want him here with her now. Not in this place.

"Mom?"

Through the floor of the hayloft, Marie recognized the sound of Zach's voice, below her in the main level of the barn.

"Up here," Marie called down, and in a few boyish, vertical reaches, her son pulled himself up onto the floor, where he stood, looked around, and seemed pleased with whatever it was he saw. Dust motes in shards of sunshine, maybe. But those were ordinary enough.

"What are you doing—How did you get up here?" Zach asked.

Marie swallowed. "It wasn't easy. And I guess I don't know how I'm going to get down." Down, in Marie's experience, was always the more difficult direction. A person could climb halfway to the sky and not have any trouble, because you could always be looking up. But down required you to see how far you'd gotten away from the ground. How far there was to fall.

"Come sit by me," Marie said, patting a space next to her on a hay bale.

Zach took another look around before he accepted Marie's invitation. When he did, he sighed and leaned into her, and she into him, her chin tucked over his head like a goose.

Somewhere behind them, a litter of kittens began to mew out a chorus of discontent.

"You know we can't stay up here forever," Marie said.

"Of course not. There's nothing to eat except hay and, unlike Uncle Henry's cows, we only have one stomach each," Zach said. "Besides, me and Aunt Toots made dough for *rollkuchen* today, and you have to come down for that. She said I can help with the frying if I'm really careful and listen to everything she says."

"Yes. She would like that. But I mean here, on the farm. We can't stay here forever."

"Oh."

"Don't you think your dad needs us back? And your friend back at Stillwater. You can stay away from him. You can forgive him first, for making you do things with him. But after that, you can just stay close to me and your dad."

"That's not what I want," Zach said, pulling away. "Thomas didn't make me do anything."

Marie was about to argue when a mother cat crossed their path, belly swaying, on her way to the sounds of kittens mewling in the corner of the loft. She was carrying a mouse in her mouth, limp as a rag, and paid no attention to the two strangers who watched her go

by. A minute later, returning the way she'd come, she crossed in front
of them again, this time carrying a single kitten. "Don't say that. I
know you," Marie said as a second mother cat arrived with a mouse.

"Mom?" Lizzy called up the ladder.

Marie had been about to shush Zach, but the codeine had
reached her mind now, and she was too slow. Lizzy's head appeared
through the same hatch that she and Zach had come through.

"What are you guys doing up here? Mom, how did you get up
here?" Lizzy pulled herself up until she, too, stood and looked
around in the same kind of unnecessary wonder.

"We just needed to get away," Marie said and she could hear
the sharpness in her voice. She almost apologized by inviting her
daughter to sit with them. There was enough room on the bale if
they squished together, the way the four of them used to do on their
too-small couch back in Kelowna sometimes, when the kids were
little and Daniel agreed to bring the TV out of the hall closet for a
special movie from the church library.

But that couch, the TV, their life back there was gone. And if
there was anyone to blame, she was standing in front of Marie now.
Instead of making room, Marie spread herself out and Lizzy sat on
the floor.

"Mom," Lizzy said, her voice uneven as she sunk to the floor and
looked up at Marie. "I didn't mean to hurt you, you know. I didn't
mean to do any of this without asking you." Her voice broke off
and she looked down toward the triangle of space created by her
own crossed legs. Marie watched as she picked up and sifted into it
a handful of hay, broken into shards by being stepped on so many
times.

"Kids," Marie said. "I honestly don't know what you expect from
me. And I don't know what we're doing here. I'm sorry if you don't
think I'm a good enough mother to know what's best for us, and
you two go off deciding everything for yourselves."

"Mom, you know what the director was going to do with Zach, don't you? And what Joel did to that poor rabbit, right?"

Marie's thoughts had begun to stretch like dough inside her head. "So you say. But what does that have to do with us?"

"He killed it for me. As a gift. He thought I'd want to dissect it."

"Sounds like he knows you pretty well, then. Joel might have gone too far with that, but that's the way boys can be. Right, Zach? You just tell them not to do it again and make sure to give them better ideas in the future." Marie caught herself from slipping off the hay bale. "Honestly, Lizzy. If that's why you dragged us here, I think there's something wrong with you that you should think about."

"You're one to talk," Lizzy said. "You have no idea what Dad might be capable of at all."

"What's that supposed to mean?" Marie said. "You're the one who doesn't know what all that man puts up with for us and for you."

"Mom," Zach said. "Lizzy didn't mean—"

"No, I meant it," Lizzy interrupted. "You have no idea what either Dad or Joel are capable of. Neither of you."

"Your father is a good man."

"I think he wants to be, Mom. He just has no idea how. Like with everything else, like with this stupid virus. He just makes things up as he goes along."

"And what about you, Lizzy? Does kidnapping your own mother make you good?"

"At least I didn't almost let you die. Twice."

Marie's fingers trembled as the silence lengthened between them. "I don't know what you're talking about. Your father pulled us all from that lake. And he took me to the hospital when I was sick."

"He didn't, Mom. He didn't pull you from the lake. And Zach was the one who called the ambulance to Stillwater when your skin turned blue and you couldn't breathe."

"What's up with all these cats?" Zach asked as a third momma, a calico, led a small litter of puff balls away from the far wall of the loft. "Mom, do you know?"

Marie, who had clenched down hard on her teeth, loosened her jaw and looked away from Lizzy. "There's a babysitter cat over there," she said. "There's always one of those around so the other mothers can go off to work."

"That's nice of her. And the mice are payment?"

"Come here." Marie got up and made her way over to the wall. "There, look," she said, when Zach followed her to a nest full of kittens.

"Look at this one," Zach said, picking up an all-black baby that had been ambling around with its fat tail stuck straight up in the air.

"Black is bad luck," Marie said and made him put it down. "Now look here. These will be hers." Next to the babysitter cat, Marie moved aside a cluster of larger kittens to reveal three sickly ones, starved-looking, and too weak to even raise their heads. One was all bones and loose fur. "She takes care of herself and everyone else and forgets all about her own kids." Lizzy was close enough to hear her speak. "Is that how you think I am, Lizzy? I just think of myself and not you?"

Lizzy joined them over by the wall, where she scooped up the suffering kittens, the worst of them last, and nestled them into the front of the hoodie Henry had bought her in town. "Zach, can you help Mom get down?" she said and quickly disappeared back down the hole.

"We should go, too," Zach said. "Uncle Henry and I picked out a watermelon from the store yesterday. It's to go with the *rollkuchen*."

"I know what it's for," Marie snapped, then softened. "I'm sorry. I just don't like being here the way you do."

"Maybe you would if you tried. The last time you were here, you were really sad about something. Aunt Toots said so. She said you left too soon."

Marie didn't speak.

"Uncle Henry said that watermelons only ripen if they stay on the vine."

Marie, who could already taste the slightly salty dough, together with the sweet crispness of a perfectly picked watermelon, didn't know what to say. The memory was delicious in her mouth, and she spat it out onto the floor.

"When did Toots say I was here last?"

"I don't know. She just said you were here."

"I don't want you listening to anything she says about me. Learn to fry dough. Go ahead. But that woman doesn't know a thing about me," Marie said, coughing as she batted Zach away for offering his hand. She could feel the barn dust in her throat, constricting her lungs as she croaked, "I can get myself down."

With Zach gone, silence fell around Marie like a shroud. It was heavy, and she slumped beneath it as though an invisible hand was pressing her down.

Lizzy couldn't possibly remember being here, but she knew something. That much was clear. Almost three years they'd spent here, with Daniel visiting when he could between school and work. Marie had hated doing that to him, keeping him away from his daughter, who cried every time he came.

Henry had wanted to go out every few minutes to help settle her down.

"She's fine. Let them have their time," Marie would say. But she had wanted to go to Lizzy, too.

ROLLKUCHEN

3 eggs
¾ cup cream
1 cup milk
2 ½ tsps salt
3 tsp baking powder
4 ¾ (approx) cups flour

Whisk together eggs, cream, milk and milk. In a separate bowl, whisk together flour, salt and baking powder. Add dry ingredients to wet and bring together until a ball begins to form. Turn out onto a lightly floured surface and knead to form a soft dough. Place in a bowl and cover with plastic wrap; let rest in fridge for an hour.

Heat a few inches of canola oil in a deep, wide pot, to 375–400°F.

Meanwhile, roll dough out, one third at a time, to ¼-inch thickness. Cut into rectangles, approximately 3 x 5 inches. Cut a short, lengthwise slit in the centre and fold one end through. Place, two at a time, in the hot oil, turning to cook both sides to a light golden brown. Remove to a baking sheet covered with paper towel to drain and cool slightly. Serve with spears of watermelon.

Note: Rollkuchen go stale by the next day, but the dough freezes well, and can be pulled out for small fresh batches all summer.

BABA GHANOUJ

"Just stop here a minute," Daniel said as a wave of grasshoppers lifted in the wake of the car. It had been a month since Lizzy, Zach and Marie had left Stillwater. A month, during which time Director Schlant had counselled him to let the Lord bring his family back to him.

Daniel himself had left Stillwater only three days ago, without telling anyone. He had been afraid of being told not to come back if he found his wife and kids unchanged in their hearts. *Too much trouble.* That's what he had imagined the director would say.

"You've come a long way to turn back now," said the man in the front seat. Ibrahim and his wife were the last of a series of drivers who had stopped to pick him up.

The first, just outside Stillwater, had been a good Christian trucker. A Sunday-keeper who Daniel had taken the opportunity to witness to. "It will be the Mark of the Beast, I tell you. Those passports they're talking about. Next thing, they'll activate whatever's in those shots to keep track of us all, just like in Revelations."

He went on to talk about the Sabbath, and the driver described how he and others had plans to shut down Ottawa if things went too far.

Not long after, the trucker dropped Daniel off near Vernon. A lone woman had pulled over once, but Daniel waved her away. Besides being a woman, she had offered him a mask. Four more drivers had gotten him to Medicine Hat. Three of them yapped about their families, which was fine for a while, but tiring.

"We're going to take back our country," said one man in cowboy boots, who drove a sports car with running boards. Daniel was in Alberta by then, which he liked. Alberta, to him, had always had a way of making sense. When the Tribulation came, which looked to be soon, and Sabbath-keeping Christians were persecuted, a lot of SDAs would flee here to their mountains.

Now here he was, out in the farmland surrounding Maple Creek, and Ibrahim's wife had recently taken over the wheel. They lived in town here and owned the only restaurant that wasn't either a diner or a Chinese smorg. Back near Medicine Hat, Sara had not seemed at all pleased to let Daniel into their car, but now she obligingly flicked on the turn signal for no one to see and pulled over to the side of the gravel road.

"I haven't changed my mind," Daniel said. "I just need a minute to pray."

That, at least, was something he and Ibrahim had in common, although it pained Daniel to admit it. A while back, Ibrahim had stopped the car and gotten out, turned toward the east, and knelt down on the cold, hard ground to pray. If only he had been praying to the One True God. But neither of them had wanted to hear.

In the backseat, behind Ibrahim and Sara, Daniel bowed his head. His mind, though, felt hollow and he couldn't find the words. Instead, all he could hear was the occasional grasshopper strike the outside of the car. "I should pay you for the ride. I know it's out of your way," Daniel said when he lifted his head.

Daniel felt Sara shift the car into park, and when he looked up, he saw that she had unwrapped a pita from a crumple of foil. He could tell it was falafel and the smell brought an audible grumble from deep inside his stomach.

Sara handed the pita to Ibrahim and checked over her shoulder.

Meeting Daniel's eyes for less than a second, she reached into a cooler between her and her husband and passed a foil-wrapped package to Daniel.

"Isn't this one for you?" Daniel said, even as he accepted, anticipating the first bite of chickpeas, hummus and tzatziki. Maybe Sara would even have something halvah in that cooler. Mostly sesame seeds, it could hardly be considered a sweet.

"I can eat when we get home," she said with a shrug, adjusting a bright orange scarf shot through with gold thread.

"Thank you," Daniel said, making a mental note to talk to Director Schlant about scarves or kerchiefs for the Stillwater women, so they could cover their hair. Plain, of course. Like women would have worn in Jesus' time.

Daniel knew that Marie's mother and grandmothers had covered their hair to leave their homes. Toots had done as much when he'd first met her. Although Marie had said it was because of the wind.

Daniel peeled back an edge of foil. He should have refused the food, even if just to prove to his stomach that he was in control. Ahead of him, though, was Toots' cooking, and even the food that wasn't unclean would be dripping in some kind of grease.

Mrs. Schlant's cooking, of course, was everything he had come to expect from a good Seventh-day Adventist woman. If Daniel was honest, though, he preferred a more global menu. The kind he and Marie enjoyed when they first moved to Kelowna and relied mostly on takeout or food from the mall. Falafel back then as well. Italian meatballs, which he convinced a restaurant to make with nuts instead of meat. Teriyaki tofu with vegetables. Curries. And sushi rolls filled with avocado or tempura yam.

Back then, both he and Marie had worked—she as a piano teacher and a fruit picker in the summer, he as an orderly while going to college—and spent money whenever they had it. They had even talked about adopting children from overseas, the country of choice changing with whatever spice palate they'd brought home to eat. India. Thailand. Russia. Vietnam. Ethiopia. He had reasoned that neither he nor Marie had families whose legacies needed to be carried on. Adopted children, he believed, would never need to bother with where they came from. The five of them—they would adopt three—would be the start of something separate and new.

Then Lizzy had come along. He had named her Elizabeth, which meant "pledged to God." Somehow, though, whenever he looked at Marie, and later, at Lizzy her in her crib, he had only seen someone who never needed to be born. In her, he had seen his own parents, and she seemed just as disappointed in him as he was in her. His plan to become a doctor was over.

Daniel's mind drifted over the memory of his infant daughter as he took a bite of his pita. He chewed and swallowed before he realized that what he was eating was not what he'd expected. "Is this chicken?" he said, alarmed. "I can't—I don't—thank you, but—" Quickly, he tried to cover the missing bite with the foil he had peeled back. "Shit," he said when the foil tore and a clump of heavily sauced meat fell into his lap.

"Goat," Sara said, taking the package from him and folding it back up.

"My God." *What kind of people eat goats?* "I think I'll walk from here," Daniel said. He reached into his pocket for a few dollars he had borrowed from the director's office and handed them to Ibrahim. "Thank you for the ride."

"I apologize," Ibrahim said, stepping out of the car and returning the bills Daniel had given. "If I had known, I would have offered you mine."

Daniel was aware that he had just been rude. "It's all right. Neither of us knew."

Sara joined them, holding a tiny box of apple juice that she punctured with a straw and handed to Daniel.

"It's cold. It will help you feel better. So will a little walk," she said and returned to the car.

Daniel rinsed and spat, and with the goat cleansed from his mouth, he continued to sip at the juice as he walked. It would take another hour or so before he reached the small cluster of farms where Toots and Henry lived.

The last time Daniel had been there was to pick up Marie and Lizzy. Before that, there had been a number of visits to see them.

It had been partially his fault that they had ended up there. He could admit that. But Marie had promised she would be able to keep Lizzy quiet early in the morning, when Daniel needed to sleep after work and before going to class, now that he was reduced to nursing school.

"Why won't she sleep?" Daniel had half-shouted, half-growled. He had gotten out of bed, two hours before he needed to, to see why a six-week-old couldn't be bothered to give her own father a little peace when he needed it.

"She's colicky," Marie said. "Her stomach bothers her."

"Well, what are you eating? It all comes from the milk, you know."

"I don't eat anything different from you," Marie said, jiggling a wailing Lizzy up and down. "She just won't settle."

"Put her in her crib. She needs to learn."

Marie set Lizzy down. "It's not going to work. She's a baby, Daniel. Babies cry when they need something."

He had been so tired. The kind of tired that creeps up on a man like a wild animal and threatens to devour him if he doesn't lie down and play dead for at least five hours. "If she can't learn like the rest of us, then maybe what she needs a good slap."

Later that morning, Daniel had woken to get ready for classes. When he did, it was to an empty house and an empty crib.

Daniel kicked a clump of dirt on the road and pushed his tongue against the roof of his mouth to unlock his jaw. He ground a few grasshoppers into the dirt to let them know he could and slowly moved on.

From anywhere in the village ahead—a hamlet, really, no more than a dozen homes—it would already be possible for people to see him coming. Even at a single glance, anyone, everyone, would know he wasn't from around here. And thanks to Toots, the whole village would probably be on high alert to watch for a man coming to see his own family. Again.

Although Daniel expected Toots to be the first to come out and stand in his way—honestly, that woman was a human Canada , always hissing and flapping at him—it was Henry who appeared on the gravel drive that led to the farmhouse. A kernel of anxiety popped inside his chest, and he touched his fingers to a sore rib. The rib he believed all men were missing, and that in his case made Marie the Eve to his Adam.

Confronted with his brother-in-law, Daniel looked down at the driveway beneath their feet. The gravel had been oiled recently to keep down the dust. At the same time, he noticed a glob of *baba ghanouj*, all garlic and eggplant, slipping down the front of his own shirt.

"The *dotter* is in the house with Marie and Toots. The boy, too. That one's a good cook," Henry said, without removing his hands from his pockets.

The *dotter*, Daniel thought, feeling his jaw ratchet tight once again. The *dotter*. As though Lizzy was everyone's. Henry's. Toots'. The whole damn village, maybe. Everyone's but his.

"What's Zach been cooking?" Daniel asked, to keep from speaking his mind.

"*Varenyky* and the *schmaundt fat*," Henry said, then added, "That's cream gravy. Cheese pockets and cream gravy." As though Daniel had never been here before.

Schmaundt fat was the thick, fatty sauce Marie's family liked to put on everything. On *varenyky*, which were just Mennonite *perogies*. And also on potatoes, noodles or even just warm Saskatoon berries or prune plums that had been simmered down with sugar into a sort of sweetened stew.

"Lots of grasshoppers this year?" Daniel asked when Henry didn't turn to lead him toward the house.

"Not so many, but enough."

"Enough for what?"

"Enough to keep a man from being too pleased."

Daniel hated how much he appreciated what Henry had just said. In fact, if he could get past who it came from, he would offer it to Director Schlant for one of his Vespers sermons. Although maybe he would replace grasshoppers with something more common to their area. Aphids, maybe. Caterpillars. Or hail that came and smashed bruises into all the delicate tree fruits. Maybe he would write that sermon himself, and deliver it, too. If the director didn't mind.

"I've come a long way to see them, Henry," Daniel said. He was losing patience now, with Henry and with himself for not simply stepping around his brother-in-law and going where he wanted. Henry wouldn't even even bother to stop him. It wasn't his way. *Turn the other cheek.* That's what the Mennonites believed. As though a man—as though Daniel—hadn't already run out of those.

"I'm going to the house," Daniel said, but didn't move. He still waited until Henry nodded thoughtfully, then finally turned to lead the way.

BABA GHANOUJ

1 lb eggplant
1 tsp salt
3 tbsps olive oil
2 cloves garlic, chopped
2 tbsps tahini
3 tbsps fresh-squeezed lemon juice
½ tsp cumin
Salt/pepper to taste

Heat oven to 350 °F. Cut tops off eggplant(s) and slice lengthwise. Place, cut sides up, in a baking dish. Drizzle with 2 tbsps of the olive oil and sprinkle with salt. Roast for 35-40 minutes, until flesh is soft and browned. Let cool until easy to handle. Scoop out flesh into the bowl of a food processor (discard skins). Add garlic, tahini, lemon juice, cumin and remaining oil. Process until smooth, adding salt and pepper to taste. Let rest for about an hour (overnight would be better) in fridge to let flavours mingle.

SCHMAUNDT FAT

From her customary spot at the kitchen table, Marie saw Zach looking out the kitchen window. He liked to watch the chickens peck at seeds and grapefruit peels. The cats that stalked mice from behind a rain barrel. And he liked to watch for Henry to come out of the barn, carrying a pail of milk, pouring the warm froth over slabs of stale bread and buns for the kittens and cats.

Lizzy was usually wherever Henry was as well. But not today. Today Marie could see her through the window, coming from the direction of the henhouse, with a gathering of eggs, which she carried in a blue ice cream pail that dangled from her hand.

"Should we do some scrambled eggs for night lunch before bed tonight?" said Toots.

Zach turned from the window. "Could we do poached instead? I like cracking eggs into the water."

"Anything you like. Don't forget to stir your *schmaundt fat*," Toots said and left the room to fold the laundry she'd just brought in from the line.

Zach, who had nearly forgotten about the pot of cream gravy on the stove, dipped in a wooden spoon and gave it a thorough stir. On the back burner, meanwhile, a stock pot simmered away with the Saskatoon berry and plum *varenyky* he and Toots had spent the entire morning kneading, rolling, stuffing and pinching closed.

The cream gravy, when Zach checked on its progress, did not yet coat the back of his wooden spoon. He tasted it with a swipe of his finger and added a little more salt.

"No wonder they got the idea you're a little woman," Marie muttered under her breath.

Zach returned to the window, his shoulders hunched.

"What's so interesting out there?" Marie asked.

"It's just Lizzy coming with Kanga Sue." Kanga Sue—the sickest of the three kittens from the hayloft, who Lizzy had brought back to life with eyedroppers of warm milk and drips of honey—often rode in Lizzy's front apron pocket. "I think the kitten should stay in the house while she's still so little."

"It's a barn cat. Better it learns to like it outside," Marie said.

Zach ignored her, suddenly focused on the scene outside. He lifted himself up a few centimeters and balanced on the edge of the sink, see-sawing there with his feet in the air. A moment later, his elbows gave way and his belly scraped against the edge of the counter as his feet slammed to the floor. He turned to face her.

"Dad's here. Did you call him?"

"Shouldn't I call my own husband?" Marie said and rushed over to see for herself.

By the time the door to the summer kitchen opened, the cream gravy was scorched on the bottom. Zach turned off the burner, while Marie, who had gotten to her feet, now found she couldn't move.

Lizzy was the first one inside. Henry followed, and then Daniel.

Still by the stove, Zach quickly scooped the last of the Saskatoon pockets out of the stock pot and into a buttered dish, where he dotted each one with a little more butter before sliding them into the oven to keep warm. As he did, Toots came into the kitchen from the other side of the house.

"I see you're teaching my son to be a housewife. And my daughter, the scientist, is an egg collector, now," Daniel said, seeming to grow in confidence as he stepped farther into the house.

"And who do you have there?" Daniel nodded toward Lizzy's apron, where two lilac-point ears suddenly appeared.

"We don't know where that colouring came from," Henry said. "We have mostly black-and-whites. Tabby cats. But you know how old toms like to roam when they're in season."

Marie noticed Daniel's shoulder twitch, but he was quick to straighten himself back up. "Can't just rely on cousins," Daniel said, his tone flat.

"Zach, why don't you and your sister put Sue in your room. We'll call you both when it's lunch," said Toots.

Lizzy turned toward to go, as though she had suddenly been released, but Zach stopped and took Marie's hand. "Mom," he whispered. "Come with us. Just for a second, okay?"

Marie stiffened. "Your dad came a long way to see us," she said, trying to keep Zach with her.

"Your hair, Mom. Let me help you with your hair," Zach said quietly, and Marie, embarrassed, moved to follow.

"I'll just get the kids settled," she said and allowed herself to be led away.

"What's he doing here?" Lizzy said, dropping to sit on her side of their bed. She scooped Kanga Sue out of her apron and handed the kitten to Zach, who considered Kanga to be more his than his sister's.

"He's your father. Does he need a reason?" Marie said, sitting down on a wooden chair.

"Did you call him?" Lizzy's voice was quiet. "Did you tell him to come?"

Zach, having tucked the kitten into his own apron pocket, began to carefully pull pins out of his mother's hair.

"Maybe when you have a husband and a family, you'll know better than to ask me that. But no. I couldn't get the number. Stillwater is unlisted."

"Try to stay still," Zach said, smoothing her hair. He twisted and pinned it back up into the bun she always wore.

"Does Dad really think he's going to just come here and take us back there?" Lizzy asked.

Toots came to the bedroom door and let herself in. "The men are talking. We should let them."

"Talking about what?" Lizzy's voice was guarded. "We should be out there. We're not suitcases to be carried off whenever and wherever anyone decides."

"Is that right, Lizzy?" Marie snorted. Her hands fluttered up to her head, where she touched the shape of Zach's handiwork, satisfied that enough of her usual pins were in place.

"They're talking about the weather," Toots said evenly. "Men need to do that. They talk about the weather, or the crops, find something to agree on, and then we can all sit down to eat."

SCHMAUNDT FAT

    2–3 tbsps butter
    ¼ cup flour
    1 cup milk
    1 cup cream
    ½ tsp salt

In a small saucepan melt butter over medium heat. Add salt and flour and whisk to form a paste. Whisking constantly, slowly add milk. When mixture thickens, slowly add cream. Continue cooking/whisking until the flour is cooked. Adjust consistency with flour and milk or cream as desired.

VARENYKY

Lizzy felt sick. Not just to her stomach, but with a sickness deep in the marrow of her legs, which she rubbed with the flats of her hands. She looked to her aunt, trying to read what Toots might or might not know. She suddenly wondered if Toots and Henry would be glad to be rid of them. They had shown up uninvited, after all. Her aunt and uncle's kindness had convinced her they were welcome, but neither had actually ever said as much.

Zach moved toward the door. "We should at least go and say hi to Dad."

"You just want to know about Thomas," Lizzy snapped, immediately sorry.

"Enough, the both of you," Marie's eyes lingered on Zach. "Lizzy, you should go out there and thank your father for coming. I'll bet he's had an awful time getting here."

Toots clapped her hands. "Give them a minute, Marie."

"Let's go, kids," Marie said, opening the bedroom door and letting herself out.

Zach slipped into their mother's wake, but Lizzy hesitated.

"Why does Mom hate it here so much?" Lizzy said, pulling a corner of a blanket over where Zach had left Kanga Sue on their bed. "I mean, she never once brought us here. And now, besides how we left Dad, she's so angry all the time. I don't understand."

"Ah, *mejal*," Toots said. "Have you wondered why your uncle and I are here, in this house, instead of your grandparents?"

"Not really. Mom really loved them. And they died. But—I don't know."

Toots fumbled for Lizzy's hand and held it in her own. "She was younger than you are now when it happened, you know. Just a bit older than Zach. We should have just taken her away with us. Instead, we thought it would be too much change. And so we came here to take care of her at home."

"But what happened to them? I've asked her, but she won't talk about it, and it just makes Dad angry if I want to know anything about my grandparents. Or you and Uncle Henry."

"Your mother should be the one to tell you," said Toots. "Come, let's go back to the kitchen."

When they returned, Toots joined Zach, who had installed himself back at the stove, and asked Lizzy to take down the plates for lunch.

"Do you want to do the cutlery, Mom?" Lizzy asked, leaving a handful of forks on the table before returning for the plates.

Marie seemed grateful for something to do as she began to set forks next to each of Lizzy's plates, while Toots and Zach put out the food. Everyone was doing their best to ignore the uneasy silence that had settled between Henry and Daniel, who were seated at either end of the table.

Toots brought out Mennonite sausages from the oven, and after she tonged them into a serving dish, put them beside the cottage cheese *varenyky*. Meanwhile, Zach took out an old tomato can from the fridge and added the fat from the sausages.

Inside the can was like a fat parfait. Drippings from bacon and cracklings, hamburgers and fried pieces of chicken. Sausage. All of it ready to flavour gravies or to fry fingers of bread for dipping into bright yellow yolks from still runny eggs.

Lizzy looked over at her father, whose face told her exactly how he felt.

With the table set and loaded with food, Lizzy, Zach and Toots took their seats. Perhaps out of habit from their time at Stillwater, Marie hovered nearby, waiting for the men before taking a seat herself.

"Come, Lord Jesus, be our guest," Toots started to pray. "And let this food to us be blessed."

Daniel snorted.

"Amen," Toots finished.

"Not much of a prayer."

"Here, Daniel, let me give you a cottage cheese pocket," Toots said, reaching for a serving spoon.

"Oh, but . . ." Zach said, sounding a small alarm. "Dad doesn't eat cottage cheese."

Deftly changing lanes, Toots instead fished up a purple-stained Saskatoon *varenyky* and deposited it on his plate.

"Butter. I put butter on those," said Zach, and Toots scooped the pocket back up for herself.

"*Oba.* Dairy now, too?" Toots said, then half under her breath, "How any of you had the strength to get here, I'll never know."

Zach began to squirm in his seat. "I'm sorry, Dad. I would've used margarine if I'd known. If I'd thought. I'm sorry."

Daniel, seeming to ignore Toots, tugged Zach's chair next to his a little closer. "It's okay, Zach. Nothing that's happened since you left is your fault. You know that, don't you?"

"We have some oatmeal in the fridge from this morning. I seem to recall you didn't mind a little bit of that."

"I'll get it, Aunt Toots," Lizzy said. "We have some nut milk here from the pastor's wife. She's lactose intolerant. Mom's been drinking it. You can have some of that."

"No, *mejal*, you sit."

"And some honey," Daniel said.

Until today, *varenyky* had been Lizzy's favourite of her aunt's dishes. The dough that encased the fillings was dense, almost rubbery. The cream gravy, thick and rich, coated the inside of her mouth with a luxury she had never known. She took the smallest Saskatoon and the smallest cottage cheese pockets for herself and poured out a ribbon of the velvety white sauce on top. Dark purple juice sprayed out of the berry pocket at the first touch of her fork.

"Some toast for you, too, Daniel?" Toots called out, with her head and hands in the fridge.

"You still use eggs in your bread?"

"Of course. How else should I make bread?"

"No toast, then," Daniel said.

"*Mein Gott.* No eggs, but you'll eat spit from bees." Toots sset down a jar of homemade cashew milk and a jar of honey from their own hives.

At a look from Marie, Toots pinched her lips together and emptied a sour cream container full of oatmeal into a pot. She added a little water, which sizzled at the touch of the flame, and soon set a bowl of hot oats in front of Lizzy's father. She handed him a spoon, then settled back into her seat.

Lizzy knew the expression on her father's face. One side of his mouth was twisted up into a smirk, while the other remained etched in a scowl. He was pleased with himself. But only by half.

"Lizzy, will you pass the milk and honey," Daniel said, pointing his spoon toward the middle of the table.

Lizzy handed the jars to her father. When he took them, his fingers touched hers. Their eyes met for a moment, and Lizzy saw that his were rimmed with red.

Lifting a forkful of *varenyky* to her mouth, Lizzy felt a sting of pride from knowing the flour for the pockets had come from wheat in fields she'd driven to with Uncle Henry. There were eggs from the henhouse, which she'd collected herself. Cream from cows whose names Lizzy had learned. The sausages on the table, which Lizzy left where they were, came from a pig she had helped Henry to slaughter. Although, when it came to the moment, she had closed her eyes and turned away.

Even the Saskatoons had been picked here, from wild bushes out beyond the pastures on a no-man's-land, and at the same time they were there, others from the village had come to stake out branches that were heavy with the sweet, seedy berries.

Lizzy and Zach had each half-filled an ice cream bucket soon after they'd arrived, adding them to the full milking pails picked by Toots and Henry, who had stripped the branches with such practiced hands. Almost everyone there had kept six feet of distance that day, leaving room between them and their neighbours. Although Lizzy had read in Uncle Henry's newspapers that Mennonites elsewhere were holding get-togethers to immunize themselves by getting sick.

Lizzy had met a cute boy that day, who later turned out to be their cousin. She had understood her father's joke earlier but hadn't liked it. Aunt Toots and Uncle Henry were second cousins, not first.

"Your mom and dad came out here to pick these for us once," Toots had said. "He brought back more leaves than berries."

Both Lizzy and Zach had gotten their first bee stings that day, and after pinching the stinger out of Zach's arm, she had watched the one in her own hand for a minute. Even dismembered, it had continued to pump out its poison. She loaded her fork again and swirled *varenyky* around in the puddle of cream gravy as her father raised a spoonful of oatmeal to his mouth.

A silence fell around the table and tightened like a rope. Lizzy could feel it stretching to the point where it would have to either strangle them or break.

"How did you get here, Dad?" Zach finally said, snapping the tension. "Did you get another truck?"

Daniel lowered his spoon. "No, Zach. People can't usually just buy a new truck whenever one goes missing. I hitchhiked."

"All the way here?"

"All the way here. Toots, the people who brought me the last of the way own a foreign restaurant in town, so you probably can't help but know who they are."

"Yes. Lovely people. They like my *varenyky*."

"Toots," Henry said, his first words since they had all sat down. "Maybe Daniel would like some of Lizzy's tea. That flower kind."

Thank you, Lizzy mouthed across the table, and Uncle Henry nodded, just a little.

She knew exactly which tea her uncle meant. Chamomile flowers grew wild all around, wherever the grass was thin. The two of them had picked a bucket of them one day and spread them out to dry in the sun behind Uncle Henry's garage.

As Lizzy stood to put the kettle on, she realized for the first time that she was missing something obvious. She sank back into her seat. "Mom. Since when don't you need help with that?"

Marie, who had been cutting up her *varenyky* with her own fork, let the utensil clatter onto her plate. She blotted her mouth with a paper napkin and settled her wrists on the edge of the table before she spoke. "I'm capable of all kinds of things, Lizzy. Is feeding myself such a surprise to you?"

"Yes," Lizzy said. "Because yesterday, you had me spread butter and jam on your toast. This morning you asked me to cut up your fried egg."

"And was that too much for you?"

"Mom's been going to the bonesetter lady," Zach said. "Every day except Sunday."

Lizzy felt her father stiffen.

"And you didn't tell me?" Lizzy said, as Zach plugged his mouth with a forkful of food.

"When have you been going?" demanded Toots. "I'm here all day, and so are you."

"The same way I went on my wedding day. When you sent me for a nap like I was a child. The front door."

The front door, like the couch that no one sat on, was mostly there for decoration. Until now, Lizzy hadn't even known it could open. Everyone else used the way through the summer kitchen.

"Ina didn't say a thing to me," Toots said.

"I told her I'd never come back if she did. It's nice to know she can keep her gossip to herself when she needs to."

From there, the two women erupted into Low German, and Lizzy's head began to ring.

"Stop it!" she finally said, sending her chair skidding back as she stood.

"*Feehls dü die schlajcht*, Lizzy?" asked Aunt Toots.

"*Nee, jo,*" Lizzy replied. "I feel fine. The two of you never stop, though. I'm sick of it. And Mom, you've hated me ever since I brought you here, and I'm sorry. But Mom, *bitte, horjcht*—listen, please—I wanted us to be together, and you must understand that Zach couldn't stay there. Not after—"

"Lizzy," Daniel said, almost softly. "Look at what an angry girl you've become here. Is this really the kind of place you want to be? The kids back at Stillwater, they miss you, you know. Especially the little ones. They told me you were the best teacher they ever had."

"I doubt their parents agree with them. Dead rabbit in the greenhouse. Remember?"

"They can forgive you for that."

"I don't need their forgiveness, Dad. And I don't need yours."

VARENYKY

3 large eggs, beaten
1 cup milk
½ cup cream
2 tbsps butter, melted
1 tsp salt
Flour to make a stiff dough (5–6 cups)

In the bowl of a stand mixer, whisk together eggs, milk, cream, melted butter and salt. Using the dough hook attachment add flour, a cup at a time. After about 4½ to 5 cups, turn dough out onto countertop and knead by hand, incorporating more flour as needed. (The consistency of the dough should be similar to pasta dough.) Continue kneading until the dough is smooth and elastic. Divide in half and cover with plastic wrap.

Roll out ½ of the dough to a rectangle, ⅛–¼-inch thick. Cut into 8 equal rectangles. Pinch together sides to form a pocket. Fill with berry filling and 1 tsp sugar. Pinch closed. Repeat with other ½ of the dough, filling with cottage cheese filling.

Into a simmering pot of water add 4 pockets at a time, making sure the dough doesn't stick to the bottom of the pot. Return water to a simmer and continue cooking, turning pockets occasionally, for about 15 minutes. Remove with a slotted spoon and place pockets into a casserole dish. Dot with butter to keep from sticking. Cover and place in a warm oven. Repeat with remaining pockets.

For Saskatoon berry filling (fills 8):
¾ lb approx. Saskatoons (or blueberries, prune plums, etc)
3 rounded tbsps sugar

For cottage cheese filling (fills 8):
½ lb dry curd cottage cheese
1 large egg
½ tsp salt

Process cottage cheese in a food mill/processor. Blend in egg and salt.

ZWIEBACK

Lizzy climbed into the hayloft, slipping and banging her shins on two of the rungs as she pulled herself up. Once through the hatch, she released it from the hook that held it open and dropped it into the floor, then dragged a hay bale over top to keep anyone from following. Which did not take long.

"Lizzy," Zach called through the barnboard between them.

Lizzy didn't answer.

"They're going back, you know. Mom is so upset she says she'll go with or without you. One of us has to go with her, though. Otherwise, she won't have any kids anymore."

"Zach, just—Oh, for Chrissake." Lizzy grasped the bale by its twine and let Zach up before pushing it back over the hatch again. "Has Dad said how Thomas is doing?"

"I asked before you and Aunt Toots came out of the bedroom. Dad says everyone was upset about how much he missed me. They asked him a bunch of questions, and now they're fixing him. Like you said."

A slippery cold slid down Lizzy's spine. One of the academy girls back in Kelowna had been taken away once, and then transferred to public school. She still showed up at church, though. She sat on the fringes, looking hollow, and was no longer invited to youth potlucks.

"Lizzy," came the bark of Daniel's voice, along with a sharp, single blow from the underside of the hatch.

"Just open up so we can talk to you," said Marie, sounding much farther down.

Lizzy sat on the bale and pulled up her knees.

"They just want to talk," Zach said, although he slid down to sit on his heels, wrapping his arms around his legs. "It's not like he's going to hit us or anything. He never does."

"Haven't you ever wished he would, though?" Lizzy said after a few moments. "You know, so the bruises would be real?"

"That's crazy. Why would anyone want that?"

"Because. If I had bruises, I'd make him look at them the next day, and maybe he'd see how much it hurt. Shhh."

"You're the one who's talking."

"No, I mean, I don't hear them down there anymore."

Lizzy leaned over the bale, as low as she could, and listened.

That's when they heard a rustle of hay from a corner of the loft near the open doors. Daniel, followed by Marie, stepped out from behind a stack of bales, having climbed a different ladder.

"Your dad and I used to come up here all the time," Marie said, looking anxiously between her husband and the kids. "We'd bring up a picnic of your aunt's *zwieback* when we needed to get away. See, look at this. This is what we'd sit on. We put it up here years and years ago." She gathered a dusty old rug that was leaning against the corner nearest the door, seemingly held in place as much by cobwebs as gravity. Going to hands and knees, she rolled it open; it was practically clean on the inside, except for an old smear of what looked like raspberry jam.

Lizzy got up and dragged the bale to the side so she could climb back down. She pulled open the hatch, startled at the sight of her uncle and aunt down below.

Toots held her hands, pressed together as if in prayer, up to her mouth, and Henry touched one of his to the place over his heart. Neither spoke and neither attempted to climb.

Lizzy turned back toward her parents. "I've been here before, haven't I? And don't either of you dare lie to me."

Marie, still down on her hands and knees on the rug, trying to get its ends to lie flat, stopped what she was doing, and knelt, sitting on her heels like a girl.

"Of course you haven't," she said.

"Does it really matter if it's true?"

Marie laughed, and the sound was as dry as the dust in the air.

"I don't believe you," Lizzy said. "You've been shushing everyone about it since we got here. Even the bonesetter woman. Don't tell me that isn't why you sent her away that first day here. Even Uncle Henry and Aunt Toots are keeping your secret, although I have no idea why. My birthday is the combination to Uncle Henry's safe, you know. Why would he use it if he'd never met me before?"

"It was nothing, Lizzy. Not even worth mentioning. For a little while, you and I just needed a little break. A bit of help. You were such a difficult baby until—"

"Until what?"

"Until you finally learned to sleep when you were supposed to. That's all, and that's all you need to know."

"So, you hate it here, Mom, but I was such an awful baby that you had to bring me here to sleep? You expect me to believe that?"

"That's not what I said. Don't twist my words."

"Mom," Lizzy said, struggling to control her voice. "I'm not twisting anything. I know how much you hate it here. You wouldn't have come without a good reason."

"Well, maybe we're even. I brought you here, and you brought me back."

"You know what, Mom? I wanted to leave you at Stillwater. Do you know why I dragged you here? Because Zach said he wouldn't leave without you."

"Lizzy," Daniel said, blunt as a hammer. "Stop this bullshit."

"No. You might think Stillwater is fantastic, but you never stop to think what it's like there for us. You don't even know us. You think you do, but you don't."

"Yeah? I know I have a daughter who pulled a stunt at her own baptism. A daughter who brought a dead rabbit into the greenhouse and kidnapped your mother. So, it's pretty clear to me and everyone that you're the problem, no matter how much you want to blame the rest of us."

Lizzy fought against a flood of angry tears. "You're a fool, Dad. You. The director. Everyone there if you think I'm the issue. Joel murdered that rabbit, for God's sake. And he isn't even the whole problem. You know as much as I do about what happened to him before Stillwater, and you all think that hasn't messed him up? That, what? Prayer and Mrs. Schlant's cooking are enough to fix him? It hasn't fixed you, either, Dad. I can see it. It's like your mind is wallpapered in sadness." Lizzy's voice crescendoed as she spoke. "And Mom, whatever happened to my grandparents on this farm, it hurt you so much that you won't even talk about it. And I'm sorry I brought you here, and I'm sorry your parents died here, but I didn't know what else to do to keep me and Zach safe."

"Are you finished, Lizzy?" Daniel said. "Do you think you've figured everything out and now you're the parent?"

Lizzy looked down at her aunt and uncle. Henry was on the ladder, but Lizzy nodded for him to stay.

"I'm not the parent," Lizzy said and looked back to her father. "You are. I'm the child. I shouldn't have to run away. I shouldn't have to find out that my aunt and uncle have been waiting my whole life to know me. I shouldn't have to be the one to protect my little brother."

"Stop this right now, Lizzy," Marie said.

"Really? I should stop? Tell me then, Mom. How old was I when you brought me here? And what happened to make you do it?

Because I know for damn sure it wasn't just because I wasn't a good sleeper. Dad? What happened?"

"Don't look at him. It wasn't your father's fault," Marie said. "You were—I was supposed to keep you quiet. I promised I would. And then you wouldn't stop crying. It didn't matter what I did, Lizzy, you just wouldn't stop. You wouldn't stop. And your dad. He needed to be able to rest so he could work and finish school. He couldn't do that with us there."

Daniel took hold of Marie by the wrist, and Lizzy could see that he was holding her too tight.

"It was you. You should have been able to control her," Daniel said.

Marie's wrists had been among the bones that were broken, and Lizzy watched the pain of it twist up her mother's face, bending her knees until she looked about to buckle onto the rug.

"Dad," Lizzy said, her anger draining all at once. "Dad, please let go of Mom." She glanced toward the open hay doors behind him, where bales were thrown down for the cows.

Daniel looked over his shoulder, and when he turned back, his face had fallen. "Is that what you think of me? That I'd throw your mother over the edge?"

"No, of course not. Just. We're all feeling a lot right now, and accidents can happen. Accidents . . ." Lizzy should have stopped there but finished her thought. "Like the night in the car."

Lizzy knew she had made a mistake. "I'm sorry. That's not what I meant. I just mean that—"

"That I'm some kind of maniac who can't help himself."

"No. Of course not—"

"That I lost control once and might do it again," Daniel said, taking a step back and forcing Marie to take it with him. "Like this?"

"Dad," Lizzy said, her throat suddenly raw.

"Your daughter thinks I left you to die that night, Marie. Did you know that? She's been holding it over me ever since, using it to get her way."

Marie's eyes, wide and wild, flashed from the drop behind her and locked onto Lizzy's.

"No, Dad. You said . . . You said you were thinking of me and Zach first. Just like Mom would want. But you swam back out for us when Zach was safe." She turned to Marie. "Mom. That's what happened."

"You came back?" Marie said, looking desperately at Daniel.

"He just—I meant—"

"Marie, it doesn't matter now, does it? You're here and you're fine and that's not what any of this is about."

"Doesn't matter?" Lizzy said, her voice rising again. "You told me that Mom had already swum to the shore. If I hadn't gone down to look—"

"Daniel?" Marie said, visibly shaking now, and pulling away. "Is that what happened?"

"Of course it isn't, Marie. Think about it."

"Zach?" Marie said, but Zach had covered his face with his hands. Lizzy leaned down and whispered, "Go down to Aunt Toots."

"Not without Mom," Zach mouthed back.

"Mom, just, let's all go down and we can talk on the ground. Dad," Lizzy said.

"No, Lizzy. You started this. Now it's time for you to finish it. Why don't you go ahead and tell your mother how I failed you all that night."

"Dad."

"Tell them. Let's see who they believe."

Lizzy spoke softly. "You were stuck in your seatbelt, Mom. The car was smashed up around you. I could barely get you out through all the broken glass and the metal. And the water. Look." Lizzy unbuttoned her jeans and pushed them down to her knees. As she did, she exposed the scar from the gash torn into her leg that night.

Marie crumpled and Daniel jerked her back to standing.

Lizzy, without raising her voice, pressed on.

"Dad, do you even know how fast you were driving that night? When we all knew there could be ice?"

"Lizzy, it had been a long day," Marie said. "I think everyone's nerves—"

"That's wrong, Mom. Dad was at the wheel. It was his job to be as safe as he could, not to just floor it just because he was annoyed with your singing. Or because I didn't want to go live at some crazy commune in the middle of the woods."

"That is enough, Lizzy. You'll stop speaking to your mother like that right now." Daniel let go of Marie's wrist and began striding across the hayloft to where Lizzy stood next to the open hatch.

"Dad," Lizzy said. "Dad, don't."

"Daniel!"

"Oh, for the love of God, Marie," Daniel bellowed. "Do you really think all I want to do is hurt my own kids? Just because of one stupid night seventeen years ago?"

"Daniel, stop," Marie sobbed, taking a step back. At the same time her arms began to windmill through the air. "Daniel!"

"Mom!" Lizzy screamed.

Daniel leapt back and grabbed Marie's hands as she began to slip over the edge.

Toots and Henry were up the ladder almost as quickly as Daniel pulled Marie back inside. She clung to him like a child and sobbed into his shirt as he stroked her hair. When he spoke, he choked on his words and tears fell down his face. "And whose fault is this, Lizzy? Is this my fault, too? You're the reason we're all here."

"I don't think that, Dad," Zach said, going over to Daniel and Marie.

"Zach," Lizzy said. "Dad might not *want* to hurt us. But if he ends up doing it anyway, then what's the difference?"

ZWIEBACK

1 ½ tsps dry yeast
1 tsp sugar
½ cup lukewarm water
1 cup milk
½ cup butter
1 tsp salt
1 large egg, beaten
4½ cups all-purpose flour

Dissolve yeast and 1 tsp sugar in water. Scald milk and add butter, salt and remaining sugar. Cool until lukewarm, place in a large mixing bowl, then combine with yeast mixture and egg.

Gradually add flour, mixing until ingredients come together. Turn onto a floured surface. Knead about five minutes, incorporating more flour if necessary, to form a soft dough.

Cover and set in a warm place to rise until doubled. Punch down. Pinch off balls of dough the size of large walnuts. Place on a greased pan, 1-inch apart. Pinch off slightly smaller balls, set on top of larger ones, and press down through both balls with thumb. Cover to rise until doubled. Bake at 400°F for 15 minutes. Traditionally served for *Faspa*, with cheese and preserves.

Note: *Faspa* is a lunch served around 3:30pm or later.

DRIPPINGS

I remember the first time you died. A voice in Marie's head.

It's not like I could forget. It's not as though you ever let me.

Of course Marie remembered.

She remembered how she had woken up afraid that night when she was thirteen years old. She had been in her downstairs bedroom, the same one she was in right now. Something had disturbed her, and she had sat up in her bed quick as a mousetrap. It had been so dark, and she had tripped over the knotted rag rug on the floor as she'd crossed her room. Out in the hallway, a light from the kitchen was enough to guide her to the stairs. Once there, Marie had started upstairs to find her mother.

That's how you catch a death of cold. She could almost hear her mother's voice as she turned back to fetch her slippers. Along the way, Marie had switched on every light, and finally slipped her feet into her favourite slippers, which her mother had recently crocheted.

"Mom?" Marie said, kneeling at her mother's side of her parents' bed. "Are you awake?" Across the room, a paraffin space heater clicked on.

Always, whenever Marie had been frightened in the night, for as far back as she could remember, all the way back to her crib, her mother had gotten out of bed for her. Carried her when she was little, before taking her hand in hand, the two of them going down to the kitchen, their slippered feet so silent that the only noise in the world seemed to be the sound of the refrigerator turning itself on and off in its nook beside the stove.

"I had a nightmare," Marie said and reached under the blankets for her mother's hand.

It was warm. As warm as Marie's. Still, she felt something rise inside her in alarm. "Mom," she said again, shaking her mother by her shoulder this time. "Mom! Dad. Dad! Mom's not waking up," she said as she fumbled for the switch on her mother's bedside lamp.

Click. Like the flash of a Polaroid, the image of her parents' currant-red skin burned itself into her eyes. The red, together with the peace of their expressions.

"Mom!" Marie shouted and pinched her mother's cheek.

When there was no response, she climbed onto the middle of the bed and began to breathe, one at a time, into her mother's, and then her father's, mouths.

She tried to pump their hearts, too, the way she'd been taught in gym class, but the springs in the mattress simply bounced her efforts back. And soon she was tired. So tired, and just wanting to sleep. To lie down between her mother and father and close her eyes with them. That was what she was going to do, but first, she picked up the phone.

I remember the first time you died. And now, here she was again. Having already died twice since then.

All day, Marie pretended to sleep. Finally, late in the evening, the house went quiet. Even Toots and Henry had gone upstairs and the sound of their footsteps overhead eventually stopped. The kids took turns in the downstairs bathroom and went to bed. Daniel, from what she could gather, took back his keys and went to sleep in his truck.

That was when Marie put on her slippers. The yellow and

brown ones she had been wearing when Lizzy took her away from Stillwater. The same colour her mother had made her all those years ago, when they were still a family in this house. The slippers had been in her pockets when she drowned in the lake. And in the hospital when she was sick and the doctors explained that the tube they were inserting meant she might never wake up.

Marie stole into the kitchen, took down a pot and set it on the stove. She found the jar of honey that Toots had offered Daniel for his porridge, then opened the fridge and reached for the bottle of milk. Cow's milk, this time. Like her mother had always done.

Meaning to pour it all into the pot, she instead lifted it to her mouth and swallowed. Just a little at first, to wet her tongue and throat. Again, closing her eyes at the taste of cream that had risen to the top of the glass.

When the milk was gone, Marie opened an old margarine container for the Saskatoon *varenyky* she knew it contained. There were three, and after she had eaten them cold, by the light of the open fridge door, she found the cottage cheese pockets and ate those, too.

The *schmaundt fat* Marie ate with two fingers curled into a spoon. There was a plate of sweet lemon squares. A sour cream container of green Jell-O salad. Half an egg salad sandwich that Zach had left uncovered. The last few inches of a block of cheddar cheese. A carton of orange juice. Bread and butter pickles. Pimento-stuffed olives and the brine in which they floated.

Marie slid down to the floor, already nauseated but unable to stop.

A lone farmer's sausage in intestine casing.

Marie wanted to throw up. That was when she saw the jar of fat. *I remember the first time you died.* She dipped her fingers into the congealed layers of drippings from a month's worth of Toots and Zach's pots and pans.

"Mom, you aren't eating that, are you?"

Marie looked up at her daughter and pushed her fat-slicked fingers into her mouth. She tasted bacon and sausage, cracklings and Toots' greasy little hamburgers. She tasted lard. She scooped her fingers in again.

"Mom," Lizzy said, kneeling down beside her. "Mom, please stop. You're going to make yourself really sick. Please."

Marie sucked more fat from her fingers while Lizzy went and brought back a handful of paper towels.

"I used to do this for you," Marie said as Lizzy tried to wipe Marie's hands. Her tongue and the roof of her mouth were coated with fat. She swallowed, gagged a little, then swallowed again. "You were forever coming inside with dirty little fingers."

Lizzy sat down on the floor next to Marie. "I remember."

"And I never knew if you were just playing in the mud or if you'd found some dead thing covered in disease. You could never keep yourself from touching."

"I know."

"And now, look at where that's gotten us. The butcher shop. That rabbit. You know that your grandparents died in this house, don't you? Right upstairs. Carbon monoxide. Well, I'm sure you know more about that kind of stuff than I do. But you don't know what it's like to find your own mother dead." She could hear Lizzy struggling to swallow.

"Mom," Lizzy said. "You were dead when I found you, too. *You* were dead."

"Don't be ridiculous."

Lizzy sighed, a heavy sound that made Marie stop talking. "Your heart had stopped. Do you know that? I was so cold, my arms were trembling, but I did the CPR, I tried until I couldn't push anymore. Dad only took over just before the paramedics arrived."

"I don't remember any of this," Marie said.

Liar. To protect herself from knowing, she wrapped her arms around her face. *That was the second time you died.* She remembered the spin of the car. The sudden shock of the lake. She remembered sinking in her seatbelt. Lizzy rolling down the back window and pulling her brother out. She remembered Daniel pushing open his door. The car filling with water. She remembered the watery light from the headlights. Her chest bursting with the need to breathe, and how the water, when it entered her lungs, burned with cold. Just before everything went black, Marie remembered her daughter.

"Lizzy, you should know I've decided to go back."

Lizzy nodded. "I know, Mom."

"I belong with your father."

"Okay."

"He needs me. You can come with us."

"I can't. And Mom, please don't try to make Zach go with you. He might be okay for a while. But you have to believe me, eventually, it will be worse there for him than it was for me."

"You're just saying that. It was just a mistake with him and Thomas. There's nothing wrong with him. Your brother wouldn't do that to me."

"Mom," Lizzy said. "Why can't you see it? Why can't you see that Stillwater is to me what this place is for you? I'm sorry I brought you here. I'm sorry for how I did it, and I'm so sorry, Mom, for everything that happened to you in this house. But don't ask me and Zach to follow in your footsteps."

Lizzy took Marie's hand. Marie allowed it for a moment, gave her daughter's hand a squeeze and then shook it loose.

"No," Marie said. "The difference is, my mother stayed dead, and here you are, doing everything you can to take me down again. You just don't know it. You're the reason everyone at Stillwater knows about the drugs I needed. And then you brought me here to this, this . . ." Marie flung her arms out, hit one hand against the refrigerator door, and clamped it over her mouth to keep from screaming in pain. When she recovered, she hissed, "You see?"

"But, Mom," Lizzy said, her voice falling to barely a whisper. "I need to go to school. And Joel. I think he has ideas for us. He's not okay, you know. I know he tries, but he needs help and I can't be the one to give it to him. No one knows what he might do next. And Zach—"

Suddenly, the overhead light switched on.

"I've had just about enough of you, Lizzy," Daniel said, dragging Zach out from the door where he had been listening. "You'll stop talking about your brother like that."

Marie wiped grease from her mouth onto her sleeve. "Zach, you tell her how wrong she is. Lizzy, we don't even discuss such ugly things in this family. Didn't you learn anything at that school we paid for?"

Lizzy opened her mouth to speak.

"Shut up, Lizzy. Just shut up," Zach said and broke free from Daniel's grip.

"And if you go back and you end up like Thomas?"

"What are you two talking about?" said Daniel. "Thomas told us the truth. It was all his fault. Zach had nothing to do with it. Satan got a hold of him but he's getting help. He'll be fine when he gets back."

Lizzy laughed softly, sadly, to herself. "Is that what you think? What will you do when—"

"Lizzy, don't," Zach said. "I'm serious. I'll never speak to you again. I'll hate you forever."

"Fine. All I'm saying is that Stillwater is no place for Zach, not any more than it is for me." Lizzy knelt in front of Marie and whispered. "Mom. I need you to know that I'm staying here. And you need to tell Zach it's okay for him to stay here with me."

Marie reached up and touched the heel of her hand to the side of Lizzy's face, feeling the softness and heat of her skin.

"I never guessed you could become such a terrible daughter," she said, struggling to her knees. "If I had, I wouldn't . . ." Before she could finish, Marie grasped Lizzy by the shoulders for support, and then threw up on the floor between them.

DRIPPINGS: PAN-FRIED ZWIEBACK

1 recipe Zwieback (unbaked)
Reserved fat drippings from cooking bacon, cracklings, etc

After letting the dough rise, punch down, divide and shape into bun-sized pieces.

Heat some of the fat in a frying pan over medium-high heat. When very hot, flatten a few of the buns and place them in the pan. The dough will begin to rise and bubbles will appear.

Once golden-brown underneath, turn buns over and repeat on other side. Remove to a dish lined with paper towels to drain. Repeat with remaining dough.

CREAM COOKIES

Using Zach's favourite wooden spoon, Lizzy lifted a sickly-looking skin from a pot of milk she was heating on the stove. Making a face at what she saw, she tapped the membrane into the sink and turned on the faucet to rinse it down. It was stubborn and got caught in the polished metal cross-pieces of Aunt Toots' drain.

"You'll have that burnt in another minute," Toots said softly, coming over to turn down the heat.

"I didn't know what else to do," Lizzy whispered back.

"Well, I don't know what your uncle and I just walked into here," Toots said. "But I'd say go ahead and add some honey to that. Sometimes that's about all any of us can do."

She passed Lizzy the honey jar and as Lizzy dipped a spoon into the sticky fluid, Toots moved over and opened another cupboard. From there, she took down two of her white and green mugs, along with a ladle from one of her drawers.

"How's Mom?"

"I got her to throw up a few more times, but she won't be feeling good after all that. She's sitting in her room."

"Zach, do you want to help me with this?" Lizzy said. Zach seemed rooted to the floor, which was how Lizzy could tell that Daniel was staring at him. Staring, unblinking, the way he did whenever he thought one of them was keeping a secret. Usually that was Lizzy.

How long did it take to heat up a pot of milk? Minutes? Hours?

"Zachary," Daniel said. "If what your sister is insinuating is true, the director and I can help you."

Lizzy heard her brother exhale sharply, punctuated by a squeak.

"Just leave him alone, Dad," she said and Daniel slapped his hands together for her silence.

When the milk was hot, Lizzy filled the mugs and delivered them to the table, gripping each one tightly by its handle. Aunt Toots followed with a plate of pink-iced cream cookies she took from inside a cupboard.

"Zach?" Lizzy said and pulled out a chair.

He still didn't move from his spot on the floor. "Just shut up, Lizzy," he managed to say.

"Zach, your sister thinks she's going to stay here," Daniel said. "I suppose that's what you want now, too."

"I . . ." Zach said. "I haven't decided that."

"She seems to think you don't belong back with us at Stillwater. And do you want to know what I think?"

Lizzy saw Zach shake his head, just a little.

"I think all this cooking and being in the house all day isn't good for a boy. Especially one who's already softer than he should be. I also think your aunt here isn't satisfied with getting my daughter. Now she wants to turn my son into one as well. And maybe you've decided to let her."

"That's not—"

"From where I'm standing, that's exactly what it is."

"Daniel," Marie said, holding a hand over her stomach as she returned to the kitchen. "Doing a bit of woman's work doesn't turn a boy into anything. You're a nurse and—"

"And what, Marie? Do you really want to finish that sentence?"

"And you're nothing like a woman. You've always provided for us. You've always protected us. Zach will be just the same one day."

"Mom, you don't know what you're talking about," Lizzy said.

"That's it. Lizzy. Zach. All three of you. Get in the truck. We're leaving right now."

"We're not going anywhere," Lizzy said.

"I am," said Marie.

"Mom."

"Enough. Do what your father says. Zach, if you don't want your father to think you're that way, you do what he says right now, too."

"Zach, don't."

"You're not the boss of me, Lizzy," Zach said. "And Mom, what if I am what Dad thinks. Would that be so bad?"

"Zach, no," Marie said, at the same time Daniel rushed toward him, his hands clenched by his sides.

Before Daniel could quite reach him, Lizzy stepped in between.

"There's nothing wrong with Zach, Dad," Lizzy said. "He doesn't need anyone to change him."

"I don't know if you know this, Lizzy, but I'm the father in this family. Or is everyone here mixed up about that?"

Marie rushed to the sink and threw up, then turned on the water and pushed *varenyky* vomit down the drain.

Daniel appeared unmoved. "Truck. Now."

Lizzy was still standing between her father and brother. "You really think now is a good time to drive? You? In the middle of the night?"

"We're all upset," Marie said, rinsing the sink before vomiting into it again. "Maybe let's wait until morning. After you've slept, Daniel."

Toots had been quiet until now. "Everyone, please. Why don't we all go back to bed. We can talk in the morning when we've all had a chance to sleep on things. I'm sure this is all just a misunderstanding."

Lizzy saw her father draw back his hand. "I've had about all I can take of you, woman. Tonight. Tomorrow. For the rest of our goddamn lives."

"That's enough," said Henry.

"You do understand what's going on here, don't you?" Daniel

said. "You understand why Zach has to come back with us. Or are you going to deal with that here, in front of your little village?"

"What is he talking about?" Toots said, turning toward Lizzy.

"Zach?" Lizzy said.

Zach turned toward Toots. "I'm sorry. I'm sorry."

"*Oba* . . . what are you saying?" Toots said, taking a step back. "*Oba.* no."

"I'll get my things, Dad," Zach said. "It's okay if you want to leave now. Aunt Toots, Uncle Henry, it's okay if that's what you want me to do too."

"Lizzy," Daniel said. "Are you coming?"

Lizzy shook her head. "Zach," she said. "Please. Stay. I need you here. *I* need you."

"Not everything is about you and me. I told you. Someone has to stay with Mom."

Lizzy spent the next year with Toots and Henry, studying on her own. The University of Saskatchewan had accepted her application. So had UBC in the Okanagan.

Now she unzipped an old suitcase from Toots and Henry's attic and began to fill it with clothes. Toots had taken her shopping, all the way to Regina. Uncle Henry had come along and decided that Lizzy should be the one to drive.

"Now that you have a license, you need the practice," he'd said and given Lizzy the keys to his second-best car: a Chrysler with heated seats.

Later, when they were home, Henry had kicked the tire. "It's a good, safe car. It will take good care of you." That had been his way of giving it to her.

"You'll come visit me, won't you?" Lizzy said when she, her aunt and uncle were finally all standing around her car.

"Of course," Toots said. "We might even come out for apples in the fall. Take a look at that new place of yours. Don't forget to get your boosters whenever they say."

"Drive safe," Henry said and pressed something small and black into Lizzy's hand. An iPhone that flashed on when Lizzy touched its face. "You call us on this when you stop for things." Toots handed Lizzy a brown paper bag full of pink-iced cream cookies, and *zwieback* stuffed with both cheese and jam and cheese and meat. Inside the bag was a Ziplock stuffed with cash.

"Take this, too," Henry said next, patting Lizzy roughly on the cheek before giving her his favourite set of butchering knives from the Quonset. "In case you catch a chicken."

At first, Lizzy listened to the radio as she drove, tuning into the different frequencies for the CBC as she travelled in and out of range. "Quirks and Quarks" was her favourite, but she found herself leaning toward the voice of Shelagh Rogers and her guest, a novelist who'd grown up Mennonite in Manitoba. Like Lizzy's mother, the author, too, had needed to go away.

Later, when the programming began to repeat itself, Lizzy turned the radio off and drove in silence, eating cookies first, then a sandwich to settle her nerves.

Hours passed. Medicine Hat, then Calgary, Canmore and Banff. Finally, after travelling through the Shuswap and stopping for ice cream at D Dutchmen Dairy and the fifth phone call of the day, Lizzy arrived in the valley.

On the west side of Vernon was Kalamalka Lake. Then Duck. Then Wood. That was where Lizzy stopped for the last time before Kelowna.

It had been Henry's idea to buy the tiny condo near the campus, with a second bedroom for Zach. Henry had called the real estate agent himself, made an offer, and Lizzy had helped him sign the legal documents with the lawyer over Zoom. "That brother will come to you one day. You make sure."

That, Lizzy knew, would take time.

Maybe it would never happen at all.

But as she parked the Chrysler on the shoulder by Wood Lake and walked down to the water, Lizzy looked in the direction of Stillwater and knew she would wait.

CREAM COOKIES

4 large eggs
2 cups heavy cream
3 cups granulated sugar
1 tsp pure vanilla extract
pinch salt
9 cups all-purpose flour
2 tsps baking powder
1 tsp baking soda

In the bowl of an electric mixer, whisk together eggs, cream, sugar, vanilla and salt. In another large bowl, sift together flour, baking powder, baking soda and salt. Add dry ingredients to wet, one cup at a time, mixing to form a soft dough (do not over-mix). Divide dough into four equal parts. Wrap each in plastic wrap and refrigerate for a few hours, or overnight, until well chilled.

Preheat oven to 350°F. On a well-floured surface, roll out dough to ¾-inch thick. Cut out cookies using a medium round cutter. Place 1 inch apart on a baking sheet, lined with parchment paper or Silpat. Bake 12–14 minutes, watching carefully in last few minutes to be sure the cookies do not brown (they should remain white, but be set in the centre). Allow to cool completely.

For frosting: Cream together 2 cups confectioner's sugar with 1 tbsp cream, 2 tbsps softened butter and ½ tsp vanilla. Add a few drops red food colouring for a soft pink. Spread over cooled cream cookies. Dip each in shredded coconut.

EPILOGUE

Dad, I've been thinking about our old washing machine some more. I'd never seen you so happy as when we all came down to the basement. And, for a minute, you let us in. I think that's who you are inside. Who you could have been, anyway. Laughing while riding a washing machine. That's how I want to remember you.

You should know that Zach is here. I think it's important for him to stop thinking of you as so much bigger than him. Seeing you like this made him cry, Dad. We both did. But it also made him stand a little taller. I wonder if you'd be proud of either of those things?

I sent Zach to sit downstairs with Mom. She's the one who called an ambulance for you. Just like Zach did for her. Zach is going to come live with me. He's finally decided, and the people at Stillwater want him to go. He has a lot to work through after what you and the director did to him. Did he ever tell you about that place? How they kept him isolated like a criminal? Did you know they showed him pictures of men—pornography, Dad—and gave him electrical shocks?

All for nothing. And now I have to help him become whole again.

If you don't recover, Dad, I'm going to take the slippers from under your bed, the ones Mom knitted for you when you were first admitted. I'll keep the slippers instead of my *Messages to Young People* so I have something better of yours to remember you. I'll keep the slippers, and I'll go and knock on the door of our old house. And if the new family will let me, I'll dig a hole and bury Ellen White under the rhubarb. Next to my old shoes.

ACKNOWLEDGMENTS

This novel took a village.

Back in February 2012, just more than a year after the publication of the *Mennonites Don't Dance* short story collection, I broke my back.

That is the easiest way to say it.

Except that it wasn't a fracture.

Instead, the bilateral rupture of my sacroiliac joints was due to adenomyosis, a gynecological condition that goes undiagnosed in far too many women and often takes decades to finally name and treat.

Gradually, and then all at once, the stress from my uterine ligament twisted my sacrum like a jam jar until something—the joints—finally had to give.

I can say that my doctor at the time tried to manage my pain. I can say that he sent me to see every possible specialist while tossing out diagnostic darts at my chart.

I can also say that Marie's prescription history in *Stillwater* is my own, but only in part. And I can say that these prescriptions, combined, were a sustained act of malpractice. There is a consensus that my brain should have stopped telling my lungs to breathe.

After two years, much of it spend on my hands and knees, silent screaming into the carpet on my bedroom floor, a pain specialist in Vancouver diagnosed and began to knit my joints back together with prolotherapy. A gynecologist performed a complete hysterectomy.

I tapered off the fentanyl.

The Dilauded, the Ativan, the Zopiclone.

The Cyclobenzaprine. Lyrica, too. Prescription NSAIDs left my stomach lining damaged and I spent a year in spasms, vomiting in and out of emergency rooms.

Finally, though, I had my body's permission to heal. And with the help of various professionals, including pain specialist Dr. Pam Squire, physiotherapist and functional medicine practitioner Angela Simpson, pilates instructor Suny Samson, RMT Cheray Brandt and Jolene Albrecht, Doctor of Chinese Medicine, I began the one-day-at-a-time process of coming back to life.

Three years after that February, I dusted off my laptop and opened up the first draft of *Stillwater*, which I had not quite abandoned, at least in my mind.

Having started off as a NaNoWriMo project, however, the draft was a mess and so was I. I soon realized I would need help to find my way back to who I was before the injury.

This time, where Sandra Birdsell mentored me through *Mennonites Don't Dance*, Gail Anderson-Dargatz walked with me, Lizzy, Marie, Daniel and Zach through this novel. And as she wrote notes on storylines and character development, not only did the novel come to life, but Gail slowly brought me back to life as a writer as well.

With monthly pages and conversations for more than a year, Gail became more than my teacher. She became one of my most cherished friends and sister-writers, and I hope she knows how much I love her.

At the beginning of the pandemic, Betty Jane Hegarat read the next draft of *Stillwater* and declared that it was good! Her coming alongside this project, at exactly that difficult time in the world, gave me so many kinds of courage.

Vicky Bell, a friend from the Humber School for Writers, read the draft after that and helped me refine the text and keep believing. I have no doubt that her own novel, an unforgettable story set in Apartheid-era South Africa, will find its way to bookshelves next.

Diana Manole introduced me to my agent at Transatlantic Agency, Rob Firing, who signed me to his list of authors before even reading this book. When he did, he became its champion and mine, and I am grateful every day for his support and guidance.

Diana, I don't know what I did to deserve you.

Lynn Duncan at Tidewater Press saw further potential in the original manuscript and became the wind at my back until that potential was realized. Kilmeny Denny at Tidewater parsed through the timelines and created the cover for the book you now hold. I have perhaps never loved an image more! Kilmeny, I apologize for the trauma caused by my banana and tomato sandwich recipe. If I figure out how to forget the taste of it, I'll let you know.

Marthese Fenech, Misty Hawes, Kim McCullough, Anne Sorbie, Sylvia Petter, Olga Stein, Sue Burge, Geraldine Sinyuy, Clara Burghelea, Susan Toy, Dew Williams, Dawn Promislow, Josephine LoRe, Sheila Tucker and many others have made up my cheering squad over the last few years, and I send squeezy hugs and buckets of gratitude to all of them.

Lori D. Roadhouse provided a final look at the manuscript after I'd revised so many drafts, I could no longer see what was on the page. More than that, Lori has been a constant support and friend.

My most profound gratitude is reserved for my husband, Dean Hossack, who some of you will know as Chefhusband.

Dean drove me to hundreds of doctor, specialist, imaging, physio, acupuncture, surgical and other appointments. He never once conceded to any of them that there might be no hope. Never once agreed I might never be myself again. That I should never hope again. Write again.

In the introductory pages of this novel, I dedicated this book to Dean because he "told me so". Not only that I would recover, when there was no reason to think I would. Not only through those silent-screaming years, but for 28 years of marriage so far.

Dean, you believed in who I am and what I do. You supported me in every possible way a partner ever could. You gave me space to grow and write. You wore an I Love My Wife tee-shirt and meant it. And then, you saved my life.

You said this book would make it into the world, and now here it is. You were right. And you told me so.

ABOUT THE AUTHOR

Darcie Friesen Hossack grew up in Saskatchewan, Alberta and British Columbia, the daughter of a Mennonite mother and Seventh-day Adventist father.

Traditions that may look similar from the outside, these faiths are oil to vinegar, mixing only when shaken. Quickly separating.

Mennonites Don't Dance, Darcie's first book, won critical acclaim and landed on multiple shortlists, including the Commonwealth Prize. It was a finalist for the Danuta Gleed Award in 2011, a year dubbed "Year of the Short Story."

Darcie lives near Jasper National Park in Hinton, Alberta. *Stillwater* is her first novel.